Bello:

hidden talent rediscovered!

Bello is a digital only imprint of Pan Macmillan,
established to breathe new life into previously published,
classic books.

At Bello we believe in the timeless power of the imagination,
of good story, narrative and entertainment and we want to use
digital technology to ensure that many more readers
can enjoy these books into the future.

We publish in ebook and Print on Demand formats
to bring these wonderful books to new audiences.

About Bello:

www.panmacmillan.com/imprints/bello

About the author:

www.panmacmillan.com/author/andrewgarve

Andrew Garve

Andrew Garve is the pen name of Paul Winterton (1908–2001). He was born in Leicester and educated at the Hulme Grammar School, Manchester and Purley County School, Surrey, after which he took a degree in Economics at London University. He was on the staff of *The Economist* for four years, and then worked for fourteen years for the *London News Chronicle* as reporter, leader writer and foreign correspondent. He was assigned to Moscow from 1942–5, where he was also the correspondent of the BBC's Overseas Service.

After the war he turned to full-time writing of detective and adventure novels and produced more than forty-five books. His work was serialized, televised, broadcast, filmed and translated into some twenty languages. He is noted for his varied and unusual backgrounds – which have included Russia, newspaper offices, the West Indies, ocean sailing, the Australian outback, politics, mountaineering and forestry – and for never repeating a plot.

Andrew Garve was a founder member and first joint secretary of the Crime Writers' Association.

Andrew Garve

A HOLE IN
THE GROUND

B E L L

First published in 1952 by Collins

This edition published 2012 by Bello
an imprint of Pan Macmillan, a division of Macmillan Publishers Limited
Pan Macmillan, 20 New Wharf Road, London N1 9RR
Basingstoke and Oxford
Associated companies throughout the world

www.panmacmillan.com/imprints/bello
www.curtisbrown.co.uk

ISBN 978-1-4472-1578-3 EPUB
ISBN 978-1-4472-1577-6 POD

Copyright © Andrew Garve, 1952

A CIP catalogue record for this book is available from the British Library.

Visit **www.panmacmillan.com** to read more about all our books
and to buy them. You will also find features, author interviews and
news of any author events, and you can sign up for e-newsletters
so that you're always first to hear about our new releases.

Printed and bound by CPI Group (UK) Ltd, Croydon, CR0 4YY

PART ONE

Chapter One

Sharp on the stroke of seven the Member of Parliament for the West Cumbrian Division drove his dusty station wagon into the Memorial Square at Blean for the "Mass Labour Rally" that was to wind up his August campaign. Already there was a fair amount of activity. Several dozen men and women—the stalwarts who formed the hard core of the Party's active workers and could be relied upon to turn up at every meeting—were chatting and laughing around Adam Johnson, the full-time agent. Close by, two youths were erecting a portable platform bearing the red-lettered inscription "West Cumbrian Divisional Labour Party." On the fringes of the open space stood a few individuals who were probably going to attend the meeting but preferred to keep in the background until the proceedings started. Farther off still there were coy indications of a wider public—heads at open windows, loungers at corners and loiterers without any apparent destination. Among all these a young girl threaded her way distributing leaflets.

"Looks fairly promising," Laurence Quilter commented to his wife.

"Not too bad," she agreed.

Although Julie Quilter had been married to an M.P. for seven years, she could never get very excited about the party political struggle. It had been the man, not the politician, who had swept her off her feet almost at their first encounter, and she had often thought since that if he'd been a Flat-Earther instead off a Socialist she'd probably have married him just the same. Of course, his sheer fervour had infected her to begin with and for a while she'd found the partisan battle stimulating and they'd had lots of fun.

Now she did gracefully what was required of her as a politician's wife because Laurence expected it and she would never have let him down. Secretly she nursed what to any politician is the worst of all heresies—that it didn't much matter which side got in!

Quilter leaned across to turn the door handle for her and as he followed her out a pleased and smiling expression began to settle on his face. He was good-looking in a rather boyish way and appeared much younger than his thirty-nine years. A lithe, vigorous walk, a slim figure, unruly brown hair and heavy horn-rimmed glasses increased the suggestion of an eager undergraduate.

As they crossed the Square together there was a stir of welcome among the group of supporters by the platform. Adam Johnson swivelled round on his one leg with a practised shove from his crutch and stumped towards them. He was a white-haired, rubicund man of sixty with a rugged face, an open candid expression and the inner guile of a lifetime spent in professional politics.

"Evening, Laurence! Evening, Mrs. Quilter!" Johnson shook hands with them, though the three had met every night that week in similar circumstances. "Well, what do you think of it?" He eyed the square with the satisfaction of a man whose labours were about to be rewarded. "Not too bad for Blean, eh?"

"I've seen worse," said Quilter, and both men smiled at the understatement. The fact was that they had held some heart-breaking meetings on this square in days gone by—nothing but noisy children and dogs and stony adult indifference. In those days Blean had been less a town than a strip of coast dotted with cheap bungalows, their inhabitants dull and self-centred and lacking any vestige of corporate spirit. The place had had no focal point, no community of interest, and Quilter had found it politically inaccessible. However, all that was changed, now. A huge plutonium-producing plant—the largest source of atom-bomb material, it was said, between America and the Iron Curtain—had been built beside the little river Blea, and now every house in Blean and almost every thought was dominated by the pale pink chimneys that towered five hundred feet into the sky. In the past few months workers had come crowding in from Birmingham and London as production swelled, occupying the great new prefab estate that made the original bungalows seem no more than a suburban fringe. And politically the place had come to life.

"We're expecting quite a big contingent from the plant," Johnson said, following the direction of Quilter's gaze. "Should be here any minute now. And the whole town's been well billed. With luck, we'll make fifty new members to-night."

"Good work, Adam." Quilter patted the agent's shoulder and began to circulate among his supporters, greeting each by name and chatting in an easy, natural manner. Johnson, leaning on his crutch, looked on approvingly. He knew that organisations could be made or marred at such moments; a hint of condescension or too much heartiness from a Member could be as fatal as aloofness. There wasn't any danger of that here, though. Quilter had just the right touch—he appeared genuinely interested in people and knew how to inspire them with his own keenness. He was an agent's dream!

Julie, too, was mixing in her more personal, discriminating way. One of the compensations of her public life was that she had come to know and like many of these devoted people and rightly counted them her friends. It wasn't difficult for Julie to make friends, for she had a naturally happy disposition and a most attractive appearance. Her sepia eyes were usually bright with laughter and her lively features had a piquant, elfin quality that was matched by her smallness and lightness of movement. This evening she seemed a little subdued, but her manner had an added sweetness. Several mothers of large families thought what a pity it was that the Quilters had no children.

With the arrival of the Member, the atmosphere in the square had become expectant and the crowd was visibly swelling. A bus deposited the first batch of workers from the plant and a party of miners from Coalhaven in the north of the constituency added to the solid nucleus by the platform. There were many more townsfolk about now, too, and the pavements were becoming well-lined. The local constable wheeled his bicycle on to the square and took up an unobtrusive position against a tree.

"If you're ready, Laurence, we'll make a start," Johnson called. Quilter nodded and moved towards, the platform. "Right, up you go, Joe."

A heavy, balding man climbed carefully on to the stand. Joe Halliday had been for forty years the signalman, porter and general factotum at various stations on a branch line near Blean, an unexacting job leaving him with a good deal of surplus energy which he had devoted unsparingly to the Labour cause. A slow-witted man, he might normally have expected to live out his political life doing the most menial, of party chores, but it so happened that he had a voice of loud-hailer strength which in the general view ideally fitted him for open-air chairmanship. To-night as always he had prepared his introductory remarks with laborious care and now proceeded to unload them with the stolidity of a town crier. Even when some misguided wit called out, "Speak up, Joe!" and a gust of laughter swept the square, he paused only long enough to dab his moist face and then resumed his discourse without a smile.

Quilter stood close beside him, following his banal words with every appearance of interest and backing him up from time to time with an earnest "Hear, hear!" Inwardly, he wished that Joe would cut it short. The foghorn voice might be all right in theory but in practice it seemed to keep the crowd at a distance. Quilter felt keyed up and impatient to get started himself. Although he had been in public life for fifteen years and had made more speeches than he could remember, he always felt acutely nervous just before he was called upon. His irritation increased as Joe shouted, "Finally, my friends . . ." for the third time and embarked on yet another peroration. One or two people on the outskirts were starting to drift away and Quilter longed to tug at his jacket. Johnson, too, was beginning to get restless when the welcome-words came at last—"And now, my friends, it gives me much pleasure to ask our Member to address us."

Quilter helped the chairman down, murmuring congratulations, and mounted the stand to solid applause from the hard core and some good-natured booing from the middle distance. Once up, he seemed in no hurry to begin. He took off his coat and gave it to Joe to hold and then he leaned nonchalantly over the front of the platform. "Suppose you all come a little nearer," he said in a conversational tone, beckoning the audience towards him with both hands. Almost unconsciously they closed in, forming a corporate whole with himself as the focal point. "That's much better. Well, now, as you know the Government's been having a rather difficult time with its small majority . . ."

It didn't take him long to capture their interest. He began telling them the inside story of the session, explaining the issues in homely terms, drawing lively little word pictures of members who had taken part in the debates, salting his account with amusing episodes. He was completely in command and obviously enjoying himself. Every now and again, as he found some happy phrase, he would look down and catch Julie's eye and smile. His manner was intimate, as though he were chatting over a glass of beer, yet confident and authoritative, too. Occasionally he slipped in phrases like, ". . . so I asked the Prime Minister about it and he told me . . ." People liked that sort of thing—it was almost as good as hearing someone talk who had had dinner with Clark Gable. Politics without tears!

As the crowd continued to grow, Johnson mentally rubbed his hands. Laurence was doing well to-night, better than ever. A first-class speaker, full of charm and personality. A first-class Member, altogether. Mature, now—very different from the too-clever, verbally violent young man who had somehow managed to snatch the seat in 1935 and had become the "Baby" of the House at twenty-three. In those days Johnson hadn't expected him to last, but he'd survived two elections and was better-liked now than ever. Of course, he had all the advantages—the prestige of belonging to a famous local family, the kudos of going against that family's political traditions, great wealth, good looks, an attractive wife—those things all counted. But he'd earned his popularity, too—he'd never spared himself and he'd always had the interests of the constituency at heart. Even so, it would be a near thing next time. The Government had lost ground, there was no denying that, and it was just a question whether the influx of new workers into the district would make up for it. Perhaps an early canvass would be a good idea . . .

Julie, also, was thinking about Laurence. "Now that he had got into his stride she had moved away to the edge of the crowd and was watching him appraisingly from a distance. There was no doubt, she thought, that he was wonderfully effective on a platform. He responded to the limelight—and he was at his best in the limelight. At least—she wanted to be fair—it showed up one of his best facets and threw all the contradictions of his complex character into shadow. On the platform he always appeared as she had first seen him—as a man of conviction and integrity and vision, with the fire and intelligence to communicate his message to others. Yet she sometimes wondered. After all these years she still wasn't sure what kept him in politics—whether it was high principle and the desire to serve, or ambition, or vanity, or just the usual mixture.

She strolled away out of earshot of the too-familiar speech and made a circuit of the square. She felt restless this evening. Presently she stopped by a seat, smiling at a burly, heavily-moustached man who was wearing a ginger sports jacket and flannel trousers as though he wasn't really comfortable in them. "Hello, Mr. Barratt," she said.

"Evening, Mrs. Quilter." The man's rather stem features relaxed in an answering smile and he moved along the seat. "How about resting your feet?"

"Thank you," said Julie. She liked Barratt. He was a sergeant at the police station in the square and was usually to be seen behind the counter taking particulars of lost dogs and handbags. It was actually a handbag that had brought them together. Off-duty, he was a Labour supporter in a discreet way and a great admirer of Laurence Quilter.

"Quite a good meeting," he said, motioning towards the crowd. For a policeman he sounded almost wistful.

"Not bad, is it? We've been hard at it all week, you know. Mr. Johnson thinks we're going to have a very close fight, next time."

"Does he?" Barratt stroked his moustache judicially. "Can't say I agree with him. Mr. Quilter's done well—he'll get back. That's what all the chaps in the Force think, anyway, and they keep their ears open."

"You're most encouraging."

"Well, Mr. Quilter's very highly thought of, particularly just now. Fine gesture of his, handing over the Hall and all that property to the Trust! Not many would have done it."

"Perhaps not. But I'm sure he'll get a lot of pleasure from seeing the place put to a good use."

Barratt nodded. "I dare say. Still, it must have been a wrench." Suddenly he broke into a chuckle. "I reckon old Lady Quilter would just about turn in her grave if she knew of it. She was a tartar! I remember going up there as a young constable to get some papers signed—she was a magistrate, of course . . ."

The sergeant, who was inclined to be terse behind his desk, became quite expansive. His reminiscences were so amusing that Julie would have much preferred to stay and listen, but her sense of duty told her that she'd been away from the meeting long enough and presently she bade him good-bye and rejoined the crowd.

The atmosphere had changed during her absence. Laurence was no longer describing and expounding—he'd become thrusting and aggressive and was attacking the record of the opposition with vigour. Julie knew that the climax was now impending. He recalled the situation in the thirties when the Tories had ruled—the long and deep depression, longer and deeper on this coast than almost anywhere; the endless dole queues, the heartbreak of idleness, the hungry children, the sense of desolation. His voice took on a note of passion, of quivering sincerity—it was as though the real stuff of him could no longer be contained. His face glowed, his eyes burned, and the words that poured from him had the eloquence of poetry. There was a moment of spellbound silence in the square.

Julie, too, was moved in spite of herself. It was always the same, she found—she would watch him for some time, admiring his technique and his patter, appreciating his knowledge and wit, but feeling completely detached herself. Then he would suddenly bare his soul—or seem to—and she would become an ardent girl again, stirred to the depths, ready to follow him in any crusade.

He was finishing now, for he was too good an artist to blur his exit line. As he got down from the platform, his face rigid with emotion, there was a burst of applause such as Blean had rarely heard. Joe Halliday climbed up to make a few announcements and the edges of the crowd thinned a little as someone began to take up a collection. Then questions were invited.

Quilter returned to the stand with the assurance of one well-practised in the cut-and-thrust of question-time. He expected an onslaught from the Tories, but to-night it was the Communists who proved most persistent and awkward. There was usually a sprinkling of them at his meetings and their attitude to him was bitter, perhaps because in his political adolescence he had been well-disposed towards them, and they now regarded him as a bit of a renegade. One of the most troublesome was a man who didn't look at all like the popular idea of a Communist—though, as Quilter knew, it was impossible to tell from appearances where a man's loyalties lay. He was a quiet, well-educated man of about thirty who always put his questions with a slightly lop-sided smile and went on smiling disconcertingly while they were being answered. At earlier meetings he had pursued Quilter with faintly insolent, faintly derisive queries about his family estates and the ethics of being a wealthy socialist. Since Quilter's arrangement with the Lakeland Trust, however, he'd had to change his ground, and for some time he'd been plugging away about the atomic plant. The Communists could do nothing effective to hold up production there, beyond fomenting an occasional strike, but at least they could spread alarm and despondency about the plant's safety. Quilter had already done his bit in helping to dispose of the rumours after a short briefing by the Minister of Supply. The air of Blean, he had explained, was quite harmless, since the factory chimneys had been built specially high in order to disperse the dust. The sea was quite safe for bathing, because the effluent was carried away in pipes a couple of miles long and there was a routine check on the water at every tide. Nor was there the least chance that all the men in the district would become sterile!

Those things had all been dealt with, but now the man, whose name was Granger, had thought up a new approach. "I am told," he said in his rather sneering voice, "that the milk yield is falling off in the dale farms. Can the Member say definitely that this is not due to some radio-active cause?"

Quilter ridiculed the notion. Everybody except a few cranks, he said, knew that no ill-effects came from the plant at all. The place was as safe as Blackpool.

"Pity it's not as cheerful," said Granger, earning his laugh.

Darkness was falling now, but the crowd still stayed. Julie knew how worn out Laurence would be, and longed for the end. She was sick of argument, sick of the sound of disputing voices. When one of the Communists raised the subject of re-armament and it looked as though an entirely fresh debate was going to start she felt like going in and dragging Laurence away. But even he seemed to be flagging now, and presently he stood down and allowed Joe to close the meeting.

Quilter's task was still not quite finished, for a few people were anxious to tackle him about personal problems. One had a pensions query, another a son in Malaya of whom he'd had no news for some time. The leader of a Boys' Club wondered if the Member could possibly address them in the autumn. Quilter listened and advised and said he'd try, while Julie scribbled down details in her diary by the light of someone's bicycle lamp.

At last they were free to go. Johnson, who had made twenty-four new members and was very cheerful, was as usual given a lift home to his semi-detached villa near the sea front.

"Well, good-bye, Adam," said Quilter as the agent struggled with his cratch. "A most successful campaign—congratulations!" He slipped the car into gear and then leaned out of the window again. "By the way—no more politics for a couple of months. I'm definitely in purdah till October."

Johnson laughed. "All right, Laurence, you've earned your holiday. Enjoy yourself. Good-bye, Mrs. Quilter."

Julie waved, and leaned thankfully back against the seat as the car moved off.

Chapter Two

The cottage where they lived was on rising ground about two miles from the sea and was approached by a narrow lane with many bends. Quilter drove slowly, his eyes straining to pick out the grass verge.

"God, I'm tired," he muttered.

"Would you like me to drive?" Julie asked hesitantly.

He gave a short laugh. "I wouldn't find that much of a rest."

Julie said nothing. After a while Quilter became impatient at her silence. "Well, how did it go?"

"Splendid, darling. You were marvellous."

His mouth, that had been curving downwards, relaxed. "It would be a pretty bad show if I couldn't handle an audience after all this time. Still, I *was* in good form tonight. I can tell at once, you know, how it's going to be—whether I'm going to hold them or not. To-night I could have done anything with them." For a time he drove with a contented look on his face, savouring again his little verbal victories. Then he gave an exaggerated sigh. "I wish to God it was going to lead somewhere, though."

"It will probably lead back to the House when the election comes, and that's the main thing, surely."

"You think so? It's not going to be much fun being a back-bencher all my life."

"Oh, darling, don't be absurd—you're only thirty-nine."

Quilter swung the wheel sharply as a small animal shot across the road. "I'm damn nearly forty, and that's a hell of an age, as you'll realise in ten years' time."

"Perhaps so, but it's different for you. A lot of men do their best work between forty and sixty."

"A lot of men die between forty and sixty! Anyway, other people get their chance. Clarke got the Dominions Office at thirty-six and Grigson became Parliamentary Secretary to the Ministry of Defence at thirty-two. And it isn't as though either of them is any bloody good. Clarke's just a rubber stamp—does exactly what his officials tell him."

"At least you haven't got T.B., as poor Grigson has. I wouldn't envy *him*—you said yourself he wouldn't last."

"No, he'll resign before the new Session. But I won't get the job, you'll see. Or any other job. It's pretty sickening when I think of the work I might be doing."

Julie fell silent again. She was accustomed to seeing Laurence with this sort of hangover after a particularly exhilarating meeting and there was nothing to be done except wait until it wore off. Of course, it *was* very frustrating to have been passed over so often. She often wondered why he hadn't been given a big job, instead of being palmed off with committee chairmanships and minor missions all these years. No one could doubt his capacity, and he had a fantastic store of nervous energy which could surely have been directed into useful channels. All the same, by political standards he *was* still young and his chance would probably come. If only he could be a bit more patient!

She sat gazing out of the window at the splendid park which the Quilter family had owned and cherished for three hundred years. The large round chimneys of Bleathwaite Hall were silhouetted against the rising moon.

"The ancestral home looks quite something to-night," said Quilter in a slightly mocking voice. He was often inclined to sentimentality, but never about the Hall. It reminded him only of an unhappy childhood, a dominated adolescence, a pattern of unwanted luxury and social rigidity which he had rejected the moment he could break free.

"It always looks lovely," said Julie, but she, too, spoke without regret. It had been a shock to her when Laurence had told her that he had decided to make over the estate to the Trust—had decided without even consulting her—but she had had to admit to herself that she didn't really mind. Living in one wing of the great house, with all the rest of it closed and untended, had never been very cosy. Besides, Laurence was so much happier without what he called "lackeys" around, and she could manage the cottage on her own. The Hall would make a splendid Youth Hostel.

Presently Quilter swung the car to the left over the ancient stone bridge that spanned the river Blea and they began to wind their way steeply through a limestone escarpment. The old station wagon made heavy going of the bill and Quilter changed down, noisily.

"This old tub's about had it," he muttered.

"I don't wonder," said Julie, her eye on the illuminated dash. "She's done close on seventy thousand. Why don't you use the Riley?"

"Oh, I can manage for a bit longer," he said with a long-suffering air.

They topped the rise and a moment later the cottage was caught in the headlights, nestling snugly in the hillside against a background of magnificent yews. It was an old farmhouse of native granite, roughcast and whitewashed, with grey-green tiles matching the fells and a squat square chimney built to defy the gales. Inside, it had been thoroughly modernised at great expense—too great, perhaps, considering how little time they spent there.

While Quilter parked the station wagon in the big stone barn, Julie went into the house and put the kettle on. When she took the tea into the living-room a few minutes later he was slumped in an armchair, brooding.

"What have you decided about to-morrow?" he asked. "Are you going to drive down?"

She sat down opposite him. "I don't think so—it's such a frightfully long way." She was going to Dorset to stay with friends for a few days. "I'll take the afternoon train and spend the night at the flat." He nodded, sipping his tea.

"You're quite sure you won't come?" Julie's wide brown eyes

dwelt hopefully on his face. "The Challoners would be so pleased, and it would be nice for me."

"You know I can't stand those people," he said almost petulantly. "Challoner talks the right stuff, but that's about all. If anything makes me sick it's to hear these comfortably-off blighters prattling their heads off about Socialism with a capital S."

"You're hardly in the workhouse yourself, darling, even if you have shed a little property."

"That's not the point, it's the attitude of mind. Challoner's a sybarite and he'll jolly well see to it that he always remains one. *I* don't give a damn what sort of conditions I live in as long as I've got work to do. In fact, I hardly notice."

"That's what you say, but there's soon trouble if things aren't just to your taste. *I* think you're rather exacting and I certainly wouldn't call you ascetic. Look at this cottage—look at the flat."

"I had the cottage done for you, as you very well know. Personally, I couldn't care less."

"Well, I wish you hadn't. I resent this idea that you're some sort of finer spirit with a mission and that I'm an earth-bound mortal who has to be indulged and pampered."

"I'm not saying that—but these things do matter to you, Julie, and they don't to me. Half the time I don't even notice what's going on around me, I'm so knotted up with thoughts of the job to be done. Challoner puts his comfort first, and there are too many like him in the Party. I'm constantly meeting men who used to spend their weekends on soap boxes at street corners and are now living off the fat of the land. The Front Bench is crawling with rich men—no, wonder we're losing support."

"You sound just like that awful man Granger," Julie said.

"It's people like Challoner who almost justify the Grangers."

Juke sighed. "If you talk like that in the House, I don't see how you can expect to get a post. It can't be a very popular attitude."

"I don't give a damn whether it's popular or not," Quilter said, scowling. "I'm fed up with keeping my mouth shut and toeing the line. If you want my frank opinion, the Party's corrupted. The whole idea of socialism is that people should get what they earn, including politicians—not what their fathers left them, or what they manage to fiddle on the strength of their office. When I hear some of these people talking complacently about the Welfare State as though they've created the Kingdom of Heaven, it makes me want to vomit. There's too much blasted charity about it, and pretty grudging charity at that. Even Challoner has begun to jib at necessary taxation, now that he's feeling the pinch. He'll probably end by joining the Tories. He's a political illiterate, anyway, and his wife's just a parasite . . ."

"All right, you needn't go on," said Julie. "I've got your point. You don't like my friends and you've no intention of trying to like them. You needn't say any more." She poured another cup of tea, turning her face away.

Laurence looked a little ashamed of his violence. "Now, darling, don't be difficult. I'm sorry if I went off the deep end, but I'm all worked up to-night. Anyway, yon know I *can't* come—I've got all this stuff to go through before we go away." He indicated a crate of old. papers and documents that had been sent from the Hall to be sorted.

"Just as you like," she said coldly.

"How about food—is there plenty in the house?"

"Yes, I think so."

"Fine! Not that it matters—I can always eat at the Plough, and anyway when I've cleared up this junk I'll probably do a spot of serious walking. The exercise will tone me up, and I'll be out of reach of that infernal telephone."

Julie nodded. "I expect you'll like being on your own for a bit. You'll behave yourself, won't you?—no solitary rock-climbing?"

"Oh, lord, aren't you ever going to forget that? Talk about an elephant . . ."

"It's just that it's so stupid to do that sort of thing." It had happened towards the end of the war, and it had been more than stupid. Laurence had brought a couple of colleagues to the Hall for the weekend—"climbing M.P.s" he'd said with a grin as he introduced them—and they'd had a shot at Scawfell Pinnacle. Laurence, an experienced and enthusiastic climber, had led the roped party, and Julie had sat on a grassy ledge below and watched their progress. At first Laurence had climbed with steady confidence—he'd been more than half-way up on a previous occasion and he'd studied the holds carefully. Then, by some piece of carelessness or misfortune, he'd dislodged a piece of rock and it had narrowly missed the head of Number Two on the rope. The incident must have upset him, for soon afterwards he had managed to get himself so precariously situated that he couldn't move and they'd all got into a frightful mess. For fifteen minutes he'd clung motionless to the precipitous rock, his nerve gone, and one of the others had had to climb past and belay higher up. It had been a humbling experience for Laurence and a terrible ordeal for Julie. But the stupid part had come later. The weekend afterwards, when Julie was in London, Laurence had gone out without telling a soul and climbed to the top of the Pinnacle alone. To get his self-respect back, he'd said.

He grinned now as he recalled the incident. "As a matter of fact," he said, "it happens to be one of the few things in my life that I've never regretted. A bit of a risk, perhaps—but other men were fighting, don't forget. Anyway, I'm really too old for climbing now—you needn't worry." He got up. "By the way, Julie, when you're in town you might ring Jane and make sure the tickets for France are in order." Jane Harper was his private secretary.

"Of course they will be—Jane doesn't make mistakes."

"Well, there's no harm in making sure. She's fixing my passport, too, and all the money business. I hate everything to be left to the last moment."

"You're telling me! You're an old fusspot."

"I know I am, but I can't help it." Quilter stretched and yawned. "Well, I'm going to bed. I think I'll go into the back room, darling—I've a feeling I'll take some time to get off and I don't want to keep you awake. All right with you?" He bent and nuzzled her cheek.

"Of course," she said in a carefully non-committal voice.

He put his hand under her chin and looked into her eyes. "Not trying to start anything, are you?" he asked with a smile.

"No."

"Well, thank God for that." He kissed her full on the lips, hugged her, and went off upstairs, his temper quite restored.

Whenever he bothered to think seriously about her, Quilter had to admit that he didn't altogether understand Julie. She sometimes had what he called "moods." For no apparent reason, she would become polite and rather strained and there'd be an atmosphere for several days until some remark of his would unleash a storm of anger and abuse and floods of tears. After that there would be a passionate reconciliation followed by a Julie all sweetness. On the whole, Quilter was inclined to put these emotional storms down to Julie's touch of southern blood, one eighth French and one eighth Italian, though he couldn't remember that she had been like that when they had first married. He didn't at all approve of the development—his idea was that the home background should be serene, so that he could give his undivided mind to the things that really mattered. Still, the outbreaks were well spaced, and he fancied that he was rather good at coping with them by now.

This time, in any case, there was no squall. The morning found Julie in a happy frame of mind—Quilter knew it as soon as he woke, for she had switched on the portable radio that he'd given her to lighten her domestic duties around the house and she never did that when she was cross with him. He also was in the best of humours it was a superb day, and he always reacted to the weather. He sang in his bath, shaved with sensual care before the open window, told Julie how well she looked in her new housecoat, and praised the coffee. As they sat over a cigarette after breakfast he read out bits from the budget of correspondence his secretary had posted on to him, adding pungent comments of his own, and even seeking her views. For Julie it was a rare pleasure to be able to linger with him at this hour, sharing the news as it came instead of having to drag it from him later when he was tired, or forgo it altogether. His good humour and evident desire to please had quite thawed her.

It was a heavy mail, for his activities and interests were wide-ranging, but there was nothing of immediate urgency and presently he threw the letters aside. "I'll deal with them after you've gone," he said. "Anyway, I've started my holiday."

For a while they sat outside in the warm sunshine, being lazy. The cottage had no garden to speak of, but it had something better—smooth grassy banks all round, sheep-nibbled and never requiring attention. Dry and fragrant, they made a perfect place for lounging. Here no sound could reach them from the valley and a shoulder of hill hid the red bungalows of Blean and the chimneys of the great plant. They might have been miles from civilisation.

It was Julie who got up at last, shaking out the folds of her housecoat. "This simply won't do," she said. "I've a load of things to clear up and then I must pack." She helped Laurence to carry the crate of papers out of doors and left him to them.

Quilter blew the dust of generations off the first packet and settled down to examine its contents. He had assumed that it would be rather a chore, this sifting of musty old family documents hoarded for no good reason that he could think of, but very soon his interest was caught. In addition to bills and estate plans, old newspaper cuttings and stock price lists, there were letters and diaries, citations and instructions, records of battles, floods and fires which in some cases dated back to the 17th century—an invaluable collection for anyone seeking source material. Most of Quilter's ancestors had helped in some way to shape the pattern of their country, as soldiers or statesmen, explorers or diplomats, and these old papers read like a roll-call of history. Quilter was fascinated. Several times he called Julie out to share some new discovery—once to read her a curious account of a civil riot outside the west wing of the Hall during which some yokels "breake into the house in the dead tyme of yesternighte with axes, handpeckes and crowes of iron . . ." There was a document, too, in the handwriting of a Quilter who had happened to be at Whitehaven when John Paul Jones had raided the port in 1778 and set fire to shipping there. It would have been easy to spend a whole morning studying such treasures, but Quilter's immediate and less exciting task was to pick out the papers which related directly to the Hall and the Estate. The Trust wanted to print a short historical review for the benefit of visitors and he had promised to let them have the relevant documents before he went on holiday.

He was still immersed when Julie announced that she was ready to go out for lunch. "Any more exciting discoveries?" she asked.

"Only that the original house on the site is supposed to have been built by William Rufus—I can't think what he was doing up here. Oh, and there's a furious account of an elopement in 1743, penned by the lady's father."

"What fun! But how is it that no one ever sorted out these papers before? I thought all old family archives were kept behind a glass case in the library."

"Evidently not. I did know one revolting family that had a record of everything every member of it had done since about 1880, and that *was* kept behind a glass case. The last half hour of each day was spent writing up little Willie's exploits in the family album. But people aren't as orderly as that as a rule. The usual thing is to stuff all the old documents away in the attic until the family's almost died out, and then the last of the line deals with them. That's me, in this case."

Julie nodded. War had taken its toll of the Quilters. Laurence's father, a professional soldier, had been killed on the Somme in 1916; his only brother, Francis, had died in the Spanish Civil War, fighting on what his mother had always sorrowfully referred to as "the wrong side." The old lady, disappointed in the end even over Laurence, would certainly never have had the heart to disinter the glorious past from a bundle of documents. She had died embittered, and totally unreconciled to the changing times.

"Well, I'd better go and clean up," said Quilter. Julie sat fingering one or two of the yellowing papers until he returned, and then they took the station wagon and drove down to the Plough to eat.

Over the meal, Quilter was full of their coming holiday. They had arranged to take the Riley across the Channel, and he was keen to make a tour of the Massif Central, which was new to him. He talked enthusiastically of places he had picked out from the Michelin guide and of possible routes, while Julie tried to look interested and kept her fingers crossed. Nothing in the world would make her happier than to have Laurence's undivided attention and companionship for three uninterrupted weeks, but she knew from past experience how politics could spoil all plans. Last summer they had been going to the Tyrol for a month, but Laurence had changed his mind at the last moment because some fellow M.P.'s were making up a party to study conditions in Germany. Julie had tagged along, and had seen lots of ruins and lots of other M.P.'s wives, but little of Laurence. Then at Christmas they had been going to Madeira, but that had fallen through too because Laurence had been made a member of a Commission that had been flown out to the West Indies to report on some troubles there. After seven years she had grown philosophical about it—if you married a keen and active politician you married his job, and it was useless to complain because you didn't see much of him except in a crowd. But perhaps this time they would be lucky . . .

Quilter suddenly became aware that she wasn't listening to him. "You do want to go, I suppose?" he asked with a touch of irritation.

"But of course!"

"I just wondered. It's going to cost a packet of money, so don't force yourself."

"Darling, don't be silly. You know perfectly well that you've quite decided where we're going, so there's no point in-my having any other ideas. In any case, I always like what you choose in the way of travelling. I shall love it, but it's not much use talking about names and places till we get there because they don't mean a thing to me."

Mollified, he gave a superior male smile. She was pretty hopeless with maps—always said "Right" when she meant "Left" and mixed up contour lines with footpaths and county boundaries with railways. The rest of the meal passed amiably.

"What about a stroll up the hill?" he suggested, as they got back to the cottage. "You've plenty of time."

For a moment she hesitated. She knew these strolls of Laurence's, that so often turned out to be exhausting half day excursions, but it seemed a pity to spoil that good humour.

"Yes, if you like," she said. "I'll just change my shoes, though."

There was really only one good way to start a short walk from the cottage. An old track, once the means of access to a lead mine higher in the hills, climbed smoothly up a protruding tongue of limestone that formed the extremity of the great mass that swept round the north of the Lakes from the Pennines. This was the way they went now, walking on the turf beside the track. Quilter was soon several yards ahead, moving with long springy strides. Every now and again he half-turned to shout some direction or warning-she must avoid a rut here, mind not to turn her ankle there. It was one of the ways, she supposed, in which he liked to mark his male superiority again, and it always slightly irritated her. However, she was glad enough of his support a few minutes later when they stopped on a steep rise to get their breath. The sudden halt after climbing made everything appear to be in movement, and for a second or two sky and green grass seemed to be swinging around her. Then the touch of vertigo passed and she was able to look out and down towards the coast. The sea was a pale blue, with a fine weather haze over *it;* the river sparkled pleasantly in its bed at the foot of the escarpment. Blean looked less garish at this distance. Only the plant seemed really out of place, a monstrosity compelling the unwilling attention. "What an eyesore!" she said.

He nodded. "Yes, they've certainly spoiled the view from here. Ah, well, I did *my* best." Quilter had been on a committee that had pleaded, but pleaded in vain, that the plant should be built farther up the coast. "We can always turn our backs on it, though. Excelsior!" He took Julie's arm and drew her snugly against his side, helping her up the slope. Her head came just to his shoulder. He seemed more aware of her now and presently stopped again and held her away from him, looking down at her.

"Well?" she said, her face tilted provocatively.

He grinned. "Not bad!"

"Do you love me?"

"You know I do."

"That's all right, then."

He kissed her, and sighed. "I wish we could do this oftener. I wish we had nothing whatever on our minds and no other people to bother about, ever. We're always happy when we're walking. Do you remember that day above Talloires ...?"

"Perfectly, my love. You said we'd just pop into the next field—and we climbed two thousand feet and walked eight miles!"

"So we did. What a brute I am! But you did damn well that day."

Julie smiled. It never occurred to Laurence that she was only pocket-sized and that the pace he set was rather gruelling, but she would always have endured anything rather than be left behind. "Anyway," she said, "it was worth it. I'll never forget that charming little chapel at the top."

"Nor I. Remember that pair of spectacles that some grateful pilgrim had left behind? Funny if he broke his neck on the way home!"

"What a macabre sense of humour you've got," said Julie. She took a deep breath. "Oh, darling, I do hope nothing happens to spoil our holiday this time ..."

"It won't. It's going to be the best ever."

They were just setting off again when a distant report reached their ears, and far below, in a field beside the Hall, a puff of smoke rose into the air.

"They must still be clearing trees," Julie said.

Like many other landowners, Quilter had been selling some of his timber to help defray the expenses of the Estate, and the stumps were being blown up to make way for the plough. "It's about time they'd finished," he said. "Still, it's the Trust's worry now, not mine."

"You know you'll think up something else to worry about," Julie said with a wry look. "Come on, if we're going to the top."

Once they were over the hump of the hill, the imperfections of the coastline were hidden and the view was magnificent. The distant fells were purple with heather and ling and far to the east the crags of Scawfell towered above the foothills. Quilter led the way to their favourite spot—a depression, a bowl in the limestone, warm and sheltered and tinder-dry, where two monolithic granite boulders, brought down by some glacier a million years ago, straddled the bed of an old watercourse now choked with scree. The Quilters called these rocks the Pikes, and on a hot day like this they gave welcome shade. Julie flung herself full length on the hospitable grass among the wild thyme and the cushions of saxifrage, stretching out her arms with a sigh of deep content. Quilter dropped down beside her and lit a cigarette. The peace here was undisturbed, for the hikers and tourists all concentrated on the more spectacular country inland and the local folk rarely had occasion to pass this way. Julie thought of it as their own special preserve, which indeed it was, for the hillside was part of the cottage freehold.

It was so pleasant lying there, and Laurence was in such a mellow frame of mind that Julie almost wished she hadn't to go away. In the end it was he who suggested that they had better make their way down again if she wanted to catch her train.

An hour later he saw her off from Blean station, settling her comfortably in a compartment which would be exactly in the middle of the train after it had been attached to the express on the main line. It wasn't likely that the train would crash, but choosing a carriage in the middle always seemed to him a sensible precaution.

The parting was casual. "Don't forget to drop me a line," he said, and gave her a perfunctory kiss. She waved once and he turned away, his mind already occupied with other things. As he drove back to the cottage, he was pleasantly aware of his freedom. It wasn't that he had any special plans, but it was a relief to be alone. Now he needn't talk or feel that he ought to talk; he needn't account for his moods; he needn't feel that he was being observed and studied and looked after; he needn't worry lest some unfortunate remark of his should touch off an explosion. Julie was fun to have around sometimes but he often found her presence irritating. Even the way she effaced herself on his account annoyed him on occasion. The trouble was, he thought, that like all women she was demanding, and the fact that he'd trained her not to show it didn't really make the atmosphere much easier. He really needed a mistress-housekeeper whom he could dismiss when he felt like it; not a wife who was always around.

He brewed some tea when he got back, and then settled down in a deck-chair to continue sorting the family papers. His first interest had waned, and the pile now seemed formidable. The sensible thing, he reflected, would have been to get Jane up here for a day or two and let her give them the once-over first. He could hardly do that now, with Julie away. Still, he certainly wasn't going to waste this fine weather—his body craved for exercise. He threw aside what seemed to be the inventory for an old sale and unfolded a sheet of stiff, parchmenty paper that crackled under his fingers.

For some time he studied it with a puzzled frown, turning it this way and that but not making much sense of it. There were two spidery drawings in faded ink—plans or diagrams of some sort—with the compass points marked in the bottom left-hand corner. In the bottom right-hand comer was a signature—"Joseph Quilter"—and below that the words "Bleathwaite Hall, September 3rd, 1855." Joseph Quilter—that must have been his great-grandfather.

He shifted his position so that the evening sun fell full on the paper. The top diagram, as far as he could make out, was a sectional drawing of a long, sloping cave with several chambers. The other one looked like a plan, a bird's eye view, of the same cave. Both were drawn without any indicated scale, nor were there any place names or reference points to show where the cave might be. Unless . . .

Quilter's interest suddenly grew. Those two jutting objects on either side of the entrance were surely the Pikes? They were very faintly sketched in, so faintly that he hadn't noticed them at first, but now that he looked carefully their shape was unmistakable. Could it really be that there was a cave like this, a whole underground labyrinth, almost on his doorstep?

He was greatly intrigued. He had never heard of any caves on the property, but then he had never heard until to-day of the rascals who had besieged the west wing with "crowes of iron!" Old Joseph would hardly have produced all this out of his head, and he had obviously gone to some trouble to preserve the record. Anyway, it would be amusing to stroll up the hill to-morrow and poke about a bit.

Quilter put the paper carefully aside and turned to a fresh bundle.

Chapter Three

The fine spell, so rare in the Lakes in August, still showed no sign of breaking next morning, and the wireless confirmed that the day would be hot and dry. Quilter breakfasted in the open, his *Times* folded against the coffee pot. Once again he felt in splendid humour—even the tenseness of the Cold War, on which he so often brooded, to-day left him quite unmoved. He chuckled over an amusing fourth leader and glanced down the correspondence columns to see if the silly season had produced anything particularly bizarre. He noticed that one of his colleagues—a Lancashire M.P. named George Walters—was making a fuss about some unprotected munitions dump in his constituency. A good vote-catching letter, but George was known to be a pacifist with a perennial grouse against the Services, so he wouldn't cut much ice higher up. Quilter poured himself some more coffee and thought for the hundredth time what a poor game backbench sniping was.

His mail was now beginning to accumulate and one or two things in the latest batch claimed his attention so that he had to postpone his walk for a while. Three constituency parties had sent invitations to him to speak in the autumn and Jane wanted instructions; a university wondered if he could lecture on "Problems of Federation in the West Indies," and a Sunday newspaper was anxious for him to review a book. Salmson, of the Foreign Policy Group, had sent a draft letter for circulation to the Press with a request for comments, and there were proofs of a propaganda pamphlet that Quilter had written for the Party's publicity department. Battersby, a left-wing colleague, wrote to say that Ames couldn't go to Yugoslavia in October after all and would Quilter like to go because if so he thought he could fix it. Quilter put that thoughtfully aside—he was far from "sold" on Tito, as some of his colleagues were, but it would be useful to see how things were shaping. In addition there was the usual batch of begging letters, formidable even after Jane had sieved them, and a considerable local post with various requests from constituents: Really", thought Quilter, it was a bit thick for August.

He dealt briskly with the most pressing matters, chiefly on the telephone, and by ten o'clock he felt free to turn to pleasanter. things. He spent a little time oiling his nailed boots, which he hadn't used since the Easter recess. Then he stuffed the one-inch map of the district into his jacket pocket, chose a stick from the rack, and set off up the hill. He hadn't gone more than a few yards before he remembered that he'd left Joseph's plan of the cave on the mantelpiece and went back to get it. The phone rang as he entered the sitting-room and he was soon caught up in a complicated discussion with the solicitors to the Trust. He got away at last, however, quite resolved that if the phone went again before he was out of earshot he would ignore it. He would have a quiet look at the site of the alleged cave, he decided, and then go on over the fells to Stickle Bridge, a comfortable nine miles before lunch.

He climbed steadily, delighting in the feel of rippling thigh muscle and glad that he could go at his own pace without distractions. For the most part he kept his gaze straight ahead—he was not one of those people who kept stopping to watch a bird or admire a flower or note some special beauty of colour or form in the hills. Walking to him was primarily a release, an outlet for his surplus physical energy. It was also a means of freeing his thoughts from the entangling worries of daily life. Sometimes he had tramped for miles in these hills without being able to remember afterwards a single detail of the route he had taken. Instead of observing he would become lost in day-dreams, composing speeches, conducting interviews, rehearsing bits of dialogue, making love and quarrelling. The life of his imagination was more active even than his real life, and far more complex. As he breasted the slope his lips moved a little, and smiles and frowns chased each other across his face. If he had met anyone he would have been thought eccentric, but he had the place to himself.

Once he reached the Pikes he became practical again. The investigation shouldn't take very long, for the crackling paper in his pocket left no doubt where the hole should be. Unless old Joseph had been dreaming, it was somewhere in the six-foot gap between those two massive stones. Now that he'd actually reached the familiar spot, Quilter thought it most improbable that he would find anything. To his eyes, no place could have looked a more unlikely site for a cave than this flat grassy expanse on the top of a hill.

He peeled off his jacket, rolled up his shirt-sleeves and began to throw aside the loose scree. It was a hot and unrewarding job, besides being hard on the fingernails, and he decided that if he found nothing in five or ten minutes he wouldn't waste any further time on it. Very soon he had quite a cairn of stones beside him and a considerable hollow at his feet. In places he had excavated to bare earth or solid rock, but in the centre there was a patch where the collection of loose stones seemed endless. This was suggestive, but it hardly promised success. It might well mean that there had been a hole there at some time but that it had become completely choked, like a filled-up well, and would take days or weeks to clear. The obvious thing was to get some of the men up from the estate and let them do the donkey-work. He was just on the point of abandoning the task when he uncovered a smooth granite boulder, some eighteen inches across. Beside this, and pressing against it, was another, smaller boulder and some big stones, all jammed tight.

He sat back on his haunches, considering the position. If only he had some sort of lever he might be able to move one of those boulders. He tried using the end of his stick but gave up for fear he might break it—it was an old friend, notched with the names and dates of various peaks and rocks he had "bagged" in his more leisurely youth. It seemed a pity not to make sure now; after all, he had plenty of time, and it would be rather amusing if he could lead Julie to a full-sized cave when she returned. In the end he went back to the cottage and found an iron bar among some old junk that the builders had left in the barn. He carried it up over his shoulder, thinking that this was an odd way to spend a morning.

Now that he was properly equipped he made good progress. Very soon he had prised away one of the stones and pushed the end of the crowbar into the soil well down under the smaller boulder. A piece of rock placed under the bar gave it leverage. At first everything seemed solid and immovable, but as he changed the direction of his thrust he saw the boulder shift a fraction of an inch and he threw all his weight on the lever.

Suddenly, the whole lot gave way. The jammed boulder jerked upwards and Quilter lost his balance and went sprawling back on to the turf. There was a long rumbling crash and a slithering of scree. When he had sufficiently recovered from his surprise to examine the results of his handiwork, he saw with a thrill of pleasure and no little amazement that Joseph had been right. At his feet there was a hole about the size of a flagstone, with jagged, yellowish-white sides, and it had absorbed without diffculty the two boulders, the crowbar, and a mass of stones.

Fascinated, Quilter peered down. It wasn't a vertical drop; it sloped away at an angle that offered an easy descent to any active person and at a depth of about eight feet it seemed to flatten out and become more of a passage—as the diagram, indeed had indicated.

Quilter had never done any underground exploration and he certainly wasn't organised for it, but by now his curiosity was thoroughly aroused and he felt he couldn't leave without a closer look. Very carefully he lowered himself down the hole, his feet finding good holds on the rough limestone walls, his fingers gripping handy projections of rock. His eyes took a little time to get used to the dim light, but his confidence increased once he had made sure that there was firm standing room at the bottom. A moment later he had reached the elbow bend, having suffered no more damage than a torn shirt.

He struck a match and bent low. The continuation of the hole was very narrow, a passage no more than three feet across, but it fell away in a gentle slope and was quite dry. He could come to no harm here. Too interested now to worry about the state of his clothes he got down on to his stomach, his head a little lower than his feet, and worked his way cautiously down the tunnel, stopping at frequent intervals to strike matches and see what lay ahead. The going was a little rough and the downhill position was uncomfortable but there was room enough to move without difficulty and the slope was still flattening out. Somewhere around here, if the diagram had been correctly drawn, there should be a big drop. He edged forward a few inches at a time.

Suddenly he reached a point where his outstretched hand could feel no ground ahead, but only empty space. The flickering light of a match failed to reveal anything at all in any direction. He wriggled back a little, found a loose piece of rock, and cast it into the blackness. There was a moment of silence and then there came a violent crash from the depths right beneath him, followed by the sounds of shattering and ricocheting.

Quilter drew back with a feeling of awe. This was something quite outside his experience and he wasn't at all sure that he liked it. Anyway, it was obvious that he couldn't go any farther. He worked his body round in the tunnel and a few minutes later he was clambering out into the bright sunlight.

Now that he was safely back on the surface, the thought of the chasm seemed less alarming. He lit a cigarette and sat down on the grass to study Joseph's diagram. The place must be of tremendous size, for the second drop indicated on the paper was shown as appreciably larger than the first. It would be most exciting to explore down there and it was evidently possible because Joseph had done it. It wasn't a thing he could do on his own, though—he'd need an experienced companion, someone who was really at home underground. Mentally he ran through the names of his climbing acquaintances, but none of them as far as he knew had had anything to do with caves.

He was still thinking about it as he resumed his walk, for the place had stirred his imagination. There were, he recalled, clubs that spent their whole time exploring holes in the ground—perhaps he could get in touch with one of them. Potholers, that was what the fellows called themselves. But he'd never heard of any of them operating in the Lakes.

Potholers! Half a minute, though, that did ring a bell—there *was* someone. That young fellow—what was his name? One of his own supporters, in a quiet way. Quilter could remember his features quite plainly, he'd met him at a meeting. And there'd been a letter from him in the local paper not so long ago, about some cavern in Yorkshire that he'd explored just before coming to the district—Quilter had noticed it because it had been printed just underneath a letter of his own. He could almost see the name on the cutting—it had begun with an A, something like Askey. No, not Askey—*Anstey*, that was it. Peter Anstey. And now Quilter remembered who he was, too—he was the science master at Coalhaven Grammar School. A pleasant, intelligent young man—just the type to be interested. It might be well worth while to get in touch with him.

Quilter's thoughts switched to other matters now and it wasn't until he got back to the cottage, in the late afternoon, well-lunched and pleasantly fatigued, that he thought of the pothole again. If he was going to do anything about it he ought to get hold of Anstey right away, but the question was how to find him. Through the headmaster of the school, perhaps, or—wait—he might be in the telephone book. Quilter fetched the local directory, ran quickly through the A's and found two Ansteys, but no Peter Anstey. He was about to look up the headmaster's number when he remembered that. Anstey was a newcomer to the district and might not yet be in the book.

He took up the telephone and confided his problem to the girl at Directory Inquiries. Almost at once she supplied the information he wanted—there was a Peter J. Anstey with a Coalhaven number. "Shall I connect you?"

"If you please," said Quilter.

He listened to the ringing tone, an expectant smile on his lips. He was wondering what sort of view Julie would take of pot-holing as an alternative to rock-climbing. In imagination he was already exploring the hole and triumphantly overcoming all its difficulties. He'd probably get quite a bit of local publicity out of the exploit—and that always helped. People liked their M.P.s to be physically active. That chap who sat for South Leicestershire—what was his name, Fothergill—his majority had shot up three thousand after he'd jumped into a canal to rescue a child from drowning. But that was a bit different, of course.

The ringing was interrupted by the girl's voice. "I'm sorry, there's no reply."

"All right," said Quilter, "I'll try later." He made a note of the number on the telephone pad and went out to the barn. He'd better do something about covering up the hole in the meantime—it wasn't very likely that anyone would walk up there after dark but a sheep might fall down it and anyway it was best to be on the safe side. He prodded about among the tools and timber, cement and paint, and presently found what appeared to be an old loft door, about two feet six square, which would just do the trick. He slung it in the back of the station wagon and drove slowly up the bumpy track. It proved to be an excellent lid and a couple of heavy stones placed on top of it ensured that it wouldn't be kicked or blown away.

Back at the cottage, Quilter tried the Coalhaven number again, and this time his luck was in.

"Peter Anstey speaking," said a crisp pleasant voice.

"Ah. This is Laurence Quilter. We have met, I think."

"Mr. Quilter! Why, hello, sir!" Anstey was friendly, but obviously puzzled.

"You're wondering why I've rung you. The fact is, Anstey, I seem to remember that you're interested in potholes ..."

"In what? I'm afraid I didn't quite get you."

"Potholes—you know—holes in the ground—caves and things."

"Oh, *potholes!* Sorry, I couldn't believe you really said that. Yes, I am, very interested. Why?"

"Well, I've found one. Practically in my own back garden."

"Really?" Anstey sounded a trifle sceptical. "You're sure it's not an old well or something like that?"

"Oh, no, it's the real thing all right. I found an old plan of it among some family papers—it's got several big chambers and it looks as though it might run for miles. I've been down the first bit of it but I got held up by a precipice. I wondered if you'd care to explore it with me—it's really a job for an expert."

"You bet I would—it sounds terrific. I knew there were some small caves over near Glaramara but I'd no idea there was anything of interest round your way. When would you like mine to come, sir—to-morrow morning?"

Quilter smiled at his keenness. "Why not?—as early as you like. You'll have no difficulty in finding me—my cottage is the only one above the Plough Inn."

"Right, I'll be there . . . By the way—have you done any potholing before, Mr. Quilter?"

"No, but I've done plenty of climbing—you'll find me quite safe."

"I'm sure of that," said Anstey apologetically. "I only asked because there *are* some people who lose their heads a bit—quite naturally if they're not used to it. What about equipment—shall I bring everything?"

"I'm afraid I've nothing here except a few lengths of nylon rope and an old torch. If you like, I'll bring the car over."

"No, that's all right, I've got a sidecar. I can pile all the stuff into that. Leave it to me. Now about this precipice . . ."

"There are two of them, actually, according to the plan."

"I see. Does it give any idea how deep the drops are?
I'd like to know because of the ladders."

"No, it doesn't give any measurements at all."

"M'm. Well, they can't be all that deep, I shouldn't think, We'll see how we go, Right, I'll be over about nine, then, Mr. Quilter."

"I'll pack up some food and be all ready for you."

"There is just one other thing—have you told anyone else about the hole?"

"Not yet. Don't you want me to?"

"Well, if it's all the same to you I'd like to keep it dark until we've explored the place. Once these things get around you never know who's going to barge in."

Quilter chuckled. "All right, Anstey, we'll keep it to ourselves."

"And thank you for ringing me, sir."

"It's a pleasure," said Quilter. "Thank you."

Chapter Four

He was beginning to wonder next morning whether something had delayed Anstey when the crackle of a motor cycle engine outside the bam announced his arrival.

"Hello, sir," he called, as Quilter went out to greet him. "Sorry I'm late—the bike developed a slow puncture and I had to stop and pump." He was an impressive-looking young man in his late twenties, dark and strongly-built, with a square cleft chin. His manner had a trace of shyness, but the older man soon put him at his ease.

"That's all right, Anstey, we've got all day. Nice to see you again. How's schoolmastering?"

Anstey grinned. "The holidays and weekends are pretty good."

"Yes, that's something I envy you—we politicians never seem to stop. Have you always been a schoolmaster?"

"Good lord, no. I was in corvettes, for six years." His glance followed Quilter's to the heavily loaded sidecar. "Lot of stuff, isn't there?"

"Staggering. Shall we really need all that?"

"We shall if the hole is anything like your description of it."

"You must have been up all night getting ready."

Anstey laughed, showing white teeth. "No, as a matter of fact most of it was already packed up when you rang. I was going over to Ingleborough to finish exploring a passage some of us opened up last week."

"I hope that doesn't mean I've upset your plans?"

"Oh, not at all, there was nothing fixed—just a casual arrangement that I might join the others if I were free. But this is new ground—I'm really looking forward to it."

"Well, come inside and see what you think of my greatgrandfather's drawing first of all. There's a spot of coffee left, too—we might as well finish it." He led the way into the sitting-room. "Here you are—this is the thing that put me on the scent. I'll leave you to study it."

When he returned with the coffee a few moments later, Anstey was still scrutinising the yellow paper, his eyes bright with interest.

"Yes, it could be quite a place," he pronounced at last. "Pity we don't know the scale, of course. I'd say it was a very rough drawing—we'd better not rely on it too much. Still, it's impressive—*most* impressive. Mind if I hang on to it for the time being?"

"By all means."

Anstey put the paper away in his wallet and gulped his coffee as though he could hardly wait to start. "How far away is the entrance and what's the going like? I suppose we'll have to do it, on foot and that'll probably mean two journeys."

"On the contrary, there's quite a good track all the way. I suggest we transfer the stuff to the station wagon as your bike's out of action. We'll be up there in a couple of minutes."

"Wonderful! A lot of holes are terribly inaccessible, you know, and the portage is often the heaviest part of the trip. I once had to borrow a donkey in France. Well, now, in that case we can change here—I've brought you a full kit. Half a minute, I'll get it." He went quickly out to the sidecar and was back almost at once with an armful of gear that included a couple of boiler suits of thick grey canvas.

"I think this one should fit you, Mr. Quilter. They're a bit clumsy, you'll find, but anything lighter gets cut to pieces. They're good for keeping water out, too, when there is any—see, they fasten at the wrists and ankles." He demonstrated. "What about footwear?" He glanced down at Quilter's rock-climbing boots and nodded. "Yes, that's the idea."

"How do you come to have all this stuff?" asked Quilter, working a patent fastener. "Spares?"

"It's club property, actually. I'm still the secretary of an outfit in Yorkshire." He turned Quilter round and inspected him. "Fine. Now the helmet." He picked up a steel helmet, rather like the ones that miners wear, with an electric lamp in the front. "The battery fits snugly inside," he pointed out, "so there's no chance of getting it wet."

Quilter looked at himself in the mirror. "It's a formidable kit, isn't it? I feel more like a commando than a politician amusing himself on a day off."

Anstey laughed. "You wouldn't go rock-climbing in carpet slippers, would you?"

"I wouldn't go rock-climbing at all at the moment—my wife's forbidden it. I'm afraid she'll hold you answerable if we don't emerge from this cave."

"Oh, that's all right, sir. Potholing's safe enough if you treat it with respect—it's the people who don't who give it a bad name." He tested the battery of his own helmet and slipped it on. It made him look very tough and businesslike. "Let's see, you've got the food, have you?"

"Right here," said Quilter, patting his haversack.

"Mind if I take a look? Sandwiches, chocolate, coffee—yes, that should keep us going. I've brought a bit myself, too. You can never be quite sure how long these trips are going to take."

"That sounds ominous. What's the longest you've known?"

"A hundred and sixty-eight hours," said Anstey. Quilter stared. "You're joking!"

"No, it happened. Don't be alarmed, though—that was quite exceptional. We were trying to link up two underground systems and it needed a full-blown expedition."

"Oh, I see—it was all planned?"

Anstey grinned. "All except the last sixty-eight hours! Well, sir, shall we go?"

Rather thoughtfully, Quilter followed him out to the sidecar and helped to transfer the remaining gear to the station wagon. "I should push the bike into the barn," he said. "It doesn't look as though it'll rain but you never know."

Five minutes later they jolted to a standstill at the top of the hill. Quilter scrambled out, walked quickly across to the Pikes and raised the loft door with the air a chef inviting inspection of a dish. "There you are," he said proudly. "Quilter's Hole!"

"And the green grass grew all around," said Anstey, getting down on his knees and peering in. When he looked up he was beaming with pleasure. "Well, that's a nice straightforward entrance. Let's see, now. . . ." He stood for a moment gazing at the dried up beck and then walked to the edge of the hill until he could look down into the plain. "Yes, it's most promising," he said when he returned. "Of course, I can see now—it's just the place for a pothole."

"Oh? It didn't strike me that way."

"Well, look at the contours—it's quite a basin we're standing in. The water would come rushing down here, with no obvious outlet, and in time it would find a way through the limestone. Carbonic acid, you know, and erosion, and there was probably some weak place to help it along."

Quilter smiled at his technicalities. "You ought to bring your boys up here some time and give them a lesson on the spot."

"Not likely," said Anstey. "They'd be down that hole like rabbits!" He took a last look round. "Right, let's get the gear out."

Quilter turned to the station wagon. Now that the moment had come he was aware of a slight reluctance. Perhaps it was something to do with the weather—it seemed a pity to leave the surface on such a perfect day, especially as the fine spell couldn't be expected to last much longer. Still, he certainly couldn't let Anstey down now. The mood soon passed and he started to unload.

There seemed to be more stuff than ever when it was spread out on the turf, and Quilter inspected it with interest and some surprise. There were three lengths of steel-wire ladder done up in separate bundles; three coils of nylon rope; some iron pitons with circular heads for the rope to go through; a small sledgehammer; a couple of sacks, and two powerful waterproof torches with spare batteries.

Anstey smiled at Quilter's expression. "Potholing isn't like rock-climbing, you know, sir—no aids are barred. I've even known people use tubular scaffolding." He stowed a host of smaller objecte into the capacious pockets of his boiler suit. Then he divided the bulkier stuff into two lots on what appeared to be some carefully thought out plan, and they took a sackful each. "Right, let's go," he said.

A moment later he had lowered himself into the hole, letting the sack drop as soon as he saw that there was a safe landing place. Quilter waited till he touched bottom and then followed him in. There was just room for the two of them to stand.

"So far, so good," said Anstey. He peered down the sloping passage. "You know this bit, of course, but I think I'd better go first." He pushed the sack ahead of him and wriggled his way head foremost into the tunnel as Quilter had done, his headlamp brilliantly illuminating the gradual descent. Quilter switched his own light on and found it most satisfactory. The going was very easy and he was close on Anstey's heels when the first precipice brought them up sharp. "This is where I stopped," he said, rather unnecessarily.

Anstey grunted and flashed his torch around, trying to find the opposite walls. "It's a big place," he said, "I can't see a thing." He took some old newspapers from one of his pockets and screwed them up into long spills. He was humming quietly—Oh for the wings of a dove! "Presently he was ready. "Can you squeeze a bit nearer," he said, "just in case there's anything worth seeing?" He lit the spills and dropped them one after another into the void. For a moment or two, as they flared, they lit up one side of the chasm, showing rough serrated edges of rock, horribly uninviting. For a while they wafted on air currents, burning brightly, and then they gradually flickered out.

"Not much help," said Anstey.

Quilter was still staring down, the smell of burned paper in his nostrils. "Horrible place! If there were steam rising I'd expect to see tridents!"

"I'll try for depth," said Anstey, who was now intent on the job.

40

He produced a coil of thin cord with a lead weight attached to one end, which he lowered carefully over the edge and slowly paid out.

"I threw a piece of rock over," said Quilter.

Anstey nodded. "I've had to rely on that method sometimes when I've had no plumb-line, but it's not very satisfactory. Somebody worked out quite a good formula—a Frenchman, I think it was—that gave pretty accurate results, but there's always the human element. The trouble is that the rock may hit something on the way down and then it slows up on the rebound and puts the timing out. Also it may dislodge other stones and then you don't know where you are. Of course, this doesn't always work, either—it depends which way the wall slopes." He was still paying out the cord, counting the knots at measured distances. Once the lead stopped as it caught on some projection but Anstey swung it free again with a jerk of the line.

"Sixty feet, so far," he said.

"Perhaps it's bottomless," murmured Quilter. "We'd be in a fine hole then!"

Anstey gave a little chuckle, but said nothing. A moment later the lead touched again and this time no shaking could dislodge it. "About sixty-eight feet," he announced calmly. "How do you feel about it, Mr. Quilter?"

"I'll tell you when we get to the bottom," Quilter said. Anstey rolled up the lead line and carefully stowed it away. All his movements were precise and unhurried. "We'll have to drive in some pitons to hold the ladder," he said. "Two, if possible. Can you go back a yard or two?"

Quilter gave him room and Anstey began to examine the rock floor. Presently he found a crack that satisfied him and drove one of the short steel wedges deep into the cleft, wielding the sledgehammer with difficulty in the confined space. Quilter, watching him testing the piton for firmness and then repeating the whole process in another cleft a little farther back, began to understand why exploration below ground took such a long time. Even the unrolling of the wire ladder, the avoidance of tangling, required deliberation and care. At last, however, it was in position, its top end made fast to both pitons so that if one gave way the other would hold. Anstey weighted the other end with a stone and lowered it into the darkness until it touched bottom.

Then, for the first time, he hesitated. "There's a bit of a snag at this point. If you went first, Mr. Quilter, I could lower you on a safety line—it's a sound precaution whenever possible. On the other hand if I go first I can hold the ladder for you and prevent it swinging, and if there are any unexpected difficulties I can let you know. What do you say?"

"I'm in no hurry," said Quilter. "Frankly, I think I'd sooner you did the reconnoitring. There's no danger of these ladders breaking, is there?"

"I've never heard of it happening. I wasn't thinking of that—it's just that the rope's a support if you happen to get a bit panicky. Still, I'm sure you'll be all right. I'll lead, then. Now here's the drill. I'll go down and take a look round. If everything's straightforward I'll give one blast on this whistle. When you hear it you'll let down the gear on a rope—you've got a ninety foot length in your sack. Make sure it's tied securely. I'll detach the gear and we'll leave the rope hanging. The second whistle will mean that you can came down yourself."

Quilter nodded.

"Don't hurry it. Oh, and be very careful how you move about near the edge—the biggest risk in this job is that who-ever's below may get knocked out by something, falling on his head."

"I'll be careful," said Quilter grimly. That was something he didn't need telling—the incident on the Pinnacle was much too fresh in his mind.

"I'm off, then—see you in the depths!" Anstey wriggled round so that for a moment his headlamp dazzled Quilter, and then he had grasped one of the rungs, found a foothold on the ladder and dropped below the edge. He seemed to have no nerves. Soon his lamp was no more than a pinpoint in the blackness.

In what seemed to Quilter a remarkably short time—a matter of minutes only—the first whistle came up eerily out of the chasm.

He had just finished knotting up the sacks. As he lowered them they swung once round the ladder and there was a check, but they soon came free again and reached the bottom in safety. The weight came off the rope and a second blast on the whistle gave him his signal.

He felt his pulse quicken a little and once again he almost wished he hadn't come. He was accustomed enough to sheer drops on the mountains in daylight—he had hung over many a precipice of more than sixty feet with nothing but the skill of his hands and feet to rely on. But it was a bit different trusting yourself to three millimetres of steel wire in a pit of darkness. He thought of what would happen if the ladder broke or the pitons became dislodged—he *had* to think of it. It was his way to suffer in imagination all the pangs of disasters that never happened. It was the same when he was driving a car or travelling by plane—he always had to live through the crash that might come as a way of insuring himself against fear. Once he had done that, he was all right. The thought that always troubled him was that he might be caught off guard, mentally unprepared, and fail in a crisis. That was what had happened on the Pinnacle.

It would never do, though, to let Anstey sense his hesitation, and in a moment or two he had braced himself. The pit could do its worst. He turned as Anstey had done till his legs overhung the edge, groped for a rung, and committed himself to the ladder.

It felt much safer than he'd expected, once he'd accustomed himself to the thinness of the wire and the very slight swaying motion, and for the first few yards he made good progress. Then he ran into a bit of trouble. For some distance the rock wall bulged outwards like a nose so that the ladder pressed close against it and made toe-holds difficult. He took his time, and presently cleared the hazard as the wall turned in again. The point of light that was Anstey was getting larger every moment and as his confidence increased his pace quickened. Four minutes after his take-off he stepped down on to the floor of the chasm, pleasantly conscious of a sense of achievement.

"Nice work," said Anstey approvingly. "Now let's see where we are." Both men flashed their torches round the chamber, probing the rough rock surfaces with strong beams of light. They appeared to be at the bottom of a funnel-shaped hole which narrowed where they stood to no more than ten feet. The walls were jagged, with a dry yellowy-white hue. The silence was absolute. Quilter was surprised to find that the air, though fresh and cool, was not unpleasantly cold.

Anstey began at once to make a tour of the chamber, inspecting every crevice. "There's always a chance we might find something that your great-grandfather missed," he said hopefully. However, there seemed to be no exit except the one marked on the plan and presently they continued on their way.

There was a crawl ahead of them now, along a passage about three feet wide and hip-high. The sharp rock floor was hard on the knees, and the sacks that they rolled ahead of them tended to catch on jutting fragments, but otherwise the going was straightforward enough. For twenty yards the tunnel ran almost horizontally. Then it took a downward plunge, not precipitously but steeply enough to make caution advisable. Anstey, taking no risks, stopped to drive in another piton at the top of the dip and fix a rope to steady them as they descended. "We'll be glad of it on the return journey, too," he said.

As he ceased to hammer, and the echoes died, Quilter said sharply, "What's that?"

They crouched motionless, listening. From somewhere far below came a hoarse murmur, a vibration rather than a sound, which they hadn't noticed before.

"Water!" exclaimed Anstey in a tone of excitement. "A watered pothole in the Lakes! This is more than I'd dared to hope for."

A few minutes' slithering and scrambling down the slope brought them to a flattish ledge beyond which was darkness. Kneeling there, with their lights flashing ahead, they saw that they had come to the second of Joseph Quilter's precipices.

This time, it took longer to prepare for the descent. The lead, it seemed, would never touch bottom, and when finally the cord went limp even Anstey looked a little awed. "I make it a hundred and twenty-five feet," he said. "This is going to take us some time."

The ledge, though wide enough to accommodate several people, offered no crevices suitable for the pitons and Anstey had to climb back up the slope for several yards before he found a place where he could anchor the ladder. Quilter watched his assured, deliberate movements with admiration, thinking how fortunate he had been in his choice of a companion.

At last the new ladder was securely in place and Anstey lowered himself over the edge. "Same drill as last time," he said, "except that I'll wave my torch when I'm ready for you instead of blowing the whistle. At that depth you might not hear it."

Quilter lay on his belly, watching the first few yards of the descent, and then he waited as patiently as he could for the "All clear." When at last it came, lowering the gear took an age and going down himself much longer than the first time. Forty yards of ladder was far too much for Anstey to hold taut from the bottom, and the swing was most disconcerting. Quilter tried to concentrate on the rungs and forget the vastness of the space in which he was dangling, but it was difficult with that vibrating sinister buzz in the air. It was with a sense of unalloyed relief that he finally touched bottom.

Once they began to shine their torches around he lost all trace of nervousness in the thrill of discovery. This was an infinitely more exciting place than the Funnel Chamber. A stream of water gushed from a great rift in the wall some twenty feet above their heads and broke in spray on the floor of the cavern, filling the air with a fine mist that clouded Quilter's glasses. As, he turned, a cluster of stalagmite was caught in his head light. The upper chamber and passages had seemed dead, finished, abandoned, but this one was alive.

"We must see more of it," said Anstey. He groped for a length of magnesium tape and Quilter heard the scratch of a match. Suddenly a dazzling white glare rent the darkness.

Quilter caught his breath in wonder at the spectacle that suddenly opened up before them. The cavern was so vast that a church would have been lost in it. The roof, even in that brilliant light, was too high to be visible. The walls, instead of rising sheer and plain, climbed fantastically in weird limestone formations, one behind the other, higher and higher, like the scenery in a fairy pantomime. There was a whole landscape here, marvellously sculpted and infinitely varied and glowing with an amber lustre.

The two men stood rooted beside their puny ladder, drinking in the scene while the light lasted. Right ahead of them there was a great bunch of stalactite that looked like a petrified waterfall, and beside it a rock cascade polished to smoothness by erosion and furrowed from top to bottom by gigantic, flutings. From a high cleft hung a mass of snow-white curtains, wrinkled fabrics that looked as though they had been checked in motion by a magic wand. There were pedestals and obelisks and organ pipes, carved and chased into exquisite reliefs, and tortured rocks in unlikely, unbelievable shapes. The whole scene gained added impressiveness from the sense of space and utter remoteness, and from the water which had built up its own clay and pebble dams so that it lay in wide motionless pools that reflected and doubled the beauty of the rocks.

Then the light went out.

"You know, I wouldn't have missed that for anything in the world," said Anstey in a hushed voice, as though he were talking in a cathedral. "What a find! What a *terrific* find!"

"I'd no idea-there were such places," said Quilter soberly.

"It's like being on an entirely new planet. It's staggering . . ." He broke off and laughed, a shade unsteadily. "My head's quite fuzzy with adjectives."

"At least," said Anstey with satisfaction, "you know now that there's more to potholing than wriggling along tunnels on your belly. This is why it gets hold of people—this is the reward that makes all the effort and discomfort worth while. All the same, you don't see a chamber like this very often, not in England." He picked up his sack. "I can hardly wait to find out what happens next. Let's follow the stream and see where it goes. Watch your step, now."

They began to cross the floor of the chamber, walking beside the string of dammed-up pools. The ground was very uneven, with slabs of soft slippery clay lying treacherously between young growths of stalagmite that snapped and crackled under foot. Once they were held up by a grille of translucent rods and several times they had to make detours round major obstructions, but their general direction was indicated by the flowing stream and there was no danger that they might lose their way. Anstey plodded ahead, cool, observant, picking his steps. Presently they reached the opposite wall of the chamber and the stream narrowed and led them into a new passage, wide enough and high enough to permit them both to walk upright side by side. The water, for all the disturbance that it had made in falling, now lay shallow in its bed beside them, its current barely perceptible.

"This is what I call caving in comfort," said Anstey as he shouldered his sack and plunged into the runnel. The conditions were indeed not only easier now but far more interesting, for in the confined space their torches and headlamps effectively illuminated the walls and roof and they could see all there was to be seen. There was one place where the rock was sheeted with crystalline enamel; another where Anstey's torch revealed splash deposits of exquisite delicacy and loveliness. There were coral-coloured bowls gleaming with limpid water and opaline limestone flowers glistening, and sparkling in rock niches. At every step one or other of the men would brush away long vitreous threads that hung like hairs from the roof or snap the slender spikes of purest calcite that bristled from the walls. It was like walking in an enchanted kingdom.

They had lost track of the distance they had covered when the passage suddenly opened into a third cave, much smaller than the Cascade Chamber. Anstey lit another flare, but the place was comparatively dull, or else their sense of wonder had become blunted. They pressed on along the continuation of the tunnel, which now ran almost level and seemed interminable. They had been walking for at least a quarter of an hour, never leaving the stream, when round a bend the passage widened into yet another chamber and they were brought up sharp against a blind rock face.

They dumped their gear and Anstey bent over the plan, seeking guidance. Quilter glanced at his watch and saw to his amazement that the time was nearly half-past one.

"According to your great-grandfather," said Anstey after a moment, "there ought to be two passages leading out of here. I wonder where they are." He stuffed the wallet back into the loose pocket of his overall. "Anyway, we can soon see where the stream goes." He started his familiar exploratory prowl, following the little rivulet away to the left. Presently Quilter heard him give a sharp exclamation and went quickly to see what he had found.

"It looks as though there's been a fall," said Anstey, indicating with his torch. There was, indeed, no visible opening. Instead, there was a mound of stone and rubble, into the interstices of which the stream disappeared without fuss.

"Well, there's certainly no way through there," said Quilter. "I wonder when it happened." Anstey was looking thoughtfully at the choke of debris.

"It may not extend very far into the passage, of course. It looks as though we'll have to do a bit of excavating."

"What—now?" Quilter was aghast.

"No, no, not now," said Anstey with a laugh. "We'll be quite tired enough when we get back as it is, and besides, we've no tools. Still, I should like to know what happens to that stream if it's at all possible. "He turned away regretfully and directed his torch once again at the sloping rock face. "Now where's this other exit?"

Quilter brought his own light to bear and together they swept the surface. "Hold on, I think I see something," cried Anstey after a moment. "Look—that dark patch." He started to clamber up the face, which offered quite good footholds, and almost at once he gave a shout of triumph. "It's a bit narrow," he called, "but this is it all right."

Quilter joined him on a little platform about ten feet up. There was a hole, certainly, a hole large enough at the entrance for a man to kneel in, but it rapidly funnelled until it was no more than eighteen inches in diameter.

"If you ask me," said Quilter, "we've had it."

Anstey was already investigating. "I don't see why. After all, your great-grandfather must have got through or he couldn't have drawn the plan."

Quilter made a wry face. "I'm beginning to get rather tired of my great-grandfather. Anyway, men were smaller in those days."

"I've negotiated tighter places." Anstey's tone was matter-of-fact, with no trace of boastfulness.

"Have you really? It's no bigger than a drain pipe."

"You'd be surprised what a small space the human body can be squeezed into. It's on record that seven potholers once passed through a pipe only nine and a half inches wide ..."—he grinned—"... sideways, of course."

"Pretty horrible to get stuck."

"That doesn't seem to happen in practice. You can-always wriggle out somehow. Still, it's not everyone's cup of tea, I suppose." He emerged from the entrance. "Let's have some grub and then we'll see how fresh we are."

"Good idea," Quilter agreed, and followed Anstey down the face with relief. He hadn't realised in the excitement of their progress how hungry he'd become or how much energy he'd used up. He felt anything but fresh, and found himself envying his companion's tireless vigour.

They spread the sacks on a flattish boulder for a seat and set to on the sandwiches. It was quite the strangest picnic that Quilter had ever had, but he found that the eerie surroundings gave an added zest to the meal. The air was cool and clean, the murmur of the stream a pleasant accompaniment. What a story he would have to tell Julie!

Anstey was still gazing up at the pipe as he munched and it was evident from his manner that he would leave it unexplored only with the greatest reluctance. "I imagine," he said thoughtfully, "that once upon a time the stream must have run through that passage."

Quilter looked at him in astonishment.

"Oh, it could have done, you know—a few hundred thousand

years ago. In fact there's no other way the passage could have been made. The original level of the floor must have been up there and the water must have carved the rock away and eventually found a new channel lower down. You have to take the long view at this game."

"Not a thing I was ever very good at, I'm afraid," said Quilter. "I like quick results." He poured some coffee from a vacuum flask. "I wonder where we are exactly. We must have come a hell of a long way."

Anstey nodded. "I'll do a survey on the way back, if we're not too worn out, and then we'll know."

"A survey, eh? Isn't that rather difficult?"

"Not really—just a bit wearing. It's well worth the effort, though—I'd say one of the chief pleasures of potholing is plotting the data afterwards—in comfort!" He looked inquiringly at Quilter. "How do you feel now, sir?"

"Quite restored, thanks. I'd like a cigarette, though, before we move. What about you?"

"Good idea," said Anstey. They lit up, and sat watching the smoke writhing away in the headlamp beams.

"You know," said Quilter, "what amazes me is that that tiny hole by the Pikes should be the entrance to such an enormous place. When I think of the times I've sat up there, quite sure that I was on *terra firma!*—and actually there's only a crust with all this emptiness underneath. Queer feeling!"

"Yes," Anstey agreed, "that's one of the exciting things about potholes, the tiny entrance and the huge ramifications. If ever you get a taste for speleology you should have a look at the Eastwater cavern in the Mendip. It's one of the most formidable cave systems in the country—I believe there's a total drop of something like 700 feet over a distance of three miles—but the original entrance is just a tiny sink hole with an insignificant brook trickling into it."

"Fascinating!—no wonder these places take so much finding. All the same, you know, I'm surprised that a cave like this should have been lost sight of once it had been discovered."

"Perhaps no one else knew about it except your greatgrandfather.

Cave owners can be very jealous about their little kingdoms—he may have kept the secret. Even if he didn't, local knowledge wouldn't necessarily be handed on. It's quite common for really well-known pots to be lost for generations. We know vaguely about dozens that we haven't been able to find."

"But they do come to light occasionally?"

"Oh, yes—like this one. Sometimes an old record turns up, as in your case, but more often it's some-incident that gives them away. Perhaps a farmer loses an animal and goes searching for it and finds an unexpected hole, or a heavy storm washes away debris or there's a landslip or something. One pot was discovered when a man was blasting rock for a cattle trough. It's even been known for a pothole to be given away by steam rising from the vent in winter, when the air's colder outside,"

"Really? Most interesting." Quilter stubbed out his cigarette. "Well, do we go on?"

Anstey hesitated. "Frankly, I think you've done enough for a first attempt, Mr. Quilter. I wouldn't want you to be laid up on my account. I was thinking—would you mind if I left you here for a little while and had a shot at the pipe myself? I'd be back in—well, say an hour."

Quilter looked up at the pipe. He had little stomach for it, but he certainly wasn't going to let Anstey know. "What do you think I am?" he said with a grin, "too old at forty? I'll come. At least, I'll start."

"Are you quite sure you won't be overdoing it? We've got to get back up those ladders, don't forget."

"I'll come, I tell you. Lead on!"

"Very well," said Anstey. "We'll go just a little way in. We may as well leave the gear here—we shan't be wanting it. If we have any trouble we'll call it a day."

A few moments later they were back on the little platform. "The thing about this pipe-crawling," Anstey said, "is to go slowly, keep cool, and try to prevent your clothes from ripping on the sharp bits. It's much simpler than it looks."

He got down on his knees and crawled into the hole. The floor proved to be dry and sandy, which made the going easier. Quilter followed him in. Almost at once he had to drop flat on his stomach, his arms fully extended ahead and his legs trailing behind. The roof was too low even for caterpillar progress—the only way to move forward was to push with his toes and pull with his hands, gradually easing his body along. Progress was very slow, and after five minutes of hard struggling they didn't seem to be getting anywhere. Quilter began to think of the journey back, feet first, and his fears warred with his pride. He was on the point of calling out that he'd had enough when the glow of Anstey's head-lamp suddenly faded.

"Hello," he called sharply. "Are you all right, Anstey?" A muffled voice came back. "Yes, I'm all right. There's a twist in the pipe and it gets narrower. I'll see if I can make it. Hold on!"

Quilter stopped to rest for a moment, but curiosity and dislike of being left alone in this place spurred him on. He reached the bend, and his body curved like a bow as he squeezed round on his side. The bend straightened, the pipe flattened, the rock pressed down, the walls closed in. At every point, now, the canvas of his overalls touched, and as he moved, his helmet scraped along the roof so that he had to lower his head almost to the sand. He could see nothing but Anstey's boots. This was madness! The thought that one of them might get stuck returned in full force. He should never have come!

"Anstey," he cried, "how the devil are we going to get out of this?"

"It's all right," Anstey's voice came back cheerfully, "the pipe begins to widen out here. Take it easy—we've almost made it."

After a few more feet the roof lifted and the intolerable sense of pressure eased. Anstey was moving faster now. Very soon Quilter emerged behind him into a low dry cave, ten feet high and thirty or forty wide.

Anstey gave him a slightly anxious look, "All right, Mr. Quilter?"

Quilter took a deep breath and wiped his forehead. "Yes, I'm fine. My word, that ought to be good for the waistline."

"It was a bit tight," Anstey admitted. "I expect there's more sand than there used to be." He flashed his torch around. "Well, we seem to have reached the end of this particular road."

There was, indeed, no outlet from the cave—if the stream *had* ever run through here, the exit had long ago become closed. The place felt quite cosy after the vast sonorous caverns they had passed through earlier. They seemed to have moved out of the limestone now—the texture of the rock walls was quite different here, much sandier, and of a bright red colour.

"I say—look!" called Anstey suddenly, as the beam of his torch probed the walls. Just below eye level some initials had been carved deep in the soft sandstone. "J.R.Q." he read out, and smiled. "Your great-grandfather must have been quite a chap."

"In my considered view," said Quilter, "his great-grandson is quite a chap too! I think I'll add my own initials." He took a knife from his pocket and hacked a rough "L.T.Q." underneath. Anstey, who didn't normally approve of cave defacement, watched him tolerantly. "You've done damn well, sir. I congratulate you."

They rested for ten minutes and then began the return journey. Now that all the difficulties were known Quilter no longer felt any apprehension. They moved slowly, for Anstey had begun his survey of the route. In the pipe he used the length of his outstretched body as a standard of measurement; pushing a notebook ahead of him along the sand and occasionally making an entry. Where the pipe twisted he took compass bearings. For the long tunnels he produced a surveyor's tape and where there were gradients to record he enlisted Quilter's help to take angles of sight. In the big chambers he took a straight line across the floor, leaving the more detailed survey for later. From time to time he checked the depth with his aneroid. He was completely engrossed, and Quilter almost forgot his tiredness in the interest of the work.

The climb out of the Cascade Chamber was exhausting, but without incident. At the top of the precipice Anstey looked at Quilter as though for instructions. "What about the ladders? I'd like to come back and trace that stream, in which case we should leave everything."

"Of course we'll come back," said Quilter.

It was almost more than he could do to drag himself up the second ladder. His feet felt like lead, his arms as though they would slip from their sockets. When they finally scrambled out into the warm air it was nearly eight o'clock—they had been underground for nearly nine hours. They looked it, too, for both men were plastered with clay and sand and their hands and faces were filthy.

"You'll spend the night at the cottage, of course," said Quilter as he put the lid back on the hole and climbed in behind the wheel of the station wagon. "We'll have a couple of stiff whiskies and a bath and then I'll open some tins." He let in the clutch and the car began to bump down the track. "Well, that was certainly a great experience!"

Chapter Five

Quilter's recipe for recovery proved an excellent one. The whisky revived them, the hot water soothed their aches, and Quilter's scratch meal was quite a triumph. When, at nine-thirty, he joined Anstey in me garden for a last cigarette before bed, he felt relaxed and at peace.

"So you think my pothole's a good one?" he said, sinking into a deck chair with a sigh of content.

"By English standards it's superb. Not as deep as some, of course, but it's got everything. It'll be a sensation when people get to know about it."

"You think so?"

"Undoubtedly. In fact, I'd like to bring some of my club members over before the rush. Could I do that?"

"Naturally, my dear fellow—I'd be delighted. Any time you like. After all, it's really a place for experts. I can't imagine the general public taking much interest—not with those precipices. It's rather a pity—I might have made a fortune charging half a crown a time!"

"It would certainly be worth half a crown of any tourist's money if you could get them down there."

"I suppose you don't really approve of commercialising these places?"

Anstey laughed. "Oh we don't mind—there are plenty to go round. I don't like to see them pillaged, of course."

"How do you mean—pillaged?"

"Well, people crack off the stalagmite growths and take them home. Sometimes caves are completely ruined. In Ireland in the Hungry Forties I believe people stripped quite a number and sold the stuff as ornaments. But some of these places are so incredibly spectacular that it would be a shame not to let visitors in. Electric light can work miracles down below, you know—you get the most stupendous effects. There's a magnificent hole at Padirac in the Dordogne with two lifts and boats on an underground river. It's breathtakingly lovely—quite unforgettable."

"Padirac? I must make a note of that. I expect you get around quite a lot?"

"Yes, I do. I've explored a bit in the Pyrenees and Italy, and in Ireland. It's completely gripping, you know—you simply can't stop. And the tougher the hole, the more eager you get."

"How does this one compare in difficulty with some of the others you've explored?"

"I'd say it was pretty straightforward on the whole. Of course, those drops are rather sensational and they need care, but we were never really uncomfortable, let alone in any danger. There are some shocking places, you know—pots that you can't get into without getting soaked through and where there's always a hell of a draught. Going down a ladder under a big waterfall is about the worst thing I know. Still, don't misunderstand me—I'm not saying to-day's trip was all that easy."

"No, let's not call it easy," said Quilter, who was still enjoying the feeling that he had acquitted himself pretty well. He chuckled. "Did you ever see that entry in the Visitors' Book over at Scawfell? Someone wrote: 'Ascended the Pillar Rock in three hours and found the rocks very easy.' Someone else wrote underneath: 'Descended the Pillar Rock in three seconds and found the rocks very hard.'"

Anstey laughed. "Yes, it's bad to be over-confident. These places have a way of getting back at you if you don't treat them with proper respect."

They sat silently for a while in the sultry air, watching little tongues of lightning playing over the sea. Presently Quilter said, "Are you seriously planning to excavate that passage?"

"I don't see why not. It should be a fairly simple operation."

"Is that part of the potholer's routine—digging?"

"Yes, it often has to be done. A really hard-bitten potholer will never give up until he's absolutely certain that it's impossible to go any farther. Sometimes digging isn't enough, of course—you may get held up by an obstruction of rock, and then you have to use explosive. Still, in this case it's all small stuff and pretty loose."

"What tools shall we need?"

Anstey considered. "It's really a question of what we can carry. I should think we might manage a crowbar, a pick and a shovel between us."

Quilter nodded. "I think I can supply those. When shall we go—to-morrow?"

"That's up to you, sir."

"I'd like to—I find this physical exertion a most pleasant relief from routine worries. I happen to be free just now, too—and I'd prefer to get the exploration over before my wife returns."

"That's something I don't have to worry about," Anstey said with a smile.

"Well, you're wise to make the most of your freedom. How long do you think it'll take us to clear the block?"

"That's hard to say. You can sometimes spend a whole day on a job like that and get nowhere. Still, we should have plenty of time—we shall get down much more quickly now the ladders are fixed and we know the route."

"And this time there'll be no pipe to squeeze through, thank goodness—though even that doesn't seem so bad in retrospect." Quilter drew reminiscently on his cigarette. "In fact, you know, one of the things that has surprised me most about the place is how much less frightening it is than I'd expected. Of course, it's majestic and awe-inspiring, there's no doubt about that, but when I'm there I don't feel as though I'm in a gloomy, terrifying place. Actually, it's remarkably comfortable."

"I can think of worse camping spots. I told you about that time I spent a week underground—well, we had a couple of tents then, pitched on a ledge nearly a thousand feet below the surface. We fastened the guy ropes to boulders, you know, and had sleeping bags and all the rest of it. Not bad at all."

"H'm. I think the darkness would get me down in time—and

that eternal trickle of water. By the way, have you any theories about where our stream runs to?"

Anstey shrugged. "What does the poem say? 'Even the weariest river winds somewhere safe to sea.' If we have any difficulty we'll throw some colouring matter into the water and see if we can find the exit that way. I thought at first that it might join the river Blea at the bottom of the hill, but we were actually too low for that. The limestone obviously dips below the coastal sandstone, so it's quite possible that our stream keeps underground until it's forced up into the sea below low water-mark."

"I didn't know that could happen,"

"Oh, yes, there are several precedents. Fresh water from Mendip comes up in the Bristol Channel, and several rivers emerge in Galway Bay after disappearing on land."

"We live and learn." Quilter stretched and got up. "Ah, well, we'd better get some sleep if we're going to have a big day to-morrow. You know your room, don't you? Good-night, Anstey."

"Good-night, sir."

For once, Quilter was not troubled by the insomnia of which he so often complained. He was asleep in a matter of seconds, clubbed by fatigue, and knew nothing more until morning. He awoke refreshed and pleasurably expectant. It was good to have plans, and a companion as congenial as Anstey. They should have a splendid day again.

He found Anstey already up, sitting at the kitchen table in his shirt-sleeves working on a new plan of the pothole from his survey data. Judging by the progress he had made he had been at it some time. He had also washed up the considerable accumulation of used crockery which Quilter had piled into the sink.

"My old naval training," he said. "Hope you don't mind."

"Not in the least. There'll be less for me to do on the last day!" He glanced over Anstey's shoulder. "I say, that's a very professional-looking job."

Anstey regarded his work with some pride. "Not bad—better than the original, anyway. I'm afraid your greatgrandfather telescoped some of those tunnels quite a bit."

Quilter smiled. "You know, I had that feeling when we were walking along them." He bent over the new plan. "What scale are you using?"

"Six inches to the mile. It makes it a bit unwieldy, but it does mean I'll be able to superimpose it on the ordnance sheet. Do you happen to have one?"

"I think so, somewhere."

"Good. Then to-night we'll be able to see exactly where we've been. I'll be through in another fifteen minutes."

"You go ahead," said Quilter. "I'll get breakfast. Sleep all right?"

Anstey grinned. "Can't say I remember."

Quilter boiled some eggs and made coffee while Anstey went on with his methodical measuring and calculating. Presently the postman arrived with the usual heavy mail. Quilter put it all aside except for a letter from Julie and he only skimmed through that. She seemed to be having a good time and she sounded quite cheerful.

The telephone started ringing again soon after breakfast and it was nearly eleven o'clock before they got away. Quilter managed to find a pickaxe and shovel in the barn, as well as the crowbar he had used as a lever the day he'd discovered the hole. The rest of the gear now went comfortably into one sack. With a feeling of escape, Quilter threw the stuff into the station wagon and a few minutes later they were back at the Pikes. The air was even closer than it had been the night before, and a bank of storm cloud was gathering in the west. This time, Quilter slipped into the hole without any regrets.

Familiarity with the place had bred confidence, and although Anstey set a fast pace Quilter had no difficulty in keeping close behind him. The fact that the ladders were already in position made an enormous difference to their progress and by twelve-thirty they had reached the choke. Anstey arranged two or three torches in suitable places and they were ready to begin.

"The thing to watch here," said Anstey, "is that you don't get buried by a fresh fall. Slow and steady's the motto." He picked up the crowbar and started to loosen the small stones. Quilter wielded the shovel. There was no particular difficulty—all that was needed was patience. Little by little, a mound of debris was piled up on the floor of the cavern until it was almost as high as they were. Much of it was soft cave earth. By one-thirty, when Anstey called a halt for lunch, they had succeeded in laying bare the entrance to the passage and had even advanced a little way into it. It seemed to be about five feet high and six wide, and it fell away in a fairly steep gradient.

After a short break, they continued their navvy's work. Anstey had the more exhausting task, for he was working farther in and he had to hack and prod while bending low under the roof. He was still going at it, though, as if there were someone to be rescued on the other side. By now, both men were filthy. Their boots had become soggy from standing in the stream and they were sweating profusely under their boiler suits. Quilter's hands-were beginning to blister.

"Some people," he said, scrambling out of the passage for a short rest, "would think we were crazy to be doing this for fun. How much longer, do you suppose?"

Anstey heaved at a piece of rock and jerked back quickly as there came an ominous slither of debris ahead of him. Then he gave a shout of excitement. "I believe we're almost through—there's a gap just under the roof."

They both set to work with new vigour and very soon only a pyramid of loose stones lay between them and the continuation of the passage. Another half-hour's back-breaking labour and the last of the block was cleared.

Quilter dropped his shovel and sank back against the pile of debris, pretty well all in. Even Anstey looked as though he'd had about enough. "Well, we've done it," he said a little breathlessly. "At least we'll get as far as your greatgrandfather did."

Quilter wiped the sweat from his forehead with the back of his hand. "We ought to have brought a camera. A few pictures of myself with a shovel would have been worth votes!"

They had some more coffee and a cigarette and then Anstey became restless again and began nosing about in the entrance to the passage. Quilter, who had become very lethargic, watched him without enthusiasm.

"Look, Anstey," he said, "I've done all the exploring I can take for the moment. You go ahead if you want to. I'll be glad of the rest."

"Really? Sure you don't mind?"

"Not a bit. I shan't even mind if you decide to name the place Anstey's Burrow! It's all yours."

"Right you are," said Anstey with a laugh. "I'll just take a peep. See you later."

Quilter nodded. "So long—and good luck!" He watched Anstey bend and disappear into the tunnel and then he settled himself comfortably against the mound, working his shoulders until he had made himself a nice soft back-rest. He was still pleasantly warm after his exertions and rather drowsy. The gentle murmur of the stream was like a lullaby. He switched off his torch and closed his eyes and almost at once he was sound asleep.

He woke in what seemed total darkness and it was a moment or two before he could remember just where he was. Then he sat up with a jerk of alarm. His headlamp battery was almost flat and the bulb barely glowed, so Anstey must have been away some time. He groped around for his torch and his fingers closed over it thankfully. The strong beam was reassuring. He looked at his watch and saw that he had been asleep for more than an hour.

Then he became aware of a subtle change in the cave. It seemed noisier. He scrambled to his feet and flashed his torch on the stream. There was no doubt about it—the flow had increased. Instead of running quietly in its channel it was rushing and gurgling over the cavern floor and pouring in a small cataract down the passage which Anstey was exploring. Even as Quilter stood and watched it its volume seemed to grow. He needed no one to tell him what had happened. The weather must have broken, as it had been threatening to do, and the storm waters were pouring into the pothole. He and Anstey ought to get out quickly—who could tell what might be happening up there? What the devil could Anstey be up to? Surely he must have noticed the change in the stream?

Grasping his torch, Quilter peered down into the passage. "Anstey!" he shouted at the top of his voice. "*Anstey!*" The echoes mocked him. He ventured in a few steps, bending to clear the low roof. The floor shelved rapidly and the water swirled noisily past his feet. There seemed to be a twist in the passage ahead and he clambered down to it, his heart hammering. Round the corner the tunnel flattened out and seemed to run straight for as far as he could see. The water here was almost up to his knees, but he no longer had the impression that it was flowing.

Suddenly terror smote him—not in any metaphorical way but as a flash of fight and pain in the head and an unbearable constriction of the chest and throat. The place was filling up like a bath! The water couldn't get out quickly enough and was flowing back and soon the tunnel would be full! At that moment a light winked somewhere ahead. "Anstey!" he yelled. "Come on out, quick! *Quick,* man." He splashed forward a step or two and stopped.

There was an answering shout now, an encouraging shout, and the fight grew bigger. Quilter felt a surge of relief—he was coming, it was all right. There had been nothing to worry about really—Anstey was too old a hand to be caught like that. He'd noticed, of course. But why the hell didn't he hurry? The water was almost half way up the wall. What was he waiting for, the fool?

A moment later Anstey's whistle shrilled along the passage, urgent, insistent. The light had stopped moving.

"Help!" The cry came echoing over the water. "Quilter! Help!"

"Come out!" yelled Quilter, rooted by leaden feet. "Come out, you bloody fool!" He could feel the slap of the icy water against his thighs, the tug of fear at his heart, and scarcely knew what he was saying.

"I'm stuck!" came the voice—more like a cry of despair now. "Quilter! For God's sake, hurry!"

Quilter began to whimper. Crouching as he was, the water was surging round his chest, only a few inches from his face. He couldn't go through that—he *couldn't.* He'd be drowned like a rat. In a few moments now the tunnel would be full to the roof. Blind panic seized him. Suddenly he turned and started to fight his way back through the water, sobbing, oblivious to everything but the need to escape. He reached the bend and struggled up the slope, crashing his head against the roof, gashing his clothes. He felt the water against his skin, cold as death.

As he scrambled out of the passage he had only one thought—to get out of this ghastly trap while there was still time. Abject terror filled his mind. In the long stretch of high straight tunnel, he ran. He was still running when he reached the Cascade Chamber, now a bedlam of noise. His breath came in great choking gasps and the blood pounded in his ears. The ladder!—once he was up that ladder he would be safe. He lurched and plunged across the uneven floor of the chamber. Suddenly he slipped on a bed of wet clay and lost his balance. The torch fell from his grasp as he tried in vain to save himself; then a bunch of stalagmite came up at him and he went out like a lamp.

Chapter Six

He returned slowly and reluctantly to consciousness through a curtain of pain. His head felt as though it had been split down the middle and every muscle in his body ached. His clothes were soaked through and he was stiff and cold. With a groan he managed to struggle into a sitting position. The darkness was impenetrable. He knew he was in the Cascade Chamber because of the noise, but he didn't know exactly where. He felt a fresh pang of fear as he realised that he'd lost his torch. He fumbled for it like a blind man and knew joy when his fingers touched it, but it failed to light up when he switched on. For a moment he thought the battery had gone dead and remembered with horror that the spares were in the sack and the sack was down there beside the mound of debris. Then he discovered that the glass and bulb were smashed. Somewhere, he had a spare bulb. His fingers were so numb that it took him ages to find and fit it. At last, though, he had a light.

He looked at his watch, but that, too, had been broken by his fall and one of the hands was missing. He had no idea how long he had been lying there. He touched a throbbing centre of pain above his right ear and found that his face and neck were wet with blood. His helmet had rolled away and it was as much as he could do to retrieve it. Even with the torch he could barely see, and suddenly he realised that he'd lost his glasses. He found those, too, at last, half buried in the soft clay and miraculously unbroken. He cleaned them as well as he could with a damp handkerchief and then nausea overcame him and he had to rest.

After a while he felt strong enough to crawl over the stalagmite to one of the dammed-up pools and bathe his face and head. The cut seemed superficial, but there was a swelling around it as big as an egg. The water was deliciously cool and after he had soaked his head he drank deeply, his hands cupped.

Deliberately, he closed his mind against all thoughts of Anstey—no point in worrying about that when he himself might soon be dead. It would be a miracle if he ever got out of this fearful pit. He felt languid from loss of blood. If only he had had the sense to bring the sack, with the food and the coffee!

He sat still for a while, considering his desperate situation. If he tackled the ladder now, it was ten to one that he wouldn't reach the top. But if he waited, he might grow weaker, not stronger. The throbbing in his head made it difficult to think clearly, difficult to decide. Perhaps he'd better wait for a while.

He tried to relax, but his body was too cold for rest. A fit of shivering warned him that he must move. Waiting, in any case, was unendurable—it would be better to take a chance. He staggered to his feet and slowly made his way to the foot of the ladder. It hung motionless and infinitely inviting, a stairway to heaven if he could climb it. He thought of warm scented air and stars, of hot food and drink, of bed and sleep. He grasped the ladder and drew himself up on to the lowest rung. His head buzzed so much that the noise behind his eyes drowned the din of the cascade and he hung there unable to move. But presently the dizziness passed and he started to climb. Not having Anstey to hold the ladder made things far more difficult. It began to gyrate in the air, winding itself round the rope that still hung beside it, so that his feet became entangled. It even developed a sickening pendulum motion. The dizziness came back and he wound his arms over one of the rungs, on the verge of unconsciousness. Again the nausea passed and he straggled on. He lost all count of the distance he'd covered or the time he'd taken. He knew only that it seemed like eternity, and that will-power alone kept him from falling back into the pit. He could hardly believe it when at last his feebly groping fingers found flat rock and with a final effort he was able to pull himself up on to the ledge.

For a while he-felt too exhausted to move, but hope had begun to flow back and the climb had warmed him. He'd survived the worst bit—there was no reason now why he shouldn't manage the rest. He tried not to think of the obstacles still ahead. One bit at a time, that was the way. Presently he left the ledge and struggled slowly up the steep slope where Anstey had fixed the rope.

At the foot of the second ladder he rested again. Another seventy feet, he told himself—that was all. One more climb and then safety. One final effort! He gathered up all his reserves and attacked the ladder almost as though he were fresh, going up steadily rung after rung with his teeth gritted and his mind blank. Even so, he nearly failed at the post, for where the ladder hugged the bulging nose of rock he missed a foothold and hung for a moment by his hands alone. Then his scrabbling boot found a rung and he had reached the top and was lying in the last short passage. From weakness or relief, he buried his face in his arms and cried like a child.

He would have liked to stay there now, and sleep and sleep, but soon he felt the coldness creeping over him again and knew he must go on. He dragged himself slowly forward, clawing at the earth and rock, advancing a foot at a time. The last short climb to the exit almost defeated him but he made a supreme effort and just managed it. At last he was out on the soaking turf, drinking in great gulps of the soft and fragrant air. Night had fallen and the moon was coming up. Never before had the spacious earth and sky seemed so sublime.

He almost fell into the station wagon and drove down the track mechanically, his eyes half-closed. He left the car standing by the cottage door and staggered into the house, blind with exhaustion. Somehow he found milk and aspirin, and took six tablets and crawled upstairs. A moment later he had flung off his clothes and tumbled into bed and was asleep.

When he awoke the room was filled with sunshine. His idea of the time was now hazier than ever, but if the unfamiliar angle of the light were anything to go by it must be past noon and that meant that he had slept for fifteen hours or more. Still he had no great desire to stir. The pain in his head had quietened to a dull ache but when he tried to raise it he felt sick. His shoulders and the calves of his legs were so stiff that it hurt to move them. His mouth felt as though he had been chewing sawdust. For a while he lay still, putting off the moment of action.

In the end, thirst drove him out of bed and once he was out he stayed out. He looked in the mirror and was appalled by his appearance. His face was yellow under its grime and his eyes were sunk in shadow. Dried blood crusted his cheeks and hands. Over his ear there was a great purpling bruise around a cut that still oozed blood. He looked as though he had been beaten up, and he felt like it.

He ran a bath and soaked himself; and then he tended the cut and shaved and changed into fresh clothes. After that he felt sufficiently restored to make coffee and cook himself breakfast. In spite of his fatigue, his hunger was fierce, and he made a good meal.

Now, he supposed, he would have to do something about Anstey. He would have to report the accident to the police. His mind shied away from all the complications—it would mean answering a lot of questions, perhaps even taking them down that horrible hole. Somehow he felt he couldn't face the police yet—he wasn't ready for them. He still had to face himself. Anstey was dead, so there was no hurry.

Anstey was dead! He slumped back in his chair and gave full rein to his recollection, hating himself. Once again, he had failed utterly in a crisis. He'd done about the most despicable thing that any man could do—to save his own skin, he'd fled and left a companion to die, when ordinary guts and decency might have saved him. *Might* have—there could be no certainty. Heaven alone knew what had actually happened to Anstey. But Quilter attempted no gloss. Here, in the bright safe daylight, he hadn't much doubt that if he'd moved quickly at that first call for help he might have reached him and might have saved him. Instead he'd just stood, cursing the man for his folly, watching the waters rise, letting him drown. That was the hideous, ineffaceable truth. And this time he could do nothing to redeem himself, to wipe out the shame. This time it was no good bracing himself for a solitary effort later, no good facing up to danger and death and mastering his fears. Panic and cowardice had done their work—the man was dead.

As the full realisation of what he had done swept over him, Quilter buried his face in his hands and groaned in anguish. How could he ever survive with this memory? It would have been better if he'd been drowned too and his worthless life ended.

His worthless, wasted life! Self-pity engulfed him as he; looked back on the long unhappy struggle against his own inadequacy. Failure, that was what he had to acknowledge, failure all along the line, from the very beginning. Failure to assert himself against his doting, managing mother. Failure to do anything effective about his deepest beliefs. Failure to achieve the power and influence that his gifts entitled him to. Failure, most of all, to establish himself in his own estimation, to silence his own doubts. Failure even with Julie. She loved him, but with open eyes. She knew his weakness, his inner conflict; she saw his feet of clay. Everyone knew, everyone saw. That was probably why he hadn't been given a job; that was why his real allegiance had never been put to the test. No one trusted him, because he didn't trust himself. He was unstable, a neurotic, a man obsessed by his ego and tortured by his shortcomings, a man who craved for respect and admiration and a niche in the halls of fame, and deserved none of them. Once he had hated his brother for being all the things that he himself wanted to be and couldn't—fearless and self-possessed and inwardly tranquil. Now he envied him for having died honourably, bravely, for the cause he'd chosen.

In an hour of merciless introspection, Quilter touched a depth of misery and self-abasement that he had never known before. He whipped himself with remorse and shame and rose to some extent purged. He had painted himself in his mind with over-heightened colours, allowing himself no virtue. In fact he knew he was not as bad as that. It wasn't even true that he was a coward—not put like that, without qualification. If he could have been given another chance now, he would have proved it. Some people sprang to heroism, barely knowing what they were doing. Some people were instinctively courageous. He wasn't—he was instinctively afraid.

That made it the harder, and the slower, to be brave. If only he'd been given time! If he could have gone down now and rescued Anstey, he wouldn't have counted the cost.

Still, it was idle to dwell on that. If there were to be amends of conduct—and some day, he swore to himself, there would be a reinstatement—they would have to take some other form. Meanwhile, there were practical matters to attend to—the problem of the police, first and foremost. What was he going to tell them? Not, certainly, the whole truth. He would sooner end his life than face that shame.

With a feeling of repugnance—for to be forced to lie was itself a humiliation—he settled down to frame a plausible story, a story without too much detail. Most of it, of course, would be true enough. They had gone exploring together; Anstey, the younger and more experienced man, had continued alone when Quilter tired. That was all right. Quilter had dozed, and had wakened to the sound of rushing water. Then what? He had gone in search of Anstey, but had been overcome by the force of the stream and had only just managed to save himself. His injuries had been suffered during his rescue attempt. That sounded quite creditable and should suffice.

But suppose it didn't? Quilter tried to put himself in the position of the police and the coroner, and he knew that if he were they he would want to probe deeper. For one thing, the circumstances were so unusual. They would be interested in the pothole and in everything that had happened there. Their interest alone would lead to questions, and Quilter could imagine some of them. "Would you mind drawing us a little sketch, Mr. Quilter, just to make things clear?"

"Ah, yes, and the water was rushing in here—was it very deep when you first saw it?" "you heard Anstey call out, you say, but you didn't actually gather what the trouble was?" "How far did you go into the passage?" "How far away from him were you?" "How deep was the water when you left?" "Was his light still showing at that time?" "Was the tunnel submerged for very long?" "You don't know—you mean you didn't stay?" "Were you in any danger yourself at that time?" "Did you actually know that Anstey had been drowned?" "Wouldn't it have been possible to make sure when the waters subsided?" And so oh and so on and so on! Quilter felt the perspiration break on his forehead.

Of course, it mightn't be like that at all. It probably wouldn't be. Quilter knew that he was a respected figure in the district—there would certainly be no suspicion of him, not to start with. The coroner might hesitate to ask searching questions of the Member for West Cumbria. Probably he'd be most sympathetic. It was conscience that was building up all these difficulties and dangers—guilty imagination. But suppose it *did* happen? Suppose he muffed an answer, became confused. Suppose someone put a question that he hadn't foreseen? Suppose he contradicted himself.

The fact was—and the coroner and jury would know it—that any ordinary man, forced back by the water, would have waited, and gone in again at the first opportunity if only to make sure there was nothing he could do. Then he would have been able to give the coroner a complete picture. Quilter could give no picture. The police would recover Anstey's body and they would know more than he did. They would find out all about the stream and what it could do and couldn't do, and they wouldn't be satisfied with Quilter's story. Even if nothing were said openly, no strictures voiced, the gaps in his account would be noticed and he might leave the court an object of public gossip and contempt. In the whole world, nothing could be more unbearable or personally disastrous than that. It was a risk he simply couldn't take.

But was there any alternative? For a long while Quilter brooded, and in the end he decided that there was. It was just possible that he could keep the whole matter dark. Anstey hadn't told anyone about the pothole—indeed, he'd probably given the impression that he was going to Yorkshire if he'd said anything at all. He wasn't known in this district, and it was unlikely that anyone would have taken note of his passage up the lane. No one had been around at any time when he and Quilter had been together, either at the cottage or up on the hill. His motor-bike had been tucked away in the barn all the time. Altogether, it was most improbable that anyone would know of their brief association. Even if, by chance, some tradesman had spotted him and—less likely still—the identity of the visitor were established, Quilter could always say that Anstey had dropped in about some political matter on his way to Yorkshire. He clasped his aching head. Whether he spoke up or kept. silent, there were dangers. If he decided to say nothing he'd have to do some very thorough clearing up. He'd have to remove all traces of Anstey from the house because of Julie, and of his own activities in the pothole in case it were ever discovered. There were some of his tools still down there and various oddments that might give him away if they were found. He'd have to close up the pothole and act as though it had never existed. He'd have to get rid of the motor bike. It was a big programme. Still, there should be time enough to get through it. Julie was not due back for another three days.

He took no firm decision just then. All through the evening he continued to weigh the matter in his mind. That night, with arrears of rest still to make up, he slept deep and long. In the morning, Anstey's death had already begun to seem remote, and the decision to suppress the facts had been reached by default. If he went to the police now, it would be difficult to explain why he had delayed so long. They would say that he could at least have telephoned.

Once the choice was made, Quilter lost no time in carrying out his plan. The first and most urgent job was to put the cover back over the pothole entrance, before someone noticed it. He walked up to the Pikes and fixed the loft lid and covered it with scree. Then he returned quickly to the cottage and began systematically to remove every sign of Anstey's visit. There wasn't a great deal to do, for they hadn't spent a lot of time in the house. Apart from a slept-in bed and a few cigarette-stubs of a brand which Quilter didn't smoke and Anstey's telephone number scribbled on the pad, the only thing of importance was the notebook in which Anstey had jotted down his survey measurements and his completed plan of the pothole. Quilter burned the notebook in the boiler, but the plan itself intrigued him. He stood looking at it for a long while, and finally he locked it away in a drawer of his desk. There was nothing to associate it with Anstey and it wouldn't mean very much to anyone who found it. He could destroy it later.

As soon as he had cleared up inside the house, he set to work to mend the puncture in the front wheel of Anstey's motor cycle, keeping the doors of the barn shut and using artificial light. He would know no peace until he'd got rid of the bike. It was a long time since he'd done a repair job on a tube but there was a full kit of tools in the saddlebag and he had little difficulty. When he had finished he filled up the petrol tank, siphoning fuel out of the Riley, and checked the oil. In a pocket in the sidecar he found a one-inch map of part of the West Riding, much thumbed and marked with pencilled circles which he guessed might represent potholes: He went indoors and studied it carefully, waiting for dusk.

By the time darkness had fallen he had made all his pre-parafions for an arduous night's work and was ready for the road. It was nearly twenty years since he'd driven a motor cycle combination and it took him a little while to get the feel of it again, but by the time he'd got through Blean he was quite at ease. He drove slowly and carefully—an accident, or even an incident, would be disastrous. He circled the Lakes, keeping to the main roads, and finally turned south through Kirkby Lonsdale and Settle. The bike was behaving beautifully. Just before eleven o'clock he ran through the almost deserted town of Ingleton, stopped to consult his map, and turned left along a tertiary road that led up into the high limestone country and the Ingleborough fells. The night had become overcast and very dark and in this wild remote district he could see no sign of any living soul or habitation. Stones shot from under the wheels as the rough mountain road curved and climbed. The engine began to feel hot and to labour a little. He couldn't be far short of the two thousand foot contour now, he decided, and began to look for a suitable place to stop. A limestone quarry gleamed invitingly in the headlights, but men might be working there to-morrow and he didn't want the bike to be found too soon or in a place where the time of its arrival could be fixed. Presently he saw a promising-looking track and turned along it. The ground on either side was like a desert, dotted with slabs of rock and bare of trees, but with convenient hollows that would give temporary cover. He chose one of them and swung the bike into it. The ground was wet after the recent ram but he had no anxiety about leaving footprints—his nailed boots were not dissimilar to Anstey's, and Anstey's would never be seen again, so there could be no check. He switched off the fights and the petrol, stuffed the map back into the sidecar, and stood for a moment making sure that he had overlooked nothing. Then he set off back towards Ingleton.

He didn't hurry—his legs and shoulders were still painfully surf and he had lots of time to kill. Up on the tops there had been a strong, cold wind but as he left the bleak moors behind him it lost most of its force and walking was quite pleasant. A mile or two down the road he stopped under a sheltered bank to eat the sandwiches and drink the coffee that he had brought with him. He smoked a cigarette and then resumed his slow, meditative walk, thinking of all the things that were still to be done. The hours dragged. He knew that he mustn't be seen walking at a time when all respectable people were asleep, and that meant keeping away from places where the odd policeman might be patrolling.

Towards dawn he found a quiet haystack and snugged down on its drier side for an hour or two. His mind was too alert for sleep, but at least be could rest. As soon as it seemed safe to move again he dropped down into the valley and walked briskly through Ingleton, an early anonymous biker with a rucksack. An hour or two later, when he was well away from the district, he took a bus into Settle and a train from there. By the early afternoon he was back at the cottage.

He felt safer now, but time was getting short. In forty-eight hours Julie would be back, and he had still much to do. The worst, indeed, still lay ahead. The thought of going down the pothole again was so repellent that he made a great effort to persuade himself that it wasn't necessary. The possibility of anyone finding the place was really quite negligible—a secret that had been kept for a hundred years might easily be kept for another hundred. However, he failed to convince himself, as he had failed to convince himself that the coroner would ask no troublesome questions. There was always the risk, particularly now that the pothole had been opened. For the sake of his own peace of mind, he must remove all the evidence.

He slept badly that night in spite of his exertions, for the face of Anstey haunted him. At first light he made a parcel of his potholing clothes, threw it into the station wagon, and drove up the track, parking the car some distance from the Pikes. Then he walked back to the hole with the parcel under his arm, made sure that no one was in sight, and climbed down, drawing the loft door over the opening as far as he could from the inside. As soon as he was underground he changed into the boiler suit and helmet, stowing his own clothes just inside the first passage. Then he started the long descent. He had been afraid that some of the old terror might come back once he was in the pothole, but Anstey's death had left him in a reckless mood, and he felt inoculated against fear. Even the swinging of the ladders no longer upset him and he went down hand over hand without a pause. An hour after leaving the surface he was standing once more at the entrance to the fatal tunnel. The stream was hardly more than a trickle again, utterly without menace, and it was difficult to believe that the passage could have filled up so quickly. Difficult, too, to believe that he had fled as though pursued by demons, when for him there had no longer been the slightest danger. He saw now that there was a water mark in this cave, a high point, and that it was only an inch or two above the floor!

Now that he was here, he knew that he must find out what had happened in the tunnel. It wouldn't restore his self-respect even if he could prove to himself that he couldn't have been of any use, but it would dull the edge of remorse. The spectacle would be repugnant, but he had faced it in his imagination and would not shirk it now.

It didn't take him long to reach the spot. A dozen yards, perhaps, beyond the point where he had stood, a dozen crouching yards, and there was Anstey. An ugly, swollen figure, lying on the floor

74

of the tunnel in a strange, awkward attitude. Horribly accessible—a dozen yards.

Sick with self-reproach, Quilter crept forward and knelt beside the body of the man who had been his companion. One glance, and the cause of the tragedy became plain. A deep crack ran down the centre of the rock floor and Anstey's right boot, his strong nailed boot, was jammed tight in the cleft. He must have struggled fearfully to free himself in those last agonising moments, for one side of the boot was cut through by the rock. No doubt the lowness of the roof had impeded his efforts. His helmet lay beside him, with a broken strap, and the contents of his overall pocket were scattered pathetically around;

With set face, Quilter took his clasp knife and cut the lacing of the boot. Then he placed his hands round the ankle and heaved with all his strength. If only it would stay jammed! But little by little, as he strained, the foot began to come away from the boot, and in a moment it was free.

So he *could* have saved him! Twenty seconds to reach him, a moment's fumbling under the water, a joint pull, and they would both have been out and safe.

Quilter turned and stumbled back to the chamber. Well, that was that. Anstey was beyond aid now, and regrets were useless. Now he had to think of himself. He had to make absolutely sure that the body would never be found. The best way, obviously, was to pile all the excavated debris back into the tunnel. The shovel was still lying beside the mound, and at once he began the long, laborious task of replacing the choke. Putting it all back was easier and safer than removing it, but when he surveyed the results nearly two hours later he wasn't satisfied. The passage might be considered closed to any but a determined explorer, but it was only too plain that there *was* a passage, and explorers underground *were* determined. He stood back, sweating. No, it wasn't good enough. It would always be on his mind. He would be forever imagining someone coming down here and forcing the choke.

Suddenly he remembered what Anstey had said about opening up passages with explosive. If passages could be opened by explosive, they could be closed in the same way. Surely that was the answer—to blow up the mouth of the tunnel and bring down such a mass of rock that the evidence would be sealed up for ever? He didn't know much about the use of explosives, but he could find out. At least it was worth considering. He couldn't, in any case, do anything about it immediately with Julie coming back so soon, but later on there might be an opportunity.

He felt tired again after his long bout of shovelling but he had still a lot to do. He couldn't possibly leave those initials on the wall in the last chamber. He climbed to the pipe and wormed his way through and when he reached the cave he chipped the letters away with his knife and those of Joseph, too, for good measure. There must be nothing to fink the Quilters with this place.

Back in the lower chamber he set to work to lash up the tools They were heavy and awkward to carry single-handed, and they slowed him in the passages on the return journey. They gave trouble too, when he came to raise them by rope up the big precipice, for the sharp ends of the pick kept catching on the rock face. Stage by stage, though, he got them up, together with his rucksack, his vacuum flask, and everything else that might speak of his presence there.

He was now almost at the end of his gruelling task. All the ropes and ladders could be left in place—they had been Anstey's, not his, and if he came down again to close the passage he would need them. He changed back into his own clothes just below the exit, leaving the helmet and the boiler suit, the torches and spare batteries in a neat pile in the passage. They had been Anstey's, too.

He climbed out cautiously, replacing the lid with more than usual care and covering it thickly with scree. Looking at it gave him new confidence. The chance that anyone would stumble on his secret was indeed remote, and he felt that he had worried unduly.

He drove back to the cottage in a calmer frame of mind. This time, at least, he hadn't failed in what he had set out to do—he'd been resolute, competent and cool. Now it remained only for him ta give the house a final inspection, make himself as presentable as possible, and await the arrival of his wife.

Chapter Seven

He passed the next day quietly, dealing with his accumulated mail, answering the telephone and generally putting his affairs into as orderly a state as possible. Then in the evening he took the station wagon down to meet Julie.

In one way he was thankful that she was coming back, for the cottage had begun to seem unbearably lonely. A sense of guilt wasn't much of a companion, and at least Julie would chatter and take his mind off things. At the same time, he felt apprehensive. She had an uncanny ability to read his thoughts. Not that she would find them very easy to read to-day—he could scarcely find his way through that jungle himself. But it would be difficult to act with her as though life were normal. He found it almost impossible to tear his mind away from what had happened or to stop worrying about unpleasantnesses that might suddenly develop. Yet he knew that no preoccupation must show itself in his manner, or Julie would certainly sense that something was up.

The train was late and by the time it puffed in his nerves were pretty ragged, but the first sight of Julie did much to restore his composure. She was leaning out of the window, smiling and gaily returning his wave, and almost before the train had stopped she had jumped out and dumped her case on the platform and was speeding towards him. He held out his arms and kissed her upturned face. Her lips were warm and soft and reassuring.

"How lovely it is to be back!" she cried, beaming. "Let me look at you properly, darling—see that you haven't grown thin or anything."

Quilter's hand went automatically to the dark bruise that it was impossible to hide and he grinned sheepishly as Julie's eyes widened in disbelief.

"Darling!" she exclaimed. "What on earth have you been doing?"

"It's nothing," he said. "I walked into a door in the dark, that's all. It's nearly better now."

"It looks an awful mess. Were you tight or something?"

"No, just clumsy. Stupid thing to do, wasn't it? I smashed my watch, too—you should have heard my language." He went to pick up her case, telling himself that he'd taken that hurdle all right. "So you had a good time, did you?" he said, putting an arm round her shoulder and moving off with her towards the car.

"Wonderful." Julie tactfully followed his lead. "Hasn't it been glorious weather?"

"Not bad at all. We had one storm here—on Wednesday, I think—but otherwise it's been all right."

"We were lucky, then, we missed that. Muriel and I spent practically all our time on the beach and I'm as brown as this all over ..."—she held out a bare golden-brown arm for his inspection—". . . or nearly. I'll show you when we get home. I was sorry you weren't there—the swimming was divine. We did go into Dorchester one day, though, and I did a spot of shopping—things for France. I've bought an enchanting sun-frock—oh, but I told you, didn't I?"

Quilter threw the case into the back of the station wagon and opened the door for her, "Yes, I got your letter. I didn't think you'd expect me to reply as you were coming back so soon." He climbed in beside her.

Julie gave his leg a tolerant pat. "It would have been a miracle if you had, darling, and I don't look for miracles these days. Did you finish your old papers?"

"Papers?" Quilter had completely forgotten that pile of documents in the rush of other things. He changed down, crashing the gear a bit. "Yes. Yes, I finished them. More or less."

She laughed. "I believe you've been idling. Tell the truth, now. Haven't you been lying in the sun most of the time?"

"No, indeed I haven't. I've done a terrific amount of walking."

His mouth set in a familiar downward curve. "In fact, I think I may have overdone it a bit."

"That wouldn't surprise me—you don't do anything like a normal person. You ought to learn to conserve your energies or at least ration them out reasonably like other people, instead of flinging yourself into things with such fury and then being worn out afterwards."

Quilter grunted.

"Anyway, where did you go?"

"Oh, the usual rounds. Up Scawfell one day—circuit of Derwentwater on the tops—Grisedale and Helvellyn. Nothing very sensational, but I must have averaged about fifteen miles a day."

"That *is* a lot. Have you seen anyone we know?"

"Not a soul. Apart from the odd hiker I've hardly seen a human being since you went away."

"What bliss for you! Did you manage all right about food?"

"Yes, I ate out, mostly. Had plenty, anyway."

She nodded, satisfied, and watched him negotiate the turning out of Blean. Suddenly she gave a little exclamation. "Why, I'd almost forgotten—wasn't it odd about Grigson?"

He shot her a swift glance. "How do you mean?"

"Well, his resignation—coming practically the very day that we'd been discussing him."

Damn! thought Quilter. That *would* happen! He made a non-committal sound. "The P.M. isn't being in a hurry to get in touch with me."

"That doesn't mean anything. It's August, after all—I don't suppose he's in a mad rush to fill the post."

Quilter grunted again. He had no feelings at all about Grigson at that moment. Instead, his mind was feverishly occupied with a glaring omission of his own. He'd been so busy that day with his stack of correspondence that he'd quite overlooked the little pile of obviously unread copies of *The Times* on the hall table. It would never do to let Julie see those.

He stopped the car beside the barn. "Would you like to drive it in, sweetheart, while I get some drinks? Special privilege!"

She made a face at him as she moved into the driving seat. "I believe you want to get yourself a quickie first."

Quilter gave a short laugh and carried her case into the cottage. It took him only a few moments to open and fold back the papers and scatter them about the sitting room. As he came back into the hall he noticed the local weekly stuffed into the letter box and with a little spasm of anxiety he quickly paged through it.

He hardly expected to find anything so soon, but, there it was, a paragraph in the Coalhaven section headlined "Potholer Missing." Tensely, he skimmed through the text,

"Fears are entertained," he read, "for Mr. P. J. Anstey, of 12 Graham Buildings, Coalhaven, who has been missing from his lodgings since the weekend. Mr. Anstey, a science master at Coalhaven Grammar School and a well-known potholing enthusiast, left his home early on Sunday morning with the intention, it is understood, of joining an exploring party in the West Riding. Yesterday afternoon an Ingle-borough shepherd reported to the police that a motor cycle, since identified as belonging to Mr. Anstey, had been left unattended on the moors. Subsequent police inquiries elicited the information that Mr. Anstey did not in fact turn up at the club rendezvous on Sunday, and it is now feared that he may have set out alone to explore one of the many potholes in the district and become involved in an accident. Preparations are being made for an intensive search in the area immediately around the abandoned machine, but in the absence of information about Mr. Anstey's exact destination, the task is likely to prove very difficult."

Quilter felt a surge of relief. Anstey hadn't told anyone about him, and the hounds were off on the false scent. Everything was going to be all right.

A light step sounded in the hall. "What, no drinks?" He flung the paper aside. "Sorry! I was just reading a report of the speech I made at Blean."

"Narcissus! All right, don't trouble—I'll get them myself now."

She disappeared into the kitchen and he stuffed the paper into his pocket. In a few moments she joined him in the sitting-room with gin, French, and ice on a tray.

"I'm not surprised about that bruise," she said "You've almost finished the new bottle of whisky. Serves you jolly well right, you secret drinker."

Quilter made a conscious effort to control himself. Why the devil did she have to go snooping around? And how many more mistakes had he made? First the documents, and then the unread papers and now the whisky! It was just such small things that Julie noticed.

He smiled at her, switching on the charm. "I had to drown my loneliness. Any other complaints?"

"No complaints at all, darling. I think you did very well—the house is marvellously tidy. You'd make somebody a good wife."

"Now then!—no impertinence, just because you've been footloose for a few days. Cheers!" He gulped his drink. "And by the way, in case you think I've been having wild parties or something, it was I who slept in the guest room. I couldn't stand the bright sun in the mornings. I don't suppose my bedmaking's up to your standards, but I did the best I could."

Julie gave him a puzzled look and he knew he hadn't quite got away with it. "Darling, is anything the matter?"

"Matter? Of course not. Have another drink."

She gave him her glass mechanically, still staring at him.

"Oh, for God's sake, Julie, stop looking at me like that. I tell you there's nothing wrong." He ran a hand wearily over his face. "At least, nothing to get agitated about. It's just that I haven't been sleeping well—this bang on the head must have shaken me. It was a hell of a crack. In a couple of days from now we'll be off on our holiday—I'll be all right then."

"Sweetie! I wish I hadn't gone away." Julie dropped down beside him on the settee, her eyes full of compassion, her arms around him. He leaned against her and closed his eyes, wallowing in self-pity. Why had all these horrible things had to happen to him? He longed to tell her everything—to lighten his burden by sharing it. Julie loved him. No matter what he had done, she would never stop loving him. Yet this was something he couldn't tell her—not how he'd run away. He mustn't weaken about that. He must force himself to keep silent, and be forever on his guard. Suddenly he groaned, and his grip on her tightened. "Oh, Julie, don't ever leave me. I don't know what I'd do without you."

She stroked his hair, gently, reassuringly, and went on stroking it, but her eyes above his head had an anxious, baffled look. All the gaiety had gone.

PART TWO

Chapter One

They had been on holiday for nearly a week and Julie was bitterly disappointed. Everything seemed to have gone wrong.

The start hadn't been too bad by her fairly undemanding standards. Laurence always enjoyed being in control of a car and the drive down to Newhaven had been quite amicable. At times he'd seemed rather absorbed and once or twice he'd flared up about trifles, but Julie was used to his moods and more ready than most wives to make allowances for temperament. By now she had learned that she must reconcile herself to long periods of silence, fits of gloom and occasional outbursts of irritation for the sake of the utterly satisfying companion he could be in between. She had nourished the hope that when they got to France the nice part of him would come out on top.

In fact, though, it had been after they'd landed at Dieppe that the real trouble had started. Looking back, Julie had to admit that all the incidents had been very petty, but they'd been enough to cast a blight on the southward journey. On the first night it had rained hard and Julie had suggested stopping at a little auberge which had looked all right from the outside but hadn't turned out too well. Laurence had sulked, and half-way through the meal he'd gone quite white for no reason that he could explain and as always she had felt obscurely that it was her fault.

Next day they'd stopped in Rouen so that Julie could do some shopping for lunch and they'd arranged to meet again at a certain time because Laurence had said he couldn't stand shopping; and Julie had been a bit late. Laurence had been furious about that. When the tantrum had passed they'd settled down to have an apéritif at a café in the market place and Laurence had begun to talk about Joan of Arc in a morbid way, almost as though he were sorry he'd missed the chance of being burned at the stake too, and when Julie had said so, teasing him, he'd got angry again. It had all seemed so unnecessary. And they'd had another flare-up south of Chartres because Laurence had suddenly started to drive like a demon and when she'd mildly protested he'd said, "What the hell does it matter, anyway?"

Somehow they'd survived the journey and established themselves in a little old-world town called Pouillac in the Dordogne, where English tourists were only just beginning to penetrate. The district had proved to be full of interest, the scenery novel and intriguing. The weather had been perfect. They had explored old Frankish ruins and descended a most spectacular hole in the ground at a place named Padirac and examined a fascinating ancient skull at Les Eyzies. They should have been having a wonderful time, but actually it had been worse here than anywhere.

It was as though a cloud had now settled permanently on Laurence and there was no trace of the delightful intimacy which, Julie admitted to herself, was what she lived by. She had never known him so preoccupied for so long. He was going about like an actor rehearsing Hamlet, brooding, abstracted, completely cut off from her. Silence, which was usually a bridge of understanding between people who were really fond of each other, had become a gulf that divided them. Even his attempts at love-making had been so absent-minded and perfunctory that Julie had felt repelled.

For a time she had put it all down to overwork and nervous strain. He had said he wasn't very well, and he certainly wasn't himself. Sunshine and rest and good food, she had told herself, would soon bring him round. She had tried to be gay, to woo him from his melancholy by the sheer contagion of cheerfulness, but he had crushed her high spirits with sneers. Deeply hurt, she had still tried to be patient and sympathetic, as with an ailing child. But that hadn't worked either—nothing that she did was right. Her patience had begun to wear thin and there had been moments when she had felt her self-control would snap. They couldn't go on like this. At last she had suggested that he see a doctor, but that had produced a frightening display of ill-temper on his part. Now she felt baffled and increasingly resentful.

There was still tension between them when they set out, on the third morning after their arrival in Pouillac, to see the Lascaux paintings. Julie had been attracted by these prehistoric marvels ever since she had read an article about them during the war, and had been thrilled to learn that they were so accessible to Pouillac. As they drove along the unfrequented side-roads in the morning sun she made a fresh effort to disperse the cloud of gloom that hung over them. She talked lightly and unaffectedly of their surroundings and from time to time drew Laurence's attention to sights she thought might interest him. When he showed some signs of responding, her own heart lightened and she began to feel happier than she had done for days.

They stopped in the pleasant little town of Martignac to buy a long crusty loaf, some cheese and a bottle of red wine, and then they drove through plantations of sunflowers and up the white, poplar-lined road that led to the famous cave. There was a turning circle at the top with a parking place for cars, but there were only three or four there just now—a fact which Julie noted with relief, for Laurence in his present misanthropic mood would be certain to shy away from a crowd. One of the cars was an old jeep with a U.S.A. rear plate, and a man was sitting on the bank beside it reading a book. He looked up with friendly interest as the Riley stopped and watched them get out.

"The cave's just closed down for lunch," he said. "It opens again at two."

They thanked him and Julie turned to Laurence. "Let's go and picnic up in the woods," she suggested. "They look so shady and cool."

Quilter nodded, and they strolled up through the trees, passing one or two family parties with folding chairs and tables set up in the open and. an air of having established themselves for a solid two-hour meal. "Better get away from, the kids," Quilter grunted. They went on for a bit and presently found a quiet glade. For all its fame, the place seemed totally unspoiled. Through the wood of walnut and hazel and scrub oak they could just make out a rustic café with faded blue benches and little tables in the dappled shade, but there were no other signs of commercialisation. The drawing power of prehistoric art was evidently limited.

Julie spread out their picnic lunch and they ate with good appetites. Laurence seemed to have withdrawn into silence again, so Julie read out the most interesting bits from the guidebook she had bought in Pouillac—about how the cave had been discovered because a boy's dog had disappeared down a tiny hole, and he'd gone after it, and how the paintings on the walls were supposed to be thirty thousand years old. After a while, discouraged by his apparent lack of interest, she stopped reading aloud and read for her own information.

Shortly before two they set off up the path, following the direction of an arrow that said "Grotte." The entrance itself looked rather like that of a well-kept family sepulchre, with a green galvanised iron door built into yellow stone at the foot of some steps. One of the French families was already waiting on a near-by bank, its members chattering excitedly, and a man in a beret and braces was sitting a little apart, chewing a wisp of grass. There was as yet no sign of the custodian.

Presently the American came sauntering up the path. He was a big, broad-shouldered fellow, with crisp dark hair and a pleasant, good-humoured expression. His face, deeply tanned as though he had spent months in hot sunshine, wore a look of quiet contentment, and his general air suggested that he had all the time in the world at his disposal. He stopped for a moment as he drew level with the Quilters and Julie thought he was going to come over to them. However, he seemed to sense Laurence's unsociability, for he passed on and stood smoking by the iron door.

Deliberately, Julie got up and joined him at the bottom of the steps. Laurence's gloomy presence had suddenly become intolerable to her. The American smiled at her and she thought how refreshingly casual he looked in his plaid short-sleeved shirt and his light drill trousers. She smiled back at him.

"Cigarette?" he said, holding out a crumpled packet of Chesterfields and following up with his lighter. He glanced towards the door. "I'm told this is really something."

"Yes, I'm so excited. I've wanted to come here for years."

"Well, this is the moment. Here comes the guy with the keys."

By now a couple of dozen people had emerged from the wood in little groups, and as the guide unlocked the door they trickled in behind him. Julie became aware of Laurence beside her in the dim light, but still he said nothing. When everyone had bought their tickets the guide moved off and they descended two flights of rather damp stairs and entered the lighted cave.

The paintings on the limestone walls began almost at once, and Julie was so entranced that she followed the guide's rapid discourse with only half her mind. They were much larger, much clearer, and much more dynamic than she had expected. The colours, mostly red and black, had a quite unexpected freshness. There was a frieze of deer, fleeing across a stream; a great black bull nearly six yards high with an amazingly expressive head; two horses so vigorous and full of movement that they looked as though, they might gallop away. Julie, moving slowly through the chamber, had an impression of a wild animal frolic. She tried to imagine thirty thousand years ago, and the squat ape-like men who had been moved to artistic creation, but failed utterly. Turning to comment on it all to Laurence, she found that he was away in the front as usual, a step or two ahead of the guide.

It took just over half an hour to complete the circuit. As they strolled back towards the entrance, Julie saw that the American was having language trouble. From what she could hear he was trying to find out from the guide whether the black and red paint represented different periods and if so which was the older, and after a moment or two she went to his rescue. Within a matter of seconds she had become deeply involved, for now that he had an interpreter the American appeared to be absolutely bursting with questions. Some of them were most technical, about rock strata and fossil remains. Julie's French was fluent and she had great feeling for the language, but you needed, she decided, something more than a French great-grandmother to be able to handle a conversation full of words like "palæozoic" and "cretaceous."

However, the American seemed most grateful. "That sure was kind of you," he said in his slow, pleasant drawl as they joined Laurence outside the cave and began to walk down the hill together. "I'd give a lot to talk French like that—I have quite a job getting by."

"I'm not surprised," said Julie, "if those are the sort of questions you want to ask. It all sounded horribly erudite."

He looked at her for a moment in mild surprise, and then grinned. "I guess so—it just happens to be my line of country. I'm a geologist, you see, and that guide really knew his stuff."

"Rather a busman's holiday for you, surely?" said Quitter.

"Maybe it is at that, but it suits me. I'm finding everything fascinating—never came across a place so packed with treasures. Are you folks staying around here?"

"We're at Pouillac," Julie told him.

"Is that so? I'm heading that way myself to-morrow—I'm told it's fine and central for the district. Is the town very full?"

"Not at all. If you do come, you should stay at the Lavendou. It's most comfortable, and Michelin gives it a star for food. "

"I'll remember that—thanks a lot. Maybe I'll be seeing you." He smiled at them, clambered into his jeep, and was off down the road.

"What a nice man!" said Julie.

Quilter made a faintly derogatory sound. "Not bad for an American. Individually they're often all right. Collectively, of course, they're impossible."

"You only think they're impossible because you don't happen to like what they're doing in the world," Julie said. "It's nothing but political bias on your part."

"Nonsense!" said Quilter sharply. "It's just ordinary common sense. They're going to drag us into a war if we're not darned careful. And if they win it, which God forbid . . ." He rammed the car savagely into gear and let the clutch in with such a slam that Julie gripped the door-handle in alarm.

He drove down the hill without looking at her. The sudden explosion of verbal violence had relieved him like the bursting of a boil and now he began to feel ashamed of himself. He had been behaving unpardonably to Julie, he knew that. It had been sheer sadism, the way he'd been crushing her spirit. He hadn't even enjoyed it, either—it was just that he hadn't seemed able to help himself. He'd been wretched, unspeakably wretched, and he hadn't been able to snap out of it, so he'd tried to take it out of Julie. He realised now that all this leisure alone with her had been a mistake—he'd never throw off the effects of Anstey that way. It was only in action that he could hope to forget.

Action, that was the thing! No good dwelling on the past—he must work the poison out of his system instead of bottling it up. He must make a fresh start. Julie had said that he was still young, and that was true. There was still time to prove himself, to force recognition, to re-establish himself in his own esteem. Anstey had been a defeat, a humiliation, but of so desperate a kind that it should be just the stimulus he needed. It wasn't the smug and contented who left their mark upon the world; it was the angry, the hurt, the men of stricken pride. The men who had lost so much that they had little more to lose.

After the long night of depression his mood had changed so completely that he felt almost elated, and immediately he wanted Julie to change too. He gave her a quick glance, wondering how he should approach her, conscious of her tight-pressed lips.

"Darling," he said at last, "wouldn't it be rather nice if we went back along the river and picked ourselves a quiet spot for a swim?"

"If you like," she said.

His hand reached out to hers. "Julie, I've been an awful boor—I don't know what's been the matter with me you must have had a hell of a time. But it's all over now, honestly. Please forgive me, sweetheart."

Julie tried to think of something to say, and couldn't. She turned her head away from him, her eyes brimming with tears.

Chapter Two

The American turned up at Pouillac the next evening while Julie and Quilter were sipping aperitifs on the hotel terrace. They saw him go inside and after a while he came out with the porter and had his luggage taken in from the jeep. Presently he came wandering over to the terrace.

"Hello, there!" he called cheerily as he recognised them. Julie waved, but felt slightly nervous. Laurence had been much less of a bear to-day, and she wanted to keep him that way. And after what he'd said about Americans . . .

It was Quilter himself who thrust back a chair invitingly. "Won't you join us?" he asked.

The American hesitated for a moment, but Julie's smile seemed to reinforce the invitation. "Well, that's mighty kind of you. I guess I'd better introduce myself—Benson Traill is my name."

"And ours is Quilter. I'm Laurence Quilter and this is my wife Julie."

"Glad to know you both." Traill took the proffered seat, his face puckered in a thoughtful frown. "Laurence Quilter—now that's a name I seem to know."

Julie caught Laurence's faintly smug expression and laughed. "Isn't that nice for you, darling?"

He said, "What will you drink, Mr. Traill?"

"I'll have a Scotch, if I may. I can't seem to get along with these sweet apéritifs they serve."

"I don't like them much, either," agreed Julie, who was drinking gin and French and beginning to feel very comfortable and relaxed. She was glad he had joined them—a trio was so much easier than a tête-à-tête when you were in process of making a rather difficult personal adjustment. "You managed to get fixed up, then, Mr. Traill? What do you think of the hotel?"

"It's swell—I've no complaints at all. They've given me a room with a cute little terrace all covered with flowers and vines—just like a bit of the Garden of Eden."

"But no Eve?"

"No Eve—I've still got to find her." He smiled at Julie with eyes that were deep hue and twinkling, and his glance warmed her and made her feel happy. The thought flashed across her mind, "this man likes me," and she was surprised at the refreshment it brought, as though a stream had begun to flow in an arid desert.

Just then the waiter arrived and Quilter gave the orders. Traill was still searching his memory. "It's an extraordinary thing—I could swear . . ."

"You don't have to," Julie said. "Laurence is a Member of Parliament—perhaps that's why the name seems familiar to you."

Traill's face cleared. "Sure—that's it—Laurence Quilter. You asked a lot of questions in your Parliament when there were riots in the West Indies last fall."

"I did make a bit of a nuisance of myself," Quilter agreed, "but I'm surprised you should know about it."

"That's easily explained. My company operates in Trinidad—I'm actually an oil geologist. The riots weren't far from our doorstep."

"I see." Quilter looked a bit sardonic. "Then I dare say you didn't agree with the line I took?"

"I guess not, now I come to think of it, but then I'm no politician."

"As a Labour M.P.," Julie said, "Laurence must always support the downtrodden workers." Her teasing smile robbed the remark of any malice.

Traill's gaze rested for a moment on Quilter, appraising his expensive clothes and general air of privileged well-being. Then he glanced at Julie and grinned. "Sure!" he said.

The waiter returned with the drinks and Quilter sorted them out. "Well—cheers!" he said.

"Your health!" said Traill, raising his glass to each of them in turn. "I must say this is a great pleasure."

"For us, too," said Julie. "Tell me, Mr. Traill, what exactly is an oil geologist?"

Traill laughed. "He's the guy that gets all the kicks when the company drills to fifteen thousand feet on his advice and finds no oil."

"What a frightful responsibility! Are you supposed to be some sort of diviner?"

"You could put it like that—we're supposed to work out the likely places, anyway. It's not quite as chancey as using a twig—we have some pretty slick gadgets these days to help out and they give us a good idea where the oil-bearing, strata should be. It's still true, though, that you can spend a million dollars drilling three miles of damn all and you quite often do."

"It must be a thrill when you're right."

"I'll say it is. When the old Schlumberger log's slapped down in front of you and you see it showing a nice thick layer of oil-bearing sands you feel like bustin' out all over. But the whole thing's a tremendous gamble—you can never be certain what you're going to get till you've drilled, and that's specially true of Trinidad."

"This is where I really start to show my ignorance," said Julie. "I gather Trinidad is in the West Indies but I'm sure I couldn't find it on a map. All I know about it is that it's a British colony."

"It used to be," Quilter said grimly. "A good chunk of it is now an American base. We traded the site during the war for an old destroyer or two."

Julie gave him a reproachful glance but Traill seemed unconcerned. "I guess I'll have to watch my step with you, Mr. Quilter—I see you're a man of strong feelings. Have a cigarette?"

"Thank you," said Quilter. "I meant nothing personal, of course." He leaned forward and gave Traill a light. "Have you ever thought of moving on from Trinidad to, say, Venezuela? It's much less of a gamble there, isn't it?"

"You bet! But it's a darned sight less interesting from my point of view. In Trinidad, you see, the formations are all broken up—geologically it's one of the most complex small places you could find—so there's a problem worth getting your teeth into. When there's a lake of oil stretching for miles, like in some of the Middle East fields or Texas, well, you can't miss—you hardly need a geologist."

"I suppose," said Julie, "you sit in an office with a little hammer, cracking stones?" She knew she sounded absurd, but somehow she couldn't resist drawing Traill's attention to herself. There was a depth in his voice, a friendly. warmth in his expression that affected her like sunshine after days of greyness. She felt herself thawing out, becoming human and feminine and frivolous. It was almost like the first stage of getting drunk.

He turned amused eyes on her. "Not exactly that. The office work is mostly with a microscope. You see . . ." He broke off. "Say, are you folks sure this isn't boring you?" "On the contrary," said Quilter, "it's most interesting."

"*I think so*, but millions wouldn't. Anyway, what happens is that when we drill I'm presented from time to time with "cores"—that's cylindrical bits of rock cut out at various depths for me to work on. Well, rocks often contain minute fossils, called forams, that tell us the age and nature of the strata, so we pick these out under the microscope and file them away on slides so that in time we can build up a pretty complete geological picture I've a collection of about three hundred thousand of them."

"That isn't what gave you your tan, though," said Julie irrelevantly.

"You're right there—all it gives you is eyestrain. There's a good deal of field work as well—we have to go out into the bush with gravity meters and seismograph detectors and often we're out all day and every day for long stretches. Darned hot it is, too." He looked mischievously at Quilter. "Quite hot enough without having people set fire to the wells . . ."

'Who on earth sets fire to the wells?" asked Julie.

"No one, at the moment, but it did happen not so long ago. People sent in from outside the fields to make trouble—Communists, I guess. Communist-led, anyway."

Quilter gave a snort. "You Americans see Communists everywhere."

"Well, sir, there are quite a few around."

"Perhaps there wouldn't be so many if the workers got more benefit from their oil."

"You may be right, at that," said Traill easily. "It's a big question. They don't do so badly—not in Trinidad, anyway." He grinned. "They're pretty smart. You should see them bringing out their washing when we have trouble with a well."

"Their washing!" Julie exclaimed.

"Sure. As soon as a well starts misbehaving and there's a bit of oil flying around they collect all the old clothes they've got and stick them in the way. Then they claim compensation. I don't blame them, but it's a mistake to think that it's the oil companies who get up to all the tricks. Myself, I reckon there are about eight sides to every question."

"You're very tolerant," Quilter said dryly. "One side is usually enough for me."

Julie reached for her drink. "Why is it," she demanded, "that when two men get together they must always argue?"

"You've got something there," said Traill lazily. "I guess this is no time or place to be discussing serious things, not when we're all supposed to be on holiday."

"Do you get long holidays, Mr. Traill?"

"Three months every three years, apart from short local leave. It suits me pretty well that way—I can really go places in three months."

"What are you planning this time?" Julie was almost painfully anxious to keep away from controversial subjects—she felt she couldn't bear to see Laurence become argumentative and bitter again.

"Well, I've done quite a bit already. I had the jeep shipped to Lisbon and came overland through Spain. When I've finished here I'll be going on through Switzerland, Germany and Holland."

"But not to England?"

"Yes. I'll be ending the trip there. I've got to hand back the jeep.

I borrowed it from a guy I know in the U.S.A.F., stationed near Mildenhall . . ." He broke off as sounds of a sudden disturbance came from across the street. "Say, what's going on there, I wonder?"

A man had started to blow a bugle—a man with a bicycle and a pair of lungs that reminded Julie of Joe Halliday. Presently, when he had drawn a crowd, he began to read out an announcement. Traill listened, interested but uncomprehending, and then glanced at Julie. "What does he say?"

"He says the town will be *en fête* on Saturday—they're raising money for new church bells. I should think it ought to be rather fun."

"Could be. They sure enjoy themselves when they get started. I came on a village yesterday evening where the whole population seemed to be out, dancing. Feast of the Assumption, I think they said it was. I darned nearly joined in. Well, now, how about some more drinks? Same again, Mrs. Quilter? What about you, sir?"

Quilter, who had been sitting with the old abstracted expression on his face, started. "Why, yes—thanks."

Chapter Three

Traill drifted away after dinner and they saw no more of him that evening. His impact, however, remained. To Julie it had been like a breath of fresh air to meet a thorough-going extrovert who was absorbed in a practical job and cared nothing for politics. Quilter had been stimulated by him in a different way and after a spell of taciturnity at dinner he began to talk with something of his old animation and fire. He had, he told Julie, nothing whatever against Traill personally—but that attitude of his . . .! Everyone knew that the West Indies were grossly exploited, and no man of any feeling would attempt to minimise the fact. Of course, Traill was a geologist—what with his microscope and his strata he probably hardly noticed what went on in the lives of people around him. An unconscious tool of the oil companies . . .

Julie didn't attempt to argue. Laurence could say what he liked as long as he said something—anything was better than moroseness. She found it impossible to share his indignation, but he didn't seem to mind, and it was good to see him stirred by something again—even if it wasn't by her!

Next day Traill went off early—from her window Julie saw him leave in the jeep just after nine. Laurence asked her what she would like to do and she said she wouldn't mind spending another day lazing on the banks of the Dordogne. The atmosphere of acute strain had gone, but there was still no real companionship. Julie's new role, it soon appeared, was that of audience. Laurence seemed on the point of spontaneous combustion over the Korean war, and as she lay listening to his derisive comments on the United Nations, MacArthur and Chiang Kai-shek she reflected that his views seemed to be getting steadily more extreme and hoped for his own sake that he would moderate them when he got back to England. Between his outbursts she dangled her toes in the water and read a soothing travel book by Freya Stark.

When they returned to the hotel in the early evening Traill was already on the terrace and they joined him as a matter of course.

"I'll be with you in a moment," Quilter said, as Julie settled herself in the basket chair which the American politely held for her. "I must get a paper before the kiosk shuts." He went off across the street with his usual brisk stride.

"I guess I ought to buy a paper one of these days," said Traill with a lazy smile. "Well—have you been having a good time?"

"Very pleasant, thank you—but very quiet. And you?"

"I've had a terrific day. I went down that Gouffre place they talk about so much—Padirac. It sure is impressive."

"It frightened me," said Julie. "I was glad to get out. Laurence was absolutely fascinated by it, though." She didn't add that that was practically the only time that he'd shown any interest in anything. "It was all I could do to tear him away. He had our poor boatman in a maze with his questions."

"Did you have to translate for him, too?"

"No, thank heaven," said Julie with a smile. "Laurence's French is pretty good." She turned and watched her husband slowly approaching across the terrace, reading the *Continental Daily Mail* as he walked. Suddenly he stopped, concentrating on something with an anxious frown, and then he came swiftly across to them.

"I say, Julie, there's been a bad fall at Whitehanger. Seventy-three trapped."

"Oh, Laurence!" Julie took the paper with deep concern. Whitehanger was one of the biggest collieries in West Cumbria, and she knew a great many of the miners and their wives. "Hope Fading," she read. Seventy-three men! Seventy-three families! She let the paper drop into her lap. "Oh, God, how frightful!"

"Frightful!" Quilter echoed, and sat down. "You know, darling, I think I ought to go back."

"Do you *really?*"

Traill got up. "I'm sorry about this, folks. Guess I'll see you later."

Julie gave him a rather strained smile and turned back to Quilter. "Well, if you think we can do any good, Laurence, of course we'll go. But *do* you think we can? When that explosion happened at Fotherdown and we went over I felt horribly in the way. You know how a community like that closes up when there's a disaster—they don't really want outsiders around and you can't wonder at it."

"We're hardly outsiders," said Quilter. "A colliery disaster has a public angle and I'm the M.P.—I've got responsibilities. Besides, what do you think our opponents will say if I don't put in an appearance? 'Where was your M.P.?' they'll ask. 'Gadding about on the Continent.' I can't afford to let that happen—it's going to be too near a thing as it is."

Julie looked at him in astonishment. "I see," she said. "You're not usually so frank, are you?"

"I'm being realistic," he said angrily. "Damn it, it's the usual thing to show some interest on these occasions, quite apart from feelings. It's expected. Why do you suppose the King always sends a message?"

"It's certainly not because he wants votes," she said with unusual bitterness.

It suddenly came over her again what a total fiasco this holiday had been, and she felt utterly miserable. She had tried, she knew she had tried hex utmost, to make it a happy one, but somehow it had been doomed from the start. To say that Laurence had been unco-operative was putting it mildly. He had not once, it seemed to her now, been spontaneous and natural with her. This return to England—if he had really cared about the miners and their bereaved families she would have gone with him willingly, even though she might think it a mistake. But to go with him in this mood, this hard, calculating mood—her whole nature revolted.

"Of course, if you've made up your mind," she said in a remote voice, "I suppose there's nothing more to be said. I'd better start packing."

"Now look, darling, don't go flying off the handle like that.

Please understand that I don't want to upset the holiday any more than you do, but it's part of the job and I must. That doesn't mean that there's any necessity for you to come, though."

"Of course I must come. I can't stay here without you."

"Why not? It'll only be for a day or two. I can get a train into Toulouse or Bordeaux first thing to-morrow—possibly even to-night—and I can fly from there. I'll see the trade union chaps and start a fund and say a few appropriate words and then I'll fly straight back. Let's see, where are we now? Wednesday. Why, I'll probably be back by Sunday."

"If that's how you want it . . ." Julie's face was hard and set.

"It's not a question of how I want it, sweetheart—it's the sensible thing to do. Obviously I've got to fly if I'm to be there in time to do any good—and the car will have to be driven back. You don't want to do that journey all by yourself. Besides, we're not booked to cross until the 29th, and we won't have a hope of getting the car over before then, not in August."

"So I'm to stay here?"

"Yes, darling, just until Sunday. I'm sure that's the best way—really." He bent to kiss her, but she turned her head.

"We'd better go and find a time-table," she said. "It seems as though my main function in life is to say good-bye to you on station platforms."

They went in, and Quilter explained the situation to the hotel people, who were all concern and helpfulness. Telephone calls were put through to stations and air terminals and in half an hour everything was arranged. There was a train to Toulouse at 9.40 that evening and a plane to London via Paris in the morning. The necessary reservations were made, and June went upstairs to pack Laurence's case.

They dined with time to spare, and after dinner she went with him to the station. He was laconic on the journey, his thoughts evidently far away.

"You'll look after yourself, won't you?" he said, as he hung out of the train window. "Mind how you drive! Promise?" His eyes held hers for a moment, and there was the old twinkle in them.

Julie felt like flinging herself into the carriage with him. Then the train gave a little toot and began to move.

"I'll be counting the days," she called, and stood waving and watching until the tail lights were out of sight. Then she turned and walked slowly to the car. Now that he had gone she felt quite stunned by the suddenness of it all Traill was back on the terrace when she reached the hotel and she stopped to tell him her news.

"Well, if that isn't the darnedest luck!" he said, and he looked really sorry. "Still . . . Thursday, Friday, Saturday, Sunday—it's not so long. It'll go in a flash. Have a drink, won't you, it'll cheer you up."

"Not just now, thanks. I'm a bit tired, I think I'll go to bed. Good-night, Mr. Traill."

"Good-night—sleep well. And if there's anything I can do at any time, just call on me." He smiled at her, the warm friendly smile that she liked so much. It was an anaesthetic, dulling pain.

Chapter Four

Traces of the overnight depression were still with Julie when she woke next morning to find herself alone in the big double room, but she had too resilient a nature for the mood to last. As she pushed the shutters wide open and looked out on the sunlit terra cotta roofs and heard the sounds of happy laughter from the street, her spirits rose. While she dressed, she made plans. It would be rather fun, she thought, to take a solitary prowl through the older parts of the town. She had walked round once with Laurence but it hadn't been very satisfactory because their tempo was so different. She liked to linger and he always wanted to push on. She liked to squeeze the maximum of satisfaction out of the present and he always thought there'd be something better round the corner. She still remembered an occasion in Cornwall when she'd wanted to spend some time in a village famous for its pottery works and he had insisted on pressing on to their morning's objective still many miles away. "Any climb with a view at the end of it is worth more to me than a dozen pottery factories," he'd said, and she'd toiled up the steep hillside behind him, too breathless to register even a mild protest. And then a mist had come down and they hadn't been able to see the view after all. She was still smiling at the recollection as she went lightly downstairs.

She spent a blissful morning poking about in little back-street shops, buying presents for small nephews and nieces and talking to the voluble shopkeepers. That was another thing—Laurence didn't really like meeting new people and he nearly always shied away from casual conversations so that they rarely had much contact with the locals when they were away. In half an hour she was able to learn more about Pouillac and its life than she had picked up in the whole of the previous week. When she had finished her shopping she paid a second visit to the fascinating IIth century cathedral, which she hadn't been able to look at properly before because Laurence couldn't bear the smell of incense and what he called "the tawdry trappings of organised religion."

She bought a newspaper just before lunch to see if there was any more news of the colliery disaster, but there wasn't. She lunched alone, with a book beside her plate, and spent the afternoon sitting under the chestnuts on the terrace, reading in a rather desultory way. When the sun began to lose its fierceness she took a stroll through the town to see how the workmen were getting on with the decorations. The place was already taking on a pleasantly festive air, particularly in the main square, which had been given over to sideshows and roundabouts and a large open space for dancing. The prospect of weekend gaiety made her feel lonely again and she drifted back to the hotel.

The second day was only a slight variant of the first, except that it seemed to pass more slowly. She took the car out to the quiet spot that she and Laurence had liked, but she had never enjoyed driving by herself, and picnicking alone wasn't very exciting. As on the previous evening, she accepted Benson Traill's invitation to a before-dinner drink. It would have been pleasant to pass much more time with him, for she found him attractive, but loyalty to Laurence made her ration herself where his company was concerned. It wasn't worth while getting even slightly involved merely to relieve a few days' monotony. Traill himself was strictly formal in his attitude, although it was obvious that he enjoyed being with her. He went off somewhere every morning in his jeep, full of zest and interest, and was always so cheerful in the evenings when he recounted his activities that Julie felt quite ashamed of her own insufficiency.

By Saturday morning she was able to start thinking of Laurence's return and even went so far as to borrow an air time-table to see when she might begin to expect him. That was one admirable thing about him—he was meticulous in the way he kept to arrangements.

This time, of course, he'd been necessarily vague, but he had mentioned Sunday and he'd certainly make it if he could. For once, she felt glad that he was such a hustler—she really wouldn't have been able to stand much more of this holidaying alone.

She was unable, after all, to make anything of the timetable and presently took it back to the office. As she passed the letter-rack a familiar handwriting caught her eye. She snatched at the letter in sudden apprehension and tore it open with fingers that trembled a little. If he had bothered to write, it could mean only one thing. She ran her eye quickly down the page and then took the letter out with her on to the terrace and sat down and read it again.

There was a note of haste about it, as though he were frantically busy. Adam Johnson, it said, had been most relieved when he had turned up and emphatic that he had done the right thing to return. He had been over to the pit and seen some of the bereaved relatives and the injured men, and he'd opened a Fund with a cheque for £500. Unfortunately he'd found himself more tied up than he'd expected to be, and it would probably be another day or two before he could get away. He hoped that she was enjoying herself, and was sure that the holiday must be doing her good anyway. The letter ended perfunctorily, "Love, Laurence."

Another day or two. That could mean anything. With all her heart Julie wished now that she had insisted on going back with him. He was sure the holiday was doing her good! How astonishingly insensitive he could be sometimes! Or was it that she expected too much? Wearily she wondered, and as so often happened she ended up by accusing herself. She had to remember that Laurence was more absorbed in his work than most men and that she liked him that way. She would have hated to have an uxorious husband. He couldn't be finding the atmosphere of Coalhaven very pleasant and he was probably as fed up as she was. She pushed the letter into her bag, unable to look at it again, but it was herself she was annoyed with.

So now what? How on earth was she going to pass the time? It wasn't that there was nothing to do in this place—far from it—but loneliness was a creeping, paralysing thing that froze interest and energy. A day or two was hardly long enough to make new friends, and anyway she didn't feel inclined to attach herself to any of the self-contained French families in the hotel. She could write to Laurence, of course—but at present she distrusted her mood. She would do that this evening. In the end she went out for another of her solitary strolls.

When she returned to the hotel shortly after five, Traill was sitting on the terrace. He looked up at her approach, and his welcoming grin was by far the nicest thing that had happened to her that day. "Hello, there!" he called "How are you doing?"

She subsided into the chair beside him. "I'm hot."

"That I can believe—you walk about so much. Mad dogs and English women . . .!"

"I've got to do *something*," she said.

He looked at her in surprise. "Cheer up—to-morrow's Sunday. You'll be okay as soon as that M.P. of yours gets back."

She gave a wry smile. "It seems I'm to be a grass widow for several more days. He's been delayed."

"Ah!" Traill regarded her thoughtfully. "That *is* tough." He held out a packet of cigarettes and Julie took one gratefully. "Look," he said when he had given her a light, "why don't you snap out of it and have a bit of fun?" This is no way to go on, mooning around the joint day after day."

"What do you suggest?"

"Well, suppose I take you out to dinner for a start?"

"I'd adore that," she said.

"Okay, it's a date. And look—let's get this straight right now. The way I see it, it's pretty darned stupid for you and me to go around on our own. I guess we could have a lot of fun if we teamed up for a day or two, and so far as I'm concerned it'd be strictly on the level. I've no territorial ambitions. All right with you?"

"All right with me," she said with a smile.

"Fine. Will you meet me here at—well, say quarter after six?"

She nodded happily and jumped up. "I'd better go and change. You're rather sweet, Ben—did you know that?"

She went to her room feeling ridiculously like a schoolgirl about to be taken out for the first time. After her bath she made herself up with care and put on a favourite frock of pale yellow linen, knowing how well it set off her tan. Flowery earrings in white china added a gay, light-hearted touch.

When she went downstairs at twenty past six, Traill was waiting for her. He had changed into a very light tropical suit that would have gone better with an open Cadillac than a jeep.

"Where are we going?" she asked as he helped her up.

"Not far—a place called the Langouste, or something, down by the river. I discovered it yesterday. Do you know it?"

"No, but I'd like to." She held her face to the cool breeze, enjoying the feel of it in her hair. "you know, this is the first time I've ever been in a jeep."

Ben laughed. "Baby, you just haven't lived!"

They crossed the picturesque bridge over the Dordogne and a few moments later they reached the Langouste, a little auberge with a deceptively unassuming exterior. Ben parked the jeep and led the way round to the river with the air of a man who knew his way about. Tables were set out on a flowered stone terrace just above the water, and silver and glass gleamed in the light of lanterns. A dozen people, all French, were sitting around in scattered groups., sipping apéritifs and talking in lively tones.

The maître d'hôtel came forward with a smile and held a chair for Julie. "Everything is arranged, sir," he said to Ben. His English was perfect. "Your table is over there in the corner—whenever you are ready." He bowed and departed. Almost at once, a waiter arrived with champagne cocktails.

Julie looked accusingly at Ben. "You must have rushed along here and fixed all this."

"I did just look in. This is an occasion. Besides, I need someone to hold my hand over food and wine, and this head waiter knows everything. Now we can just concentrate on each other." He handed Julie her glass and raised his own. "Happy days!"

"Happy days!" she echoed, her eyes dancing.

That was the beginning of one of the most delightful evenings that Julie could remember. Everything was marvellous, the food not least. They had *écrevisses* with a dry white wine; and chicken in a delicious tarragon sauce, with truffles and more white wine; and *Brie* with half a bottle of a specially recommended Château Latour. Ben was in the highest spirits and Julie, after her three lonely days, ecstatically gay. As the leisurely meal progressed, a sliver of moon came up over the water and threw a romantic light over everything.

About nine, the sounds of music and festivity came wafting over the warm fragrant air and they decided to go back into town and see what was happening. Ben drove with caution, easing the jeep through streets which were rapidly filling with crowds *en fête*. Bright arc lamps had been set up around the open space that had been turned into a fair ground; balloons and streamers hung from the trees; roundabouts shrieked and blared; and there seemed to be laughing, happy people everywhere.

"How about sampling the fun of the fair?" Ben suggested. He parked the jeep in a jam of cars and helped Julie down, taking her arm and steering her through the throng. They worked steadily through the side-shows, shying at coconuts, shooting at moving ducks, throwing hoops at bottles of cognac, even stopping to watch a sort of Punch and Judy show. Presently they came to the cleared area where the young people of Pouillac, and many of the old ones, were dancing to the music of three accordions.

Ben's fingers closed persuasively on Julie's arm. "How about it?"

She needed no urging, and he caught her round the waist and carried her off in a jiggy waltz. There wasn't much room to move and that suited both of them. They circled round and round in the same spot, holding each other close, completely at one with the happy, anonymous crowd.

"That was wonderful!" said Julie, flushed and a little breathless, as the music stopped at last. "You know, I can't remember when I last danced."

"No kidding! I imagined you lived in quite a social whirl back home."

"Far from it. Laurence doesn't like his fellow men very much."

"No? Now that's odd—he struck me as a pretty good-mixer."

"He does give that impression sometimes to people he meets casually, but he has to make an effort—it doesn't come naturally to him."

"Too bad for a public man! Must be quite a strain."

"I think it is. He's always worn out after a party or a meeting." She smiled up at Ben. "Sorry—I didn't mean to talk about him now. Do you think they'd start playing again if we clapped?"

"They're just going to," said Ben. The accordions went noisily into action and almost at once they were swept into a riotous French dance in which everybody seemed to be gathering the Gallic equivalent of nuts in May.

It was nearly two in the morning when the crowd at last began to thin. Ben said he'd extricate the jeep later and they walked slowly back to the hotel.

They lingered a moment in the foyer. "It's been wonderful, Ben," Julie said. "I feel so different. I can't begin to thank you."

"You don't have to, honey. It was a privilege."

She smiled. "Good-night, Ben."

"Good-night, Julie." He watched her start up the stairs. To-morrow we'll think of something else to do."

Chapter Five

From now on they spent all their waking hours together. Each morning at about ten the jeep would draw up outside the hotel and Ben would give a honk and Julie would join him. He would ask her what she wanted to do and they would agree on some general objective and set off hopefully without bothering too much about maps or routes. Ben seemed content to rely on signposts, and if they arrived somewhere they hadn't intended to and at a time that didn't fit into any schedule, it was all the same to him. In the mornings they usually just cruised along the empty secondary roads, unhurried and relaxed, stopping whenever they felt like it to admire a view or watch oxen working in a field or chat to a rustic tending his flock of goats. Then around twelve they would start to look for a shady picnic spot, which wasn't easy to find with the sun almost vertical overhead. They would lounge for a couple of hours, and sometimes all afternoon; then drift back to the hotel, have a few drinks, dine together at some place that had caught their eye, have a few more drinks, and say good-night. It was, as Ben said, a pretty good life. From the point of view of sheer companionship it was exactly the holiday that Julie had hoped for with Laurence, but she was having it with Ben instead. She had rarely enjoyed the path of least resistance so much.

It was all on a day-to-day basis, of course—that was her excuse and, she was sure, her safeguard. Any evening there might be a wire from Laurence; any morning he might arrive. They were just filling in time in a mutually satisfactory manner. When he came back it would be quite easy to resume their association *à trois*, or not, just as they liked, but in any case without embarrassment. Ben was keeping strictly to his undertaking that it would be all "on the level." Occasionally, perhaps, his smiling eyes did seem to say things that he wouldn't have voiced, but his manner was easy, natural and frank. Julie found him extraordinarily restful. However much she tried not to, she couldn't help contrasting him in her mind with Laurence, Ben was reliable and even-tempered. With him she didn't have to watch her step and guard her tongue all the time as she did with the incalculable Laurence. She didn't have to be always making adjustments to suit his changing moods—she could be herself, and know that he'd like it. She tried to tell herself that it might become dull in time if you could always rely on a person, but she never felt quite convinced. Ben would never be dull; he was too interested in everything, too appreciative, too eager to live each moment fully. Lapped in deep contentment, Julie thought how easy it would be to fall in love with him and wondered how many more days they would dare to tempt the fates.

With nothing much else to do but laze, they naturally talked a good deal about themselves and each other. Julie told Ben about her early life, about the parents who had died within a short while of each other when she was seventeen, and of the struggle she had had to establish herself financially. She told him about the dull but safe job she had held in a wartime organisation, arranging itineraries for public speakers, and how she had got to know Laurence that way and had accompanied him to many of his meetings and been completely enthralled by his eloquence and passionate sincerity. She told how she had given up her job, wanting something more active for herself, and how she'd joined the Women's Land Army, getting herself posted, she admitted with a rueful smile, to the Lake District just in order to be near Laurence when the House wasn't sitting, and how they'd had rather a clandestine affair until his mother's death because the old lady hadn't approved of the association. She told about the Quilter family, and the house at Blean, and the cottage; about the excitements and tediums of political strife about Laurence's ambitions and her hopes for him and her worries about his health. Ben was a good listener and it was pleasant to tell him about these things as they lay in the shade on the bone-dry grass, smoking and completely relaxed.

Ben did a bit of reminiscing, too, but not so much. He'd been born somewhere in the Middle West, at a place that Julie had never heard of. His father had been a small-town vet with not much money but ambitions for his son. Ben had gone to college on a shoe-string, had become interested in geology, graduated, joined an oil company, been drafted during the war and spent the best part of four years working on air-strip sites in the Far East, and then after the war rejoined the same company and gone to Trinidad.

Julie was curious to know about the life he lived there. "I know you enjoy the work," she said, "but what sort of place is Trinidad to live in?"

He grinned. "It's not bad if you like prickly heat, mosquitoes, sandflies, scorpions and tarantulas."

"Ben, I don't believe it. I'm sure that's not what the travel folders say."

"Well, and velvet skies, humming birds, coconut palms and sapphire seas."

"That sounds more like it. Aren't you forgetting the dusky beauties, though?"

"No. I'm just not telling you about them."

"Are they very attractive?"

"They're kind of mixed."

"Modified rapture, I must say. Well, where do you live, Ben—do you have a company house?"

"Yes, I have a small bungalow. Quite a civilised place, actually—I've a couple of servants and a car, and a terrace with a view over the sea, and a fifth share in a private beach, and a garden with a mango tree."

"It sounds wonderful. Is it?"

"Well, yes and no. I thought it was a marvellous life at first—every comfort, always someone around it you wanted to drink rum punch or have a game of tennis, nothing to worry about outside the job. Then after a while it got to feel kind of empty. It's an artificial, frothy sort of existence except when you're at work. I think the guys with their families out there have the best of it. I'm happier when I'm in the bush."

This conversation took place on the second day, when they were on their way to visit an ancient monastery where there was a mural that Julie rather wanted to see. On the third day they decided to drive down to a picturesque old town called Cahors and have lunch there. As Julie climbed into the jeep, smiled upon by the Lavendou's benevolent proprietress, who thought it a shame that any charming woman should ever be alone, Ben asked his usual question—"Any news?"

Julie shook her head. "I should think I'm bound to hear to-night, though."

Ben gave an uncomprehending shrug. "I don't get it," he said, as they drove away.

"What don't you get?"

"Well, I guess it's none of my business, but it seems kind of odd, leaving you here all this time and not keeping in touch . . ."

Julie tried to make light of it. "Laurence is always like that when he gets involved in something that interests him. Politics mean so much more to him than people."

"That's a heck of a thing to say about anyone."

"Oh, I don't know. Men often have to put their jobs first."

Ben grunted. "I'm darned sure of one thing—if I'd had the luck to marry a nice girl I'd want her around."

"Watching you break stones?"

"Sure! It'd be twice the fun."

"Politics and geology aren't quite the same thing."

"I'll say they're not. I may be talking out of turn, but I distrust these men who get so keen on ideas that they've no time to be human. They're dangerous—always making trouble."

Julie laughed. "Laurence would call that a very reactionary remark. He thinks the only way you get progress is by making trouble."

"You get a lot of other things as well. I'm not saying we'd be better off without any politicians, but it would help if they'd take a bromide now and again. I've seen them operating at close quarters. They've stirred up plenty of grief in Trinidad."

"Wasn't it necessary?"

"I don't think it was—not in our business, anyway. We provide good jobs for hundreds of coloured workers, pay them far better than anyone else does or ever did, build them decent houses, look after their health, help to educate their. kids, give them a standard of life they couldn't dream of without us. What's more, we get along well with them if we're left alone. We know them and we like them."

"Benevolent capitalism! That's what Laurence would say."

"I guess he would, but from my point of view it's just a good human relationship. When I go out into the bush on a field job it's with a native team, mostly, and it works fine. I know their names and their interests and how many women they're keeping and what they do Saturday nights, and when we talk it's all down to earth and simple and mighty satisfying. They know I've got a chichi bungalow and a car and a private beach, but they don't envy me, and why should they?—they're as happy as I am. Then the politicians come along, full of big words and always in a hurry. They tell the workers they ought to be better off, ought to emancipate themselves, ought to get the full fruits of their labour, whatever that means. Next thing someone's inciting a mob to demonstrate, the good relationship's spoilt, the men strike and riot, the families go hungry, oil's set on fire and wasted, drillers are attacked and finally people get shot. Everybody's worse off. What's the point of it all?"

"You know," said Julie teasingly, "I think you could be a politician after all—you're quite angry. You'll probably be a Senator one day."

"Not me—I'll stick to stone-breaking." He gave her a rather shamefaced grin. "I guess I'm all steamed up on account of that inconsiderate husband of yours."

She made no reply to that and he didn't pursue the subject. For a while he looked a bit grim, and then they came to a closed level crossing, and his interest was caught by what was going on there. A very large, very fierce female who seemed to be in charge was telling a party of impatient French motorists, with much flamboyant gesture, that if she let them through before the train her employers would cut her into three separate pieces. She indicated precisely where the incisions would be made. Ben said, "Gee, isn't she a honey?—let's go and join in," and a moment later he had jumped out, all his annoyance forgotten.

They had a grand day at Cahors, lunching on the ramparts of the old walls, taking photographs of the 14th century bridge and of each other and climbing afterwards to a fine viewpoint just outside the town. They stayed out late, making the most of the day in case it should be their last together, and when they got back to Pouillac Julie said goodnight and went straight upstairs to bed. There was no letter in the rack, but as she entered her room the first thing that caught her eye was a telegram on the dressing table.

She opened it and read: STILL DETAINED HOPE TO GET AWAY SUNDAY LAURENCE.

She went over to her open window and sat there for a long while, her mind full of disturbing thoughts. She had always known that Laurence had an unusual capacity to detach himself from ordinary human feelings—to concentrate on what he was doing regardless of everything else. It was one of the things she had rather admired in him—but only, she now realised, because she had never herself felt the full impact of his ruthless single-mindedness. Now that she had, it was like a blow in the face. She couldn't imagine what was detaining him, but that seemed almost immaterial. What was important was that he could be so indifferent to her; that he didn't even bother to explain; that he could leave her alone like this on their long-awaited holiday with nothing to sustain her but these curt uninformative messages.

She found it hard to sort out her feelings. She wanted to rush home and ask him what he thought he was playing at. She wanted to stay away from him and show him that she didn't care. She was deeply hurt and angry and humiliated—and yet, at the back of her mind, was the assuaging thought of Ben. The more she raged inwardly at the absent Laurence, the greater comfort she found in the recollection of Ben's gentleness and understanding. And that in itself infuriated her. Damn it, if Laurence had *wanted* her to have an affair he couldn't have arranged it better.

It was a long time before she slept, and all her thoughts were of the two men.

Chapter Six

They had planned to go to Rocamadour next day if by any chance Julie was still without word, and Ben was waiting with the jeep as usual. He greeted Julie with his customary air of detached cheerfulness, but for the first time she found it hard to respond. She had pretty well come to a decision, but it wasn't going to be easy to tell him or to carry it out. Sensing her mood, but mistaking its cause, Ben refrained from his usual "Any news?" Obviously there wasn't any, and that was why she was looking so blue. For a moment his arm rested consolingly across her shoulder as he lit a cigarette for her, and then they were away and he was talking fast, so that she wouldn't have to.

Julie found herself more conscious of him to-day—more conscious of his close physical presence. She noticed his hands on the wheel. They were smaller than she would have expected in a man of his build, and beautifully-shaped, with slender fingers and delicately-boned wrists. Sensitive hands—more suited certainly to the microscope than the mallet. She noticed, too, the fineness and smoothness of his brown skin where his short-sleeved shirt ended above the elbow. She realised, with a sense of something missed, that in all these days she had hardly touched him—not since they had danced in the square, and that seemed years ago.

The knowledge of what she had to do oppressed her, but she had no intention of spoiling their last morning and as they reached the plateau that commanded Rocamadour her interest sounded unforced. They left the jeep and walked through the fantastic perched-up village with its real and pseudo relics and its air of commercialised pilgrimage that scarcely detracted from its fascination. They climbed to the château and from its ramparts gazed down in awe at the diminutive rooftops of the cottage hundreds of feet below, Julie drawing back a little with a gasp of dismay at the height, and glad of Ben's reassuring grip. They refreshed themselves with *vin blanc* on a terrace swathed in bougain-villea and then made an unsuccessful search for, what the guidebooks said was Roland's Sword.

When they had had their fill of sight-seeing they returned to the jeep and drove out on to a deserted road till they came to a place where a solitary juniper threw enough shade for lunch. It was a wild and arid spot, with a view over immense empty hills and no sign of life anywhere. There was a gentle heat murmur, and when they moved through the short sparse grass myriads of huge strange grasshoppers flew up with bright wings of blue and red, as pretty as moths. It was a place that Julie felt she would always remember.

When they had finished the meal and were lying back with cigarettes alight, looking up at the blue sky through dust-coloured leaves, Julie said: "I thought you were going to tour Switzerland, Germany and Holland, Ben?"

He turned his face lazily towards her, and grinned. "I thought your husband was coming back last Sunday!"

"That hasn't anything to do with it. What I mean is . . . Ben, you're not going in for knight-errantry on my account, are you? Because . . ."

"*I* know," he said. "Because you're not anybody's lost property and you can look after yourself perfectly well . . . Isn't that what you were going to say?"

His teasing smile was so full of affection that her eyes dropped before his glance and she felt the pricking of tears.

"Look, Julie," he said, sitting up, "we don't have to pretend with each other. I stuck around here because I liked being with you, and if you think it was out of pity for a poor lonely girl you're crazy." Then he added: "Of course, if what you're really trying to say is that you want me to go—well, for Pete's sake, honey, just say it. I'm a great awkward clod but I'll understand." He saw her turn her head away sharply and frowned. "Maybe it isn't that either. Something special's upset you to-day, hasn't it? Come on, honey, tell Uncle Ben. What's happened?"

Julie was fiercely stubbing the end of her cigarette into the grass. At the gentleness in Ben's voice her self-control suddenly broke and she gave a little sob. In an instant Ben's arms were round her shoulders, tender and comforting. That was her undoing. Her over-wrought nerves gave way and: she buried her face against him in an abandonment of weeping, while he murmured soothing, indistinguishable things into her ear.

It didn't last long. Presently she struggled free from his embrace and sat up, blowing her nose fiercely. "I'm a fool" she said crossly, "a perfect fool!" She sniffed. "It's partly your fault, too—don't you know you should never sympathise with a hysterical idiot? You ought to be telling me to snap out of it, not encouraging me to cry on your shoulder."

"I guess I haven't had enough practice. C'mon, then, snap out of it. And now tell me what's eating you."

"I—I've had a telegram from Laurence."

"About time, too! I still don't see, though . . ."

"He's not coming till next Sunday, at the earliest."

"So—o—o! And you're missing him badly—is that it?"

"No—I'm not. That's part of the trouble. I'm not missing him, Ben, I'm having a wonderful time, but . . ."—Julie's voice shook—". . . oh, Ben, I'm feeling so terribly humiliated."

He looked at her as though he only partly comprehended. "You see—well, I suppose there *may* be something important detaining him but I can't believe it's as terribly vital as all that. And at least he could let me know what it is, but he doesn't say anything. I think he's just not caring all that much about getting back. . . . It's pretty awful to feel you've sunk yourself completely in someone else and then find you're not appreciated."

"You're telling me, honey! I've done that, too. Still . . ."—he gave her a puzzled look—". . . aren't you magnifying this thing a bit, maybe? I mean, you say yourself the guy may be genuinely held up. Or is there something else I don't know about? I guess there must be—it would take more than one isolated incident to get you into this state." Julie sighed. "There is, I suppose, but nothing specific—just an atmosphere and a lot of little things you'd think were pretty insignificant if I tried to tell you about them. Anyway, I feel horrible talking like this about Laurence when he isn't here. He's a difficult type but I know all about him and I just have to accept it, that's all. Only sometimes it gets me down."

Ben was silent for a while. He wanted to help, but it was her tangle, not his.

"Look, Julie . . ." he said at last, in the rueful tone of a man about to tell a story against himself, "here's something I didn't mean to say to you ever, but I guess I will. I think you're the most wonderful person I ever met. I've fallen for you head over heels. I didn't intend to—in fact I had every intention of not doing—but it's happened. When I found myself getting more than interested in you, pretty well right from the start, I told myself I'd better clear out – but then I figured I could keep everything under control and that anyway you didn't know, and there was your husband besides. But—well, now that you're feeling down and out over one sap who doesn't know when he's well off, maybe it'll help to know there's another sap ready to lie down and let you walk over him. I'd do anything for you, Julie. Why, goddam it, I could almost wish you happily re-united with that M.P. of yours if that's the way you want it."

She smiled through her tears. "You're so sweet, but that's one of the troubles—I'm not even sure that I *do* want Laurence, and after seven years that's a pretty shattering doubt."

Ben stared at her, incredulous hope dawning in his eyes. "Julie, what are you saying?"

"Well, I'm not at all sure that I'm not beginning to fall in love with you."

He longed to take her at her word, but the undertone of reservation warned him that this was no declaration. The rueful look came back. "Why not just go straight ahead, honey? What's stopping you?"

"Ben, I can't. It's not as simple as that. Don't you realise, I'm married. I've lived with a man for seven years and I've put everything

I have and am into that existence. I can't have the whole thing wiped out in a matter of hours, almost. It can't have mattered so little."

"Why not? It may have been a big mistake."

"Well, I don't *want* to think it has mattered so little. It's—it's humiliating."

Ben frowned. "That's twice you've used that word, Julie. I'd say it was pretty revealing. I'd say there was something badly wrong with your marriage if you're worrying about humiliation. Don't you know, honey, that love—real love—hasn't any pride? I admit I don't know much about you both, but I'd guess that what you feel for him now isn't love but—well, habit, and maybe something to do with the maternal instinct. And I just don't see how he can have any real love for *you*—leaving you eating your heart out for him here like this and not knowing all about it in his bones."

A look of obstinacy had settled on Julie's face while he was speaking. "You may be right, Ben, I don't know—but let's not talk about it any more. I shouldn't have started it in the first place. There's nothing to be done. It was only because I was upset about the telegram and knowing he wasn't coming back till Sunday."

Ben gave a little shrug of resignation. "Okay, honey, have it your own way. God knows I don't want to make things more difficult for you. What happens now, though—do I still stick around and help you pass the time?" He grinned. "Now that you know my guilty secret?"

She laughed, a little tremulously. "Ben, your secret! You know it's only because we've been together so much and had such fun and everything's been so marvellous. You're not really in love with me."

"That's just where you're wrong, Julie. I'm not kidding!"

Suddenly, as though he knew this was the only opportunity he'd ever have to show her what he felt, he seized her in his arms and crushed her to him and kissed her mouth with passion. The laughter went out of Julie's eyes and for a moment she clung to him in disbelief, staring into his face as though she had had a revelation. Then she murmured, "Oh, Ben!" and met his lips with her own.

When at last he released her she was breathless and a little pale and almost frightened at her own emotion. "Ben," she said softly, "I didn't know. At least, I wasn't sure. Darling . . . I love you."

"Honey!"

"I didn't think it possible in so short a time . . . Oh, Ben, what have we done?"

"We've fallen in love, that's all. Easiest thing in the world." His arms went round her again, but she drew away from him.

"Ben, it's no good, we've got to be sensible."

"Why? Whoever heard of people in love being sensible?"

"Don't, please! I mean it. I *am* in love with you, I want to be with you all the time, but—it's no good, we're just being absurd and romantic. It's being alone in this lovely place, it's being lonely, it's—oh, Ben, it *can't* be the real thing."

"Give if a chance, honey. I think it is. I think it's the beginning of something big and lasting . . ."

"*No*, Ben! I must have been mad . . ."

"You said you loved me, and I think you meant it,"

"But there's no future in it."

"There could be—in time. You could marry me."

Slowly she shook her head. "I can't. It isn't anything to do with what I feel, I just can't. I must go home. I ought to have gone before—I oughtn't to have let all this happen. Oh, Ben, I'm sorry—for both of us."

"You don't love him," Ben persisted.

"I don't know what I feel—I'm so confused. You may be right about him and me—perhaps the whole thing between us has been built on a false foundation. I'm not sure—I shall have to see. But in any case I must go. I must behave as though nothing has happened here. Perhaps I'll find that nothing *has* happened—that this is just an infatuation. I—I hope so."

"And if you don't?"

Her eyes met his. "I shall still stay, if I think that he needs me. And I think he does. Oh, Ben, please try to understand."

He gazed at her with hopeless longing. It was hard to be given a glimpse of heaven and then find it a mirage—but her tone was so pleading that he hadn't the heart to press her any more. She didn't want to be persuaded. Even if he could beat down her doubts and scruples, there was no fingerpost pointing to happiness that way.

"I understand, honey," he said at last. "you feel you've made a life investment and even if it's turned out badly you're not going to cut your losses. That was clear enough before—I was a darned fool to grab you and start all this." He felt for a cigarette and snapped his lighter on. "It looks like good-bye for us, then."

"Yes, I'm afraid so, Ben darling—it's good-bye." She scanned his rigid face. "I'm sorry that you're hurt—you've been such a dear."

He said wryly, "I guess we'll both manage. And after all, I didn't expect anything different—only for a couple of seconds, anyway. I thought you'd be the kind of woman who'd behave this way. Maybe that's why I fell for you in the first place."

He looked away across the empty hills. "You know, something like this once happened to me before—when I was more vulnerable. I took a header, and the water turned out to be shallower than I thought, and I was just about knocked unconscious. I never meant that to happen again. It hasn't, either—not in the same way. I've taken a header, all right, but it's turned out to be the warmest, most sparkling sea ever. I'll never regret it, honey. And I hope things'll turn out as you want them." He smiled at her. "Of course, if before we separate you get to thinking that maybe I *could* prise you away from that husband of yours—well, just let me know."

"I will, Ben—but don't expect it." Her eyes were misty.

"Okay. Now what say we go? I guess our party's about over."

Julie nodded, and they silently gathered up their things. There was only one way to deal with a situation like this, and that was to end it with speed and dignity.

As soon as they got back to the hotel Julie wrote out a telegram for Laurence. At first she said simply, "Am coming home." It was Ben who suggested she should add, "Please acknowledge." It would be too absurd, she agreed, if after all this waiting she and Laurence were to cross en route, so that he finished up in the Dordogne and she in Cumberland. Ben strolled with her down to the post office, looking pretty grim. He had reconciled himself to the inevitable by now, but the finality of the telegram was still hard to take.

They dined together as usual that evening, because it would have bean even more difficult not to, but there was no possibility of recapturing the old carefree relationship. They were actors now, struggling through banal lines to a dreary curtain. They had a last drink on the terrace and then Ben made a move.

"I guess I'd better go and throw my things together," he said. "I shall get out first thing to-morrow, Julie—I think it's best that way. You'll probably be off yourself in the afternoon, anyway."

Julie nodded. "All right, Ben. I'll come upstairs with you. We can't say good-bye here."

They went up to her room and Ben took her gently in his arms and kissed her once, without passion. "Good-bye, Julie."

"Good-bye, Ben—thank you for everything." She clung to him for a moment. "It's going to be so hard to forget you."

"It's a pity you've got to try," said Ben. "Unnecessary, I think. Still—so long, honey. Good luck." He gave her shoulder an affectionate squeeze, and was gone.

Chapter Seven

Julie lingered in her room next morning, not wanting to run the risk of an awkward last-minute encounter. Instead she watched Ben's preparations for departure from her window, wishing she had the strength not to but unable to drag herself away. She saw him standing beside the jeep, chatting to Madame, seemingly quite carefree. He was even smiling—how *could* he smile? Then his luggage was put in and he climbed up and drove away without a single backward glance.

Well, that was that! Now the sooner she followed his example the better—this place had too many memories, and partings were always worse for the person left behind. She should be getting a telegram any time. She did what packing she could and wrote some postcards that ought to have been sent off days before. Then she got out the neglected Riley and had it filled with petrol and oil in readiness for the long journey ahead.

After lunch, when there was still no word from Laurence, it suddenly occurred to her to try telephoning. A long distance call might be hard on her travel allowance but it was better than hanging about for a telegram that didn't come. Anyway, it would help to fill up the time. It took her quite a while to get through to Blean and then there was no reply from the cottage, so she left the call in. Just to be on the safe side, she also rang the flat. This time the connexion was made more quickly, but again there was no reply and she left that call in too.

She spent the afternoon with a pile of magazines, sitting on a grassy slope behind the hotel from which she could be fetched quickly to the telephone. She tried not to dwell on Ben, but her thoughts kept drifting back to him. She wondered where he had gone to, what his plans were, what he was really feeling. She missed him horribly. If only Laurence would ring!

All through the long afternoon and evening she waited, her nerves jumping every time the phone went. When, by eleven o'clock, Laurence had still not come through, she decided there could be only one explanation—he must have changed his mind and left already for France. It was a good thing that she'd curbed her impatience and not gone rushing off home as she'd wanted to do. To-morrow he'd arrive.

When the maid came in with coffee and *croissants* at nine next morning she pointed to a telegram on the tray. Julie thanked her with a smile and opened it eagerly, certain that it would tell her he was on his way. Instead, she read: NO POINT IN YOUR COMING BACK DEFINITELY JOINING YOU WEDNESDAY.

She stared at it, bewildered and incredulous. It was obviously a reply to her own wire and it had been dispatched from Blean, so he must have been at the cottage yesterday. Why hadn't he taken her phone call?

She read the short message again. Wednesday! He expected her to stay here alone for almost another week! And still there was no letter, still no word of regret or explanation. It was unforgivable.

Fury suddenly possessed her—fury at Laurence and fury at herself. What a fool she'd been to let Ben go rushing off like that! They could have been having a wonderful time together if she hadn't been so observed with the idea of doing her duty and standing by her marriage vows. It was obvious that Laurence didn't care two hoots about her any more, or he'd never have treated her in this cavalier fashion. His attitude showed an almost contemptuous indifference. Her loyalty had been utterly thrown away. And to think she'd imagined that he needed her!

Still simmering with anger, though with no clearly-formed intentions, she dressed and went downstairs to the reception desk. She forced a smile as the proprietress greeted her and hesitated a moment as she sought to frame her question without giving herself away.

"I seem to have Mr. Traill's cigarette case," she said, in as casual a tone as possible. "Did he leave any forwarding address, by any chance?"

"No, Madame. He said he was going to Switzerland, that is all."

"Oh!" Julie started to turn away. It seemed that the decision had been made for her! "Well, he'll have to do without it, I suppose." Suddenly she made up her mind. "I shall be leaving this morning, I'm afraid. I've just heard from my husband—it seems that he won't be able to get back after all."

"But of course, Madame. Such a disappointment for you!"

"Yes, isn't it?"

Julie went quickly back to her room and packed with resolution. No use thinking of Ben any more! No use being sorry for herself! She'd had her chance and missed it—now there was nothing to do but get on to the road and keep moving. She spread out the maps and studied the route. Even she could hardly make a mistake about so direct a way. Straight up the main Toulouse-Paris road for three hundred miles or more, and then north to Dieppe. More or less the way she and Laurence had come.

By eleven she was away. She drove fast, eating up the kilometres on the straight empty roads and wishing only that the car had wings. By nightfall she was at Chateauroux, too worn out to think of anything but sleep. She was up again soon after dawn and racing northwards, reaching Dieppe to find the R.A.C. port office still open. The R.A.C. man was anxious to help her but dubious whether she'd be able to get transport for the car before the reserved date, which was still a week ahead. The only chance, he said, was that some other car might fail to turn up for its appointed crossing. It did happen occasionally.

She thanked him and found a hotel for the night. If she couldn't get a passage for the car, she decided, she would leave it behind and Laurence could do what he liked about collecting it. But when she drove down to the harbour next morning, her luck was in. There was room. A few hours later she was disembarking at Newhaven.

She thought of telephoning the cottage from there but what she had to say to Laurence seemed best kept for their meeting, so she sent a telegram instead announcing she was on her way. Then she drove up to London and spent the night at the flat.

Next morning she caught the first express to the North, leaving the car behind her. By now she felt as though she had been travelling for weeks. Her body ached from the strain of continuous driving and her sustaining anger was giving way to a dull fatigue. She felt immeasurably depressed.

She was prepared for Laurence to be at the station to meet her, but there was no sign of him. She found a taxi and was soon trundling up the hill to the cottage. Not long now! It was good to be home, whatever the circumstances—good to see the familiar green hills again and feel the caress of the moist air. Good not to be still in Pouillac!

The station wagon was in the barn, but she saw at once that the cottage was deserted. A bundle of papers and letters was stacked in the porch beside a couple of bottles of milk. The front door was locked and she had to open it with her key. Inside, the first thing that met her eye was a slip of paper on the mat—a notification from the local post office that they had failed to deliver a telegram and that it was now awaiting collection. That must be the one she had sent from Newhaven.

She took a quick look over the house. This time there had been no attempt to tidy it. Some of the crockery stacked in the sink looked as though it had been there for days. There were several empty food tins lying around, and there was a good deal of mud on the tiled kitchen floor. Upstairs, Laurence's bed had been slept in but had been left unmade. It was quite obvious that he hadn't been expecting her back yet. It was equally obvious that he hadn't been here for at least twenty-four hours. Perhaps longer, she thought, remembering her unanswered calls from Pouillac.

Still, there was one person who'd be sure to know about his movements—Adam Johnson. She got out the station wagon and drove quickly down to his villa. He was at home, and came stumping to the door himself. He seemed quite taken aback at the sight of her.

"Mrs. Quilter! Why, this *is* a surprise. I thought you were in France."

"I've just got back, Adam."

"Well, come in, won't you?" He led the way into a neat parlour. Then he swung round anxiously on his crutch. "Nothing wrong, I hope?"

"I don't think so. I wondered if you knew where I could find Laurence, that's all."

He stared at her. "Laurence? Why, no!"

"Oh, dear, I quite thought you would. He's not at the cottage and he's left no message. It's very stupid, but our arrangements seem to have got tangled up.

Johnson looked as though he were tangled up, too. "Didn't you come back together?"

It was Julie who showed surprise now. "No, he wasn't able to join me—surely you knew that?"

"It's the first I've heard of it." With concern he saw how pale and strained she was. "Look, shall I ask Annie to get you a cup of tea, Mrs. Quilter?—I think you could do with something."

"Please don't trouble," she said quickly, "I'm quite all right—just a bit tired after the journey." She gazed at him helplessly. "I can't understand it—he wrote to me and said he was detained. When did you last see him?"

"Oh, it must be a week ago now."

"A week!"

"About that. We went up to Coalhaven together, just for a couple of days. He made a splendid impression there—it was very wise of you to let him come. Then he brought me back here and I gathered he was flying straight off to join you. He said nothing to me about any other business. It's very queer . . ." He frowned. "Rather worrying."

Julie suddenly wished she hadn't come. If there had been subterfuge with Adam, too, then Laurence's activities were obviously a very private matter and the less said about them the better. A private matter! God, how naïve she'd been!

She forced herself to smile. "I'm certain there's nothing to worry about—he's bound to turn up before long. Perhaps he's gone to London—I'll ring the flat." She got up to leave, and then remembered that she hadn't asked about the accident at the pit.

"A terrible thing," he said. "Terrible! They only got fifteen men out alive, you know. It's been a great blow to the district. A great blow to the Party, too—we've lost some of our best workers. Perhaps you'll be going up there yourself, Mrs. Quilter?"

"Perhaps so," she said. "I'll let you know."

He stumped to the door with her. "Well, I hope you'll soon find Laurence. What with one thing and another, Mrs. Quilter, I'm afraid your holiday must have been rather disappointing."

"It was, rather," she said. "Good-bye."

Back in the station wagon, she lit a cigarette and tried to adjust her mind to the new situation. Everything had suddenly become only too plain. History was repeating itself, and she'd been a credulous, trusting fool not to realise it before. Her thoughts went back to two other occasions when Laurence had stayed away from her and made excuses. He'd been tied up with business, he'd said, but each time it had turned out that he'd been with another woman, having a little holiday. She'd been terribly hurt and miserable, especially the second time when she'd found out it was the same woman again and had begun to think the affair might be serious. But he'd said it meant nothing to him, and she'd had to forgive him. At least, she thought bitterly, on those occasions he hadn't left her ont on a limb while he'd had his fun. She'd been blind in France, incredibly blind, but it simply hadn't occurred to her that he could do anything quite as selfish as that.

Well, there it was! She drove slowly back up the hill, wondering what she should do. She'd have to stay at the cottage to-night, of course, but she certainly wasn't going to hang about there indefinitely, waiting for Laurence to put in an appearance. Perhaps she'd go down to Norwich and stay with her sister for a few days. She turned the station wagon in beside the barn. Perhaps . . .

Suddenly her heart gave a leap. The front door was standing open—he must be back! She felt a queer surge of excitement—they would have it out, now, once and for all. Mustering her reserves, she walked through into the sitting-room.

He was standing by the telephone with the little post office slip in his hand, as though he had just rang up about the telegram. He looked a bit unkempt and his face was very-pale, in startling contrast to the tan he had had when she'd last seen him.

"Hello, Julie!" he said.

Chapter Eight

She stood with her back to the door, looking at him with smouldering, hostile eyes. He took a step towards her, then stopped.

"There really wasn't any need for you to come rushing back like this," he said uncertainly. "Didn't you get my wire?"

"Yes, and I tore it up," said Julie, her voice vibrant with suppressed fury. "What on earth do you think you've been playing at?"

"I don't understand you, darling. It took me longer than I expected to clear things up, that's all."

"You know that's not true. I've just been talking to Adam Johnson. He hasn't seen you for nearly a week."

"Well, of course he hasn't. I've had other things to do. Letters to the Press and condolences to people and all that sort of thing …"

Julie gave an exclamation of disgust. "Why do you bother to lie? I know you haven't been here—not for days. Nor at the flat. I tried to get you on the telephone from Pouillac. You might just as well tell me the truth. You've been away with someone, haven't you?"

Quilter stared at her. Then he dropped heavily into a chair. "I suppose you might as well know. Yes, I have."

"With Brenda Marlowe?"

For a moment, as he hesitated, she wondered if it had been someone else this time. Then he gave a shrug. "Yes," he said. "Look, Julie, you must try to understand. I was so tired after all the travelling and the horrible business at the colliery … I …"

"It's absolutely incredible."

"Oh, I know I promised you that I wouldn't see her again …"

132

"Stop! "Julie put her hands over her ears. "That isn't what matters. If you want to go to bed with Brenda Marlowe or any other woman I can't prevent you and I don't even care—not now. But heavens above!—you have plenty of opportunity—why did you have to do it this way? What do you think I felt like, left in France on my own and getting those horrible telegrams and knowing all the time that I practically didn't exist for you?"

"That isn't true, Julie, and I didn't mean them to sound like that. I'm terribly sorry—I ought to have thought . . ."

"You ought to have thought!" Julie gazed at him incredulously. "Laurence, I just don't know what's happened to you. It was bad enough while you were with me there, because obviously you were thinking about something else—or somebody—the whole time. But to sit here calmly admitting that you've been enjoying yourself with another woman and fobbing me off with those beastly telegrams that you mast have known would hurt me like hell!—oh, I just can't forgive you. I don't think I ever shall."

"I didn't look at it like that," said Quilter slowly. "I can see now how you felt, of course, and. I'm truly sorry, but it seemed to me then that I'd left you very happily settled in a nice place and there was that rather decent American chap . . . Traill . . ."

"For me to flirt with, I suppose. To keep me occupied while you amused *yourself!* I think I hate you, Laurence."

"I didn't mean that at all Julie—you're quite wrong." Now that the confession was over, Quilter seemed to be getting his confidence back. "I didn't plan anything. I *was* delayed for a day or two and I thought that it didn't matter all that much because you had some company and then when I saw Brenda again . . ."

"Exactly! When you saw Brenda again you didn't give me another thought."

He looked at her appealingly. "Julie, don't be so angry. I've been a cad and a swine, I know that, but honestly Brenda doesn't mean a thing to me. It was just that I felt worn out and utterly depressed and. . . . Anyway, I shall never see her again. It's all over now, I swear it."

"Not for me; it isn't," said Julie. "Not by any means. I'm going to divorce you."

"Julie, don't be a fool. You can't mean it."

"You'll see."

"For God's sake, Julie . . .!" He moved towards her, his hands outstretched.

"Don't come near me," she said tensely.

Quilter dropped his hands and stood irresolutely for a moment, as though at a loss how to deal with the situation. "Of course," he said at last, "you've a perfect right to take this line if you want to, I know that. I've asked for it. But why you should want to behave like some cheap melodramatic film actress instead of like an intelligent woman beats me."

"I suppose you think it would be intelligent of me to condone every nasty little intrigue you like to indulge in. That's a wonderful arrangement, isn't it? And what happens to my self-respect in the process? You don't know, do you—and you don't care. Well, I can tell you this—I've had enough. If I go on living with you any longer I shall start despising myself. I only wish I'd had the sense to leave you long ago."

"Julie," Quilter said with a deprecating little laugh in his voice, "you really are being melodramatic, aren't you? You know what I am—you've always known. I'm an arrogant, selfish devil—I admit it. Sometimes I've hated myself for it, but I can't help it. It's—it's because my mind's so taken up with myself and the things I've got to do. There simply isn't the time to potter around with ordinary human relationships. I tell you my brain's like a dynamo, it drives me on. Sometimes I just seethe inside—there's no other word for it. I'm carried away, I hardly notice people. I don't *care* about people—not for long stretches. I thought you understood all that. I'm an egotist, yes, but so are all men that ever do anything worth while, they've got to be. Julie, it's asking a lot of you, I know, when I beg you to stick by me—but there's another thing, too. Whatever I may be, I *do* love you—after my fashion. I've certainly never loved anyone else, not for a moment. You know that, don't you?" He smiled at her, a candid boyish smile, full of charm.

As she looked at him she wondered for a moment whether it was going to be the old story all over again. In the past, their quarrels had usually fallen into a pattern. She would lose her temper with him, provoked beyond endurance by his absorption in himself, his complete taking of her for granted, his calm assumption that she would put up with anything. In turn he would become exasperated and furious. Then, after wild words on both sides, he would begin to explain and justify himself, as though he really did care what she thought, and end by being contrite and appealing. Having roused; him, having "thoroughly upset him," as he put it, she too would be sorry. She would see him—as she was seeing him now—disarmed before her and she would feel all the indignation and anger melt away and the love she had for him come bubbling up inside her.

This time, though, it wasn't happening. Almost with disbelief she realised that she felt as hard as a stone towards him. Fleetingly she wondered if this was what Ben had done to her—if he had really broken, or caused to be broken, the tie, so slender yet so strong, that had bound her to Laurence.

"You love yourself," she said in a flat voice. "There's only one person in the world who matters to you, and that's Laurence Quilter. You think you're different clay from other men and that that gives you the right to be temperamental and egotistical. You think you can push me around and ignore me and deceive me and do anything you like and that I'll always melt happily into your arms in the end because you're such a unique person. Well, it worked for a long time but it won't work any more. I'm finished."

He shook his head. "You'll feel differently about it tomorrow. You can't break up seven years of marriage just like that."

"I can and I will." With astonishment Julie heard her own voice rejecting the very argument she had used to Ben.

"Julie," he said pleadingly, "you know how I rely on you. I may give the impression sometimes that I can get along on my own, but I can't. You're the only person in the world I can come to for peace and rest and comfort, and God knows I need that. We've meant so much to each other, Julie—it's only when you talk of going away that I realise how much. Please!—won't you give the old monster another chance?"

For a moment, Julie wavered. He looked so defenceless that it was hard not to feel compassion and concern. Somehow he hadn't the appearance of a man who'd been enjoying himself—he looked like a man who did indeed need support. His eyes were ringed with purple, his cheeks were thinner—he looked ill.

"It's no good, Laurence," she said, turning away. "You've stretched the spring so far that it won't go back any more. Something's happened to me. It may be that I've been hurt too much by you, or—it may be something else. I don't know. All I know is that if we don't break now we shall have this sort of thing over and over again. You'll never be any different and I can't stand it any more. It's not just that you put yourself and your own interests first all the time; it's the utterly ruthless way you do it. You say you need me, and perhaps just at the moment you do, but mostly you don't. You only need me as a diversion or a background. Perhaps some women wouldn't mind that, but I do. I can't live any longer as your shadow, and I'm not going to."

"That's ridiculous, Julie. You know I value your opinion. You know we always discuss things."

"I don't know anything of the sort. You make up your own mind and you do what you like. You tell me—that's all. You plan your life and I dutifully fall in with your wishes. You take decisions and I accept them. You even gave my home away without consulting me!"

"But you love the cottage," he said indignantly.

"That's not the point and you ought to know it. The point is that you think you can behave like God Almighty where I'm concerned and I've had enough of it. It's true—you know it's true. *You* decided that there was only one thing in the world that mattered and that was politics, so my life has been politics. *You* decided it would be a good thing to move out of the Hall, so we moved. *You* decided you didn't like meeting people unless it was going to be useful, so we never go anywhere. *You* decided that children would be a nuisance, so we haven't had any. And that's what happens over almost everything that makes life tolerable and pleasant to ordinary people."

Quilter was silent, brooding darkly over her words. Presently he said: "That's quite an indictment, Julie. I hadn't an idea that you'd got all that stored away. But now that you've told me . . ."

"It won't make a scrap of difference. You're incapable of behaving in any other way—I know that well enough now. Don't think I blame you entirely, though—I blame myself too. I've given way too much. I've been so weak that I've let you persuade me that what you wanted was what I wanted myself. Sometimes I've even been fooled into taking the decisions myself. . . . Oh, what's the good of talking about it any more?—we're just going round in circles."

"You're tired, Julie, that's the trouble—you need a rest."

"I *don't* need a rest. I need release. Do you hear? Release—and I'm going to get it."

"You mean that you're actually going on with this fantastic notion of a divorce?"

"Yes."

"You realise that it will probably mean the end of my career?"

"I don't see why. Plenty of politicians get divorced these days and survive. You'll be able to talk yourself out of it."

"Julie—I implore you. At least give yourself a chance to make sure—we can separate, if you insist, but don't go rushing into divorce right away. You're going to make yourself very unhappy, Julie, if you do—I warn you."

"You may be right, but it'll be unhappiness of my own choosing, not something forced on me. It's no good, Laurence, I've decided. I'm going up to town on the night train and in the morning I shall find a lawyer. Unless you've any objection I'll use the flat until things are settled."

He looked as if he were going to make one last appeal to her—then he threw up his hands in a hopeless gesture. "Very well, do as you please. But you'll regret it in the end—you'll blame yourself." He turned away with an unfathomable expression on his face.

Chapter Nine

It wasn't until she was alone in London that Julie felt the full impact of what she had done. Then it hit her hard. Her life had suddenly become a vacuum. The impersonality of the furnished flat increased the feeling that she didn't belong anywhere any more, that she had uprooted herself. For a while, loneliness and misery engulfed her. She longed desperately for Ben, but he was out of reach and would be for a long time, if not for ever. She could write to him in Trinidad, of course, but he wouldn't get the letter for many weeks. Anything could happen in between—and meanwhile she had to live.

She thought a great deal about Laurence. As the days passed, the reasons which had driven her to make her decision seemed as valid as ever, but she missed him as she would have missed an amputated leg. Seven years of shared interests and, on her part, of concentrated devotion couldn't be written off in a few hours. Every moment of every day cried out for the small familiar things.

Fortunately she was not much given to sentimentality, and there were plenty of practical problems to occupy her. The divorce, for one. Her anger had cooled and the last thing she wanted to do was to injure Laurence in any way. Divorce might not carry much stigma these days but it wouldn't exactly help a precariously-seated politician to have his amours splashed over the local papers. If Laurence lost his seat because of her it would be a stunning blow to him and she'd never forgive herself.

The only solicitor she knew personally was Laurence's, and she could hardly go to him. Instead she picked out the name of a firm from a society divorce report and made an appointment by telephone.

She was received by an elderly gentleman who listened with respectful sympathy to her story, asked her a few questions about herself, and assured her that the divorce should be quite straightforward since the name of the co-respondent was known and the suit would presuraably be undefended. When, however, she told him she would really like to arrange things so that Laurence didn't appear as the guilty party, he was horrified. He had no sympathy with erring politicians, the notion struck him as quixotic, and in any case—as he firmly pointed out—the divorce laws weren't intended to work that way. Of course, if she herself had committed adultery. . . . He became technical, murmuring of "discretion" and "collusion," but he left her in no doubt that the success of any attempt on her part to turn herself into a divorce would be highly dubious, and the process itself most distasteful to her. The interview ended unsatisfactorily, with Julie declaring she would think things over and let him know.

She felt in need of a confidante and went down to Dorset again to spend a few more days with Muriel Challoner. It was an immense relief to unburden herself, but when she came back to London she still hadn't decided what to do. She was rather surprised that there was no letter or message from Laurence—at the very least she'd have expected him to be curious about the steps she was taking, and anyway there were all sorts of mundane things to settle. She wondered how he was getting on, up there in the cottage with no one to look after him. It worried her quite a bit.

Her first task now, she decided, was to get a job and make herself financially independent of Laurence as soon as possible. She looked up one or two old acquaintances and put out some lines, and she kept a close eye on the "Appointments Vacant" column in the *Times* and the *Telegraph*. She was actually drafting a reply to an advertisement for a proofreader when, some days after her return from Dorset, the telephone rang and a man's voice, precise and slightly over-cultured, said, "Is Mr. Laurence Quilter there, please?"

"I'm afraid not," said Julie. "Who wants him?"

"This is the Prime Minister's office. It's rather urgent."

A tingle of excitement ran through her. "My husband's up in

Cumberland," she said. "I expect you'll be able to get him there. The number's Blean 124."

"Thank you very much, Mrs. Quilter. I'll ring him right away." The telephone clicked before she could frame a question. Anyway, it wouldn't have been any use—they wouldn't tell her anything.

She hung up, feeling absurdly pleased. So it had happened at last—the long-awaited offer of a job. It couldn't be anything else—mere party matters were conducted much less formally. Laurence would be so delighted, and it would help to take his mind off his personal affairs. He'd be tremendously stimulated. He'd love having to make decisions, he'd be excellent at answering questions in the House, he'd enjoy the feeling of leadership among his staff. She hadn't a doubt that he'd be a good Under-Secretary, if only he'd learn to compromise a bit. He'd certainly welcome the challenge of responsibility. She wondered if it was the Defence job he was going to be offered, or something else. Not that that mattered a great deal—the main thing was that he should get a foot on the ladder.

She was thankful now that she'd done nothing about the divorce—publicity just at that moment might have spoiled his chances. Perhaps he'd ring her after he'd had his interview and tell her all the news. He hadn't really any grievance against her, and he must know that she was still terribly interested. The thought brought back all the ache and emptiness, and she sighed as she turned again to the appointments list. What a beastly mess it all was!

It was late in the afternoon when the telephone rang again.

"I'm sorry to trouble you, Mrs. Quilter . . ."—it was the same precise voice—". . . but we're having a little difficulty in getting hold of your husband. It's seems there's no reply to his number."

"I expect he's gone out," said Julie. "Can't you try him this evening?"

"We've left the call in, naturally, but the exchange up there say they've been unable to get any reply for two days."

"I see," she said thoughtfully. She felt little surprise—it was natural that he should have wanted to get away. She was silent for a moment. "Well, I really don't know what to suggest—I should think he may have gone off walking for a day or two."

"You mean without telling anyone?" Julie could almost hear the eyebrows lifting.

"It's possible. After all, he is supposed to be on holiday . . ."

"Oh, quite so, but—dear me, this is most unfortunate. You see, Mrs. Quilter . . ."—the voice hesitated—". . . well, I can't tell you very much except that there's an appointments involved and a very urgent mission. It's quite imperative that we get hold of him by to-morrow at latest."

"I do understand that, of course," Julie said in a troubled voice. "I hardly know what to advise, though. If he is walking I should think he's probably somewhere in the Lake District, but I haven't the least idea where. His secretary might know—that's Jane Harper, Flaxman 99431. And you might try ringing his agent, Adam Johnson—it's just possible some message was left with him." She reached for her handbag and turned up Johnson's number. "Blean 2471. And if I do think of anything else I'll let you know at once."

"I wish you would, Mrs. Quilter. We've got to find him somehow." There was a sudden buzz of conversation at the other end and the man rang off abruptly.

Julie sat for a while considering the problem. She still thought her first guess was the best—walking in the hills would be Laurence's equivalent of going off to Africa to shoot lions! But it was only a guess—he might be anywhere. She picked up the telephone and rang Jane.

"Oh, it's you, Mrs. Quilter," came the secretary's voice at once. "The P.M.'s office just called me—it's thrilling, isn't it, but I do wish he'd show up, they're in an awful flap."

"You've no idea where he is, then?"

"I haven't a clue. As a matter of fact I was just beginning to get a bit bothered myself—I tried to get through to him yesterday but I couldn't and there's a terrific stack of stuff waiting to be dealt with."

"When did you last speak to him, Jane?"

"The evening before last. He rang me."

"From Blean?"

"Yes. He seemed in a bit of a hurry, I thought, and left a lot of things undecided, but he didn't say a word about going anywhere."

"Then I shouldn't think he'll be away long—we'll have news to-night, I dare say. It's very aggravating, but we'll just have to be patient. Do ring me the moment you hear anything."

"I will," Jane promised.

Julie hung up, feeling rather cross. Really, it was exasperating. Here had Laurence been waiting for a summons for years and years, and now that they wanted him he wasn't there. Of course, they could hardly expect him to sit at the end of a telephone line on the off-chance, but he ought not to be so frightfully casual, even if he was fed up. Going off like that without a word to anybody! It would be too frightful if they couldn't find him in time and the job went to somebody else. After all, they'd said something about a mission, and perhaps that couldn't wait . . .

Still, it was no good worrying—there was nothing more she could do. She passed the evening listening to a rather indifferent feature programme on the radio. It was odd, she reflected—in all her life she could hardly remember a bored moment, and yet in the past few weeks she seemed to have been constantly trying to kill time. By nine o'clock there had still been no word. She heard Big Ben strike and the announcer begin to talk and suddenly she was sitting stock still, her attention held.

"Before the news," the voice was saying, "here is a police message. Will Mr. Laurence Quilter, M.P., who is believed to be on a walking tour in the Lake District, or anyone who can give any information about his movements, please communicate at once with Whitehall 1212, or with any police station. I will repeat that . . ."

Julie snapped off the radio. Heavens, they *must* want him badly. Of course, it was the obvious way to get him—he'd be sure to hear now, wherever he was. Laurence wasn't the man to be modest about his identity, particularly in his own constituency, and anyway he was well known there, and wherever he stayed he'd have to sign the book. Somebody would be sure to tell him about the broadcast even if he hadn't heard it himself.

All the same, the announcement had upset her a little. *A police* message—well, of course, that must be the routine way, but it was a bit too dramatic for comfort. It almost made it sound as though he were a missing person, as though something had happened to him . . .

Then a horrible idea flashed through her mind. Suppose something *had* happened to him!

For a moment she felt sick with apprehension. She remembered how white and ill he'd looked in the cottage, and how desperately he'd pleaded with her. She remembered, too, the last words he'd spoken to her—"You'll regret it in the end, you'll blame yourself." And that odd look he'd given her. Oh, God, had he meant to kill himself? He had always been given to extremes, he had always seemed capable of desperate action. If he had felt as wretched as she had, and with his temperament . . .

In sudden panic she rushed to the bedroom and began to throw some things into a bag. He might be lying in the cottage at this moment! Then she took a grip of herself and tried to consider the matter calmly. Laurence was an unpredictable man, an unstable man, but she couldn't believe she'd meant so much to him that he'd feel his life wasn't worth living without her. He wasn't the sort of man to end his life on account of *any* other person—unless she were completely mistaken in him. And he certainly wouldn't have done it quietly, without fuss, as though what he was disposing of were of no value. He had too strong a sense of his importance—he'd want a good last curtain. No doubt he'd been lonely, but he'd have found some less drastic way out of his loneliness . . .

That started another train of thought. When you broke with one person, you usually went to someone else, if you could. And Laurence could have done. He could have gone to Brenda Marlowe for comfort. Of course, he'd insisted once again that that was all over and done with, and he'd looked as though he'd meant it, but he might easily have changed his mind under the pressure of loneliness.

Once the possibility had entered her head, Julie had to make sure. Brenda was almost certain to be in the telephone book. The idea of talking to her was distasteful, but if Laurence were there with her now and they happened not to have listened to the news he might not learn that he was wanted until it was too late. Quickly Julie ran her finger down the M's. Markham . . . Marley . . . Marlowe. Brenda Marlowe!—here it was. A Grosvenor number. Julie hadn't realised it, but Brenda lived in a block of flats only a few minutes away. She took a deep breath and dialled.

A woman's voice broke the ringing tone almost at once, low and attractive. "So I think we might do it again some time . . ." it was saying, finishing a sentence, and then, "Hello!"

"Miss Marlowe," said Julie. It was a statement rather than a question, for after all this time she remembered the voice.

"Yes, speaking."

"This is Julie Quilter."

There was a perceptible pause. "Oh, hello! Sorry—I couldn't quite place you for a moment, it's such ages since we met. How are you?"

"Miss Marlowe—it's not very pleasant having to ring you like this, but—is Laurence there? I've an urgent message for him."

The pause was even longer this time. "I'm afraid I don't understand . . ."

"Oh, please don't stall. It's terribly important for him—the Prime Minister wants him. If he's there, do tell him."

"I'm sorry, I don't know what you're talking about."

"Oh, yes, you do—what's the use of trying to pretend . . .?" Julie broke off as she heard a man's voice in the background. Then the telephone suddenly clicked and went dead.

Chapter Ten

So he *was* there! Rather miserably, Julie replaced the receiver. It hardly concerned her now, of course, but they might have been more open about it. In the circumstances, Brenda's attitude was ridiculous. Still, the important thing was that Laurence should have the message, and Brenda would at least pass that on.

Julie picked up the bag she had begun to pack and tossed it into a corner. What a fool she would have been, rushing up north like a hysterical wife when Laurence was consoling himself here in London! The whole episode had been too unpleasant for words. She wished now that she hadn't tried to help. Laurence would think she was weakening, and that wasn't by any means true.

She sat down to write out her application for the proofreading job. It was nearly eleven when she had finished and she was just thinking of going to bed when there came a sudden ring at the bell. She opened the door and a tall blonde woman swept unceremoniously into the room. Julie had no difficulty in recognising her. It was Brenda Marlowe, beautifully dressed, perfectly groomed, and heavily made up. She came straight to the point.

"Will you kindly tell me what all this nonsense is about?" she demanded. "What's the idea of ringing up your husband at my flat?"

Julie looked at her with icy hostility. "Because I thought he was there, of course."

"But *why?* You're not by any chance accusing me of having an affair with him, are you? It sounds very much like it."

"Well, aren't you?"

"I certainly am not," said Brenda indignantly. "I haven't set eyes on the man for years."

"I can't think why you bother to lie," Julie said. "I know all about it. I know that you and he have just been away together, *and* that it wasn't the first time. Laurence admitted it."

"Admitted it!" Brenda gave a theatrical laugh. Then she looked curiously at Julie. "I say, you're feeling all right, aren't you?"

"This isn't a joke," said Julie.

"I'll say it isn't. If you really mean what you're saying, it's serious. You see, I happen to be getting married next week, and if you're going to spread rumours like this around, some people are going to get extremely annoyed."

"Getting married! You!"

"Yes, me. Have you anything against it?"

"But . . ." Julie subsided into a chair. "But how can you? Laurence definitely told me he was with you the week before last. I—I'm going to divorce him."

"What, and name me as co-respondent? Really, this is too much. Are you mad, both of you?"

Julie stared at her. "Do you mean it's not true?"

"Of course it's not true—I've never heard such outrageous nonsense,"

"But . . ."

"My dear girl, I've just come back from a fortnight with my fiancé's people in Cornwall. If your husband was with anyone, it was with someone else. And if he's told you it was with me I think he's behaved like an absolute swine."

"What about the other times?"

"What other times? The only affair I ever had with Laurence was about ten years ago—long before you ever knew him."

"He told me twice before that he'd been away with you. Since the war."

"It's an absolute lie. Why, I haven't even seen him for at least five years. The whole thing's monstrous. To-morrow I shall go and see my lawyer." She turned angrily to the door.

Julie looked completely mystified. "I hardly know what to say—I don't understand it at all. It seems—well—inadequate to apologise, but I am terribly sorry. Please forgive me. I'd believed him, you see, and I had to find him . . ."

"If I were you," said Brenda, "I shouldn't bother!" She stalked out, and the clatter of her high heels quickly died; away.

Julie closed the door and sank into her chair again, utterly bewildered. She had no doubt whatever that Brenda had spoken the truth—her whole manner had been completely convincing. Why, then, had Laurence tried to involve her? What was the point? All Julie could think of was that he might have been trying to shield someone else, but if so he had been incredibly reckless and stupid, for he must have known that the lie would be exposed almost at once.

Her thoughts went back to the scene in the cottage. She remembered now that it was actually she who'd first mentioned Brenda's name—Laurence had simply agreed. And now that she came to think of it, he hadn't agreed very readily. He'd hesitated—and no wonder! No wonder, either, that he'd been so anxious for her not to start divorce proceedings! It made her feel a little sick to recall his emotional pleading, his certainty that they could do better in the future. It began to look now as though he'd merely wanted to prevent her uncovering the truth.

But what was the truth? Had he been away with a woman at all? Julie was beginning to doubt it. She'd been too upset in the Lakes to consider the matter coolly, particularly when he'd admitted it, but now she wondered. He hadn't looked as though he'd been having a holiday with a girl. He'd looked scruffy, and he'd been wearing frightfully old clothes—as though he'd been off on his own somewhere. But if there was no woman in the case, and he'd just seized on that as a handy explanation, what on earth *had* he been doing during all that time when he should have been in France? What was he hiding from her? And what had he been biding on those former occasions when he'd been unable to account for his movements and had confessed so humbly to infidelities that he hadn't committed?

She felt hopelessly at a loss. The trouble between them had

seemed simple and rather sordid, and now it seemed neither. It didn't look as though she had any grounds for divorce after all, but she had more grounds for worry. Something very odd was going on, and the mystery of his present whereabouts was still unsolved.

She passed a wretched night, revolving fantastic theories, and by morning she had made up her mind to go to the cottage. It was there that he was most likely to turn up and she now felt it imperative to see him again. She rang Jane, who sounded agitated. The broadcast message, it seemed, had had no result so far. All the morning newspapers, she said, had some reference to it, and she thought the "evenings" would be following up the story. One of the political correspondents had already been on the phone asking if it was true that Laurence Quilter had been offered a post. There must have been a leak somewhere. Julie told her of her own plans and left the flat before the newspapers could start worrying her. She caught the morning train from Euston with time to spare and by late afternoon she was once more back at the cottage.

Her fears for Laurence's safety had returned during the journey, and she made a quick nervous tour of the house. Her more melodramatic imaginings were soon disproved—at least he hadn't cut his throat in the bath or hanged himself from a beam. The place was in almost exactly the same condition as when she had last seen it. The bed was still unmade, the kitchen was in the same chaotic state—nothing at all had been done. The only difference was that the papers and mail had piled up again. Laurence had evidently left very soon after she had. He hadn't taken much with him, either. She could find no case missing, no coat or mackintosh, none of his suits. Indeed, after going over the cottage with a fine comb she decided that he must still be wearing the same old flannel trousers and disreputable sports jacket, and that all he'd taken was his rucksack. That seemed to settle it—he *was* walking.

She spent a busy hour putting the cottage to rights and then got the station wagon out and drove down into Blean to see if the local police had heard anything. Her old friend Sergeant Barrett was on duty behind the desk and he greeted her cordially. He hadn't any news, though. Apparently the county police had been making inquiries at all the inns and hotels in the district, but so far without success.

"I was wondering if he might have had an accident," said Julie anxiously. "I suppose it isn't possible to organise a search party?"

"Not much use till we've some idea where he is," said; Barratt. "I shouldn't worry, Mrs. Quilter—he knows his way about the hills. He'll turn up, all right."

"I hope it's soon, that's all."

The sergeant nodded. "I see from the papers there's some job waiting for him. I'm glad of that—he's earned it. Now don't bother yourself—we'll find him. I'll give you a ring directly we hear."

Julie thanked him warmly and drove back to the cottage. As she switched the engine off her eye fell on the speedometer and she gave a little frown. Surely that mileage couldn't be right? She remembered that the night they'd driven back from the meeting in Blean the speedometer had registered under seventy thousand. Now it read 72,100. Laurence couldn't possibly have done two thousand miles in that short time. She thought about it for a moment and decided that she must have misread the figure the first time. No point in making things more complicated than they were already.

The evening passed slowly. Once the sound of a car brought her rushing to the door, but the caller turned out to be a young reporter from the *Coalhaven Mercury* who said he was "on the story." She asked him in and offered him a drink, glad of his company, but there was little she could tell him and even less he could tell her. When he had gone she rang up Jane, but in London also there was no news.

Next morning the telephone started ringing before she was up and went on almost without a pause. There was a call from the Blean police, wanting to know if by any chance Laurence had turned up, and one from Jane, and one from the P.M.'s office, and one from Adam Johnson. It all seemed frightfully futile, thought Julie—everybody was asking everybody else and no one knew a thing. There were calls from the Manchester offices of three national newspapers, sympathetic in tone but with an underlying zest, as though they thought there might be good copy. Two more reporters called and one, to Julie's indignation, asked her if it could all be a "publicity stunt." In the end she got tired of explaining that she knew nothing, nothing at all, and walked up the hill to get a little peace. She took a book and some cigarettes and settled herself beside the Pikes for a quiet hour.

It was nearly lunch time when she went down again. As she approached the house she heard the sound of a car hooter from behind the barn. Another reporter, she thought. Or perhaps it was the police.... She quickened her pace a little:

Suddenly she stopped in her tracks, her heart almost turning over. It must be a hallucination, it *couldn't* be.... Then she saw him plainly, standing by the jeep, looking up at the cottage as though he weren't quite sure whether he'd come to the right place.

"Ben!" she shrieked, and raced down the grassy bank.

Chapter Eleven

He swung round, and his face broke into a huge smile. "Hello, there!" He held out his arms invitingly and she flung herself into his embrace, hugging him in ecstatic relief. "Ben!—oh, *Ben!*—can it really be you?" She Was laughing and almost crying. "Ben, I can't believe it—what are you *doing* here?—I thought you were hundreds of miles away. Oh, Ben, how did you know I needed you? Let me look at you—let me feel you."

He held her away from him. "I'm real, honey. Take it easy—I'll be here for a couple of minutes. Gee, this sure makes the trip worth while."

She still clung to him. "Oh, Ben, darling, I've missed you so much. I was such a fool—I've never stopped thinking of you. I didn't know. . . . It's been so awful, Ben, everything's gone wrong. I'm so miserable—and so happy. Oh, God. I am an idiot!"

"My, you *are* steamed up! Just relax, will you?"

"I still can't believe it's you. How did you know I was here? How did you find your way? What brought you?"

He grinned. "Seismograph! The instrument showed a pronounced disturbance around these parts, and by heck it was right."

"Oh, Ben, I don't understand—I thought we should never; see each other again."

"That was how I figured it too, honey, but the Fates seem to be working on our side."

"What happened?"

"To me? Well, I went off to Switzerland, feeling kind of low, and drifted around for a day or two trying to kid myself I was liking the scenery. It wasn't any use, though—all I could think of was the golden lights in your eyes. I reckoned I'd be better off in London where I knew a few people, so I shipped the jeep over from the Hook yesterday morning and about the first thing I saw when I got into town was this."

He produced a crumpled evening paper and she ran a nervous eye over the headlines. "MacArthur Flies to Front"—"Explosives Stolen from Army Dump"—"Meat Ration up 2d." Nothing there. Ah! "M.P. Mystery. Broadcast Appeal." She read it through, bat it was already old news.

"See what I mean? Well, I hadn't intended to look you up, much as I wanted to, but when I read that I thought it was kind of queer, especially after all that funny business in France, so I got your phone number from the London Directory and called your apartment. There wasn't a reply, of course, and then I figured that if that guy of yours had been staying up here when he disappeared, as the paper said, it was likely you'd be up here too. So I asked a policeman at Marble Arch how to get to Cumberland and he pointed this way and here I am. Quite a trip it was, too—who said England was small?"

"Oh, Ben, you must have driven all night. I am a selfish pig—can I get you anything? "

"I could use a drink, honey—I guess that's all I need. I had a snack at a roadside dump. Matter of fact, I quite enjoyed the trip." He followed her into the house and watched her get the glasses. "Gosh, Julie, it's good to see you again. I've been only half alive, and that's the truth. I kept telling myself I'd get over you in a week or two, and I knew darned well I hadn't a hope. Well—here's to our reunion!" He clinked his glass against hers. "And now suppose *you* do some talking. Has your M.P. really disappeared?"

"I don't know what's happened—I wish I did. I think I'd better start from the beginning . . ."

"It's a good place," said Ben, settling back in his chair.

"Okay, shoot!"

She sat on the arm beside him and told him everything—how she'd tried to find out where he'd gone to when she got. the last telegram in France, and how furious she'd been, and all about her row with Laurence and her decision to divorce him and her miserable days in town. Ben gave her hand a reassuring squeeze once or twice over the tough bits but he didn't attempt to hide his satisfaction at the way things had worked out. It was only when she came to her conversation with Brenda that he sat up sharply and stared at her.

"Why, that's about the screwiest thing I ever heard. What do you suppose he was playing at?"

"I don't know," said Julie slowly. "But I think now that he must have been in some sort of trouble—I think something had happened that he couldn't tell me about and that when I suggested he'd been with Brenda he jumped at it as a way out."

"She seems to have been an alibi for him all along."

"It looks like it."

"Julie, he's never actually been in trouble, has he? With the police, I mean?"

"Good gracious, no! He's always been terribly conscientious and law-abiding." She gave a rueful smile. "He even fusses sometimes over our black market whisky."

"Well, it sure looks as though he's been up to something he shouldn't."

"I'm afraid for him, Ben. He's been behaving in such a, peculiar way for so long, and it's days since anyone spoke ta him. If he were all right I'm sure something would have been heard of him by now."

Ben studied her anxious face. "And it worries you a lot?"

"Yes, it does. I can't help it. Don't misunderstand me, Ben—it's only that—well, this is something I feel I've got to see through to the end."

"Fair enough, honey. I guess we'll see it through together. He'll probably show up soon."

Julie glanced at her watch. "It's nearly one o'clock now—let's just see if there's anything about him on the wireless and then I'll take you to a nice place for lunch. I'm sure you must be famished." She slid off the chair arm. "Oh, Ben, you can't imagine how different I feel now that you're here." She bent and kissed him lightly and then looked round for the radio. "It must be upstairs," she said. "I won't be a minute."

She was away some time, and when she came back she looked puzzled. "That's queer—it's gone."

Ben's eyes swept the room. "It can't have done, honeys—what's it like?"

"It's a little blue portable—wait, I'll have another look."

She went out again and he heard her rummaging about in various rooms. She even went outside to the barn.

"No, it's definitely gone," she told him when she returned. "I've looked everywhere. What an extraordinary thing!—Laurence must have taken it with him."

"Maybe he wants to keep track of the situation wherever he is."

She gave him a startled look. "That sounds horrible—just as though he's a criminal on the run. It *is* queer, though—surely no one would go off walking with a radio set. It's really quite heavy."

"Maybe he isn't walking—maybe he went by car."

"His own car's out there now, and if he'd used any other we'd have heard about it. And he'd certainly have been noticed at the station . . ."

"What about telling the police? It might help them to find him."

Julie looked at him doubtfully. "Yes, I suppose I ought to. I know what we'll do—we'll go and eat at the Plough, that's a nice little inn just down the lane, and we'll fix up a room for you there, and then we'll go on to the police station afterwards. "

"Okay. And after that I suggest you take your mind off the whole business for a while by showing me some of this swell countryside of yours."

"I'd love to, if you're not too tired."

"Tired!—with you!" He took her in his arms and kissed her with passion.

Then, with equal suddenness, be let her go as a car engine sounded outside. "It seems like you've got more visitors," he said.

Julie glanced out of the window. A blue saloon had pulled up beside the jeep and a man was just getting out. He was big and square-built and he was wearing a raincoat and soft hat.

"I'm frightened," she said. "Every time anyone comes now I'm frightened . . ." She went out into the hall and opened the door.

The man raised his hat. "Mrs. Quilter?"

Julie nodded.

"Ah!—I wonder if I might have a word with you?" He handed her his card and she read "Detective Inspector John Ford, Criminal Investigation Department, West Cumbria County Constabulary."

"Have you news of my husband?"

"I'm afraid not, ma'am, I'm sorry. It's about another matter I'd like to speak to you."

"Oh!" Julie hardly knew whether she was relieved or disappointed. "Well, please come in." She led the way into the sitting-room. "This is Inspector Ford, Ben. Mr. Benson Traill, a friend of mine."

"How d'ye do, sir?" said Ford, with a nod and a quick shrewd look.

"I'm fine," said Ben. "Okay if I stick around, or is it private?"

Ford glanced at Julie and hesitated. "I'd like him to stay," she said.

"Very well, ma'am, I've no objection." He dropped his hat on to the settee and gave a preparatory cough. "Mrs. Quilter, I'm inquiring into the disappearance of a man named Peter Anstey."

She nodded and waited, wondering what on earth this apparent irrelevance could have to do with her.

"The name doesn't mean anything to you?"

"No, I don't think so. Ought it to?"

"Well, there's been quite a bit about him in the local paper," said Ford cautiously. "He was the science master at Coalhaven Grammar School—young fellow in his late twenties, dark, well set-up." He paused expectantly, but when Julie's face still appeared blank he went on: "He was one of those chaps who explore underground caves in their spare time—potholers, I believe they call themselves."

It was Ben, listening with close attention, who nodded.

"He left his lodgings in Coalhaven on the morning of August 8th and his landlady understood that he was off to Yorkshire to do a bit of exploring there. His motor bike was found abandoned on the moors a day or two later, but nothing's been heard of him since."

"I see," said Julie, looking more puzzled than ever. "No, I never heard about that—I was away in Dorset early in August."

"Ah, that would account for it. And your husband didn't mention him?"

"No," said Julie.

"He knew Anstey, I believe?"

"I don't think so." She frowned. "I wish you'd tell me what all this is about, Inspector. What are you driving at?"

"I'm merely trying to find out, ma'am, about Peter Anstey's last movements, and that means checking up with all the people who had dealings with him. Now apparently your husband was one of those people. At any rate, someone rang up Directory Inquiries from this house on the evening of August 7th, asking for Anstey's number to be traced, and afterwards the connection was made for him."

"Well, that must have been my husband, of course," said Julie slowly. "I'm sorry I can't help you, though—he didn't mention it. I expect it was something to do with politics."

Ford grunted. "You don't happen to know if Mr. Quilter himself was interested in potholing?"

"I never heard him say so—in fact I'm sure he wasn't. Rock-climbing, yes, but not potholing. At least . . ."

"Yes, Mrs. Quilter—you've remembered something?"

"Oh, merely that we went down a big hole in France and he was rather interested in that. But that's the only time."

"H'm! I'll tell you why I asked—it's just that a rather interesting document has come into our possession." The inspector slipped his hand inside his breast pocket, drew out an envelope, and carefully extracted a piece of paper. "Would you mind telling me, ma'am, whether you've ever seen this before?"

Completely bewildered, Julie took the stained, yellowing sheet, looked at the faded ink marks, and turned it over to see if there was anything more legible on the other side. "No," she said, "I haven't seen it before. What's it supposed to be?"

"It's a bit the worse for wear, I'm afraid," said Ford, "but it seems to be some sort of plan of an underground cave."

"Really?—I'd never have known." Ben had joined her and she held it up so that he could see it too. "What makes you think that I might have . . .? "Suddenly she stopped and gave an exclamation of surprise. "Why, our name's on it!"

"Yes, ma'am. It's hard to make out without a magnifying glass, but those words are actually "Joseph Quilter, Bleathwaite Hall, 1855." It's obviously something to do with the family, and that's why I asked you whether you'd seen it."

Ben said: "Mind if I take it over to the window, Inspector? I'd like to have a closer look."

"That's all right, sir, but please handle it carefully." He turned back to Julie. "So you're quite certain, Mrs. Quilter, that you've never come across it, eh?"

"Positive, Inspector. How did you get hold of it?"

Ford looked at her as though he were debating whether to tell her. Then he said: "It was in a wallet that belonged to young Anstey. The wallet was washed up on the seashore at Blean yesterday morning."

"Washed up! "Julie felt a sudden tug of apprehension. "You mean—he was drowned?"

"Possibly—we can't say." Ford took the document back from Ben. "I suppose, Mrs. Quilter, you've never heard of any pothole around these parts, have you?"

"No, I haven't," she said soberly.

"And there's nothing on this paper that suggests to you where the place might be. Perhaps you'd just take another look?" He held it in front of her, pointing. You see, this is obviously the section—looking *through* the pothole, as you might say—here's the surface of the ground. . . ." He glanced at her face and saw that what he was saying didn't mean a thing to her, and smiled. "No? Ah, well, I can't say I'm surprised. We'll have to see what the experts think about it. . . ."

He picked up his hat and turned to the door. "That's all then, thank you—I'm sorry to have bothered you just at lunchtime. We'll have to hope that Mr. Quilter turns up soon—perhaps *he'll* be able to help us. Good-day, ma'am. Good-day, sir."

"Good-bye, Inspector," said Julie, in a very subdued voice.

Chapter Twelve

She stood by the window as the car drove away, lost in thought. Ben waited, watching her gravely. If anyone had the key to the riddle, she had.

Presently she turned, her face pale. "So something *has* happened to him," she said.

"Easy, honey!—there's no point in meeting trouble halfway. I'd say there was darned little to go on."

"There's more than you think, Ben. The morning I left for Dorset, Laurence was looking through some old family papers and that plan was just the sort of thing he might have found. I'm certain that's where it came from—if he'd had it before I'd have known about it."

Ben nodded. "I'm with you so far."

"Well, then he rang this man Anstey—he must have known about his interest in caves, I don't know how—and they must have gone off on some stupid expedition...."

"You mean to find the pothole?"

"I should think so. If Anstey was an expert he might have known where to look for it."

"I don't see how—not from what was on that paper. Anyway, it was the other guy's wallet that was found—there's nothing to suggest your husband was there. Maybe he just loaned the plan to Anstey."

Julie shook her head. "Laurence would have wanted to go, too—he hadn't anything else to do just then, and he'd have loved it. Besides, there's something else I've remembered. I'm pretty sure now that Laurence had someone staying here that weekend—an extra bed was slept in and a lot of whisky was drunk, as though he'd had another man around. I expect he asked Anstey over and then they went off together."

Ben shrugged. "Maybe you're right, but there's still no reason to suppose your husband was involved in any accident. On the contrary, all the evidence is against it. According to that policeman, Anstey disappeared on the 7th of August—whereas your M.P. was around until about a week ago."

"I know," said Julie, frowning. "I don't understand that, either. The fact remains that they did go off somewhere together and Anstey's apparently drowned and Laurence has disappeared. There must be some connection, surely?"

Ben was silent for a while. He could understand Julie's fears—it wasn't exactly reassuring to hear about something being "washed up" when you were worried about a missing person. Still, there were all sorts of pieces that didn't seem to fit anywhere. He had an orderly mind and he felt he'd like to think it all over quietly before committing himself to a view.

"I still think there's no point in worrying at this stage," he said gently. "What say we forget it for a bit?—I could do with that lunch you promised me."

"Oh, yes, Ben, I'm sorry. I'll try to be sensible—it's just that all this is getting me down a bit. It drags on so." She made an obvious effort and smiled. "We won't talk about it for the rest of the day."

Once they were away from the cottage her anxiety soon dispersed. They stopped at the Plough and Julie introduced Ben to Joe Martin, the landlord, and they had a couple of drinks, and though it was getting late Mrs. Martin produced a satisfactory meal. After that Julie took Ben on the promised tour of the district. It was like old times, sitting beside him in the jeep with her hair blowing and knowing there were hours ahead of them. The shadow of Laurence had faded and they were happy again in each other's company. They talked about all the things that they'd had to hurry over because of the Laurence business—their parting, and their feelings, and what Ben had done in Switzerland; and when they had covered that ground they lived some of the days in France all over again in memory. The only thing they didn't talk about was the future, because the time was inopportune and anyway there was no need.

They visited Wordsworth's cottage, dined at Ambleside, and got lost in the dark on the way back over the fells, so that it was well after ten when Ben deposited Julie at her front door.

"I'll be round first thing in the morning," he said, as he kissed her good-night. "Maybe for breakfast! Sleep well, and don't worry."

Julie smiled and said that she'd do her best not to. She felt comfortably tired and pleasantly muzzy. Once she got to bed, "however, her brain became more and more active until she felt she'd never sleep. Now that she was alone, she too had begun to think about some of the pieces that didn't fit. Why, she wondered, had Laurence not, told her about Anstey and the pothole—to make a secret of a thing like that seemed ridiculously schoolboyish. Could they have discovered something important?—something so important that he could even tell that fantastic story about Brenda rather than give it away? But if that were so, why had he lied about Brenda before?

For an hour she groped for answers, wide-eyed and restless, until at last her brain grew numb with tiredness. It was no use thinking about it any more. Either Laurence would turn up soon, and explain it all, or the police would find his body as they'd found Anstey's wallet and then it would hardly matter anyway.

She must have slept in the end, for at some period of the night she had a dream. It was confused, but very vivid. She was in the jeep, with Ben and Brenda and Adam Johnson, and they were driving along a straight road lined with poplars, and Ben was saying that that must be Rocamadour right ahead and Johnson was urging them to turn back and suddenly a huge black pit opened in front of them and they went toppling over with a fearful crash . . .

Julie woke with a stifled cry, the sounds still echoing in her ears. For a moment or two she lay in a bath of sweat, listening to the beat of her heart. Then she slowly relaxed. It was all right—she had had a nightmare, that was all. Hardly surprising after what had happened. All the same, that noise had been so clear that she could hardly believe she hadn't heard it. So near, too. Almost like someone dropping something in the room. She sat up in the dark, listening, trying to see into the blackness, all her senses alert. She wasn't usually a timid person, but as she listened, motionless, she began to have a horrible feeling that someone was there with her. She felt her flesh creep. By an effort of will she made herself stretch out a hand and switch on the bed-lamp. She gave a sigh—the room was empty. She felt angry with herself—really, it was absurd to have night fears at her age.

Suddenly she stiffened. Someone was moving about downstairs—she was sure of it. She looked at her watch—it was just three o'clock. The thought of burglars flashed through her mind, but she dismissed the notion—things like that just didn't happen in Cumberland cottages. It must be Laurence!—it couldn't be anyone else but Laurence.

With pulse racing she slipped out of bed, pushed her feet into her slippers, wrapped herself in a dressing gown and tiptoed out on to the landing. There was a line of light at the bottom of the kitchen door—he was in there, walking about. She heard the soft thud of the "fridge" door being shut. Evidently he didn't realise that she was in the house. He probably thought she was still at the flat.

She was wondering how she could announce her presence without startling him when the kitchen door opened and he came into the hall and switched on the light.

"Laurence!" she called, in a low tense voice.

He swung round with a gasp and stared up at her. For a moment she could hardly believe that it was he. In the glare of the light his face was a white mask, sheet-white, with two cavernous pools of eyes. His hair was in disorder, his face bearded, his clothes filthy.

She took a step down towards him. Suddenly, without a word, he turned and bolted back into the kitchen. Before she had even reached the hall she heard the back door slam.

She rushed after him, through the kitchen and out into the: cobbled yard. "Laurence!" she cried in an agonised voice "Laurence, come back! Oh, *please* come back!"

Somewhere away to the left she could hear the noise of running footsteps and the slither of falling stones. He must be going up the bank. She stumbled blindly after him in the pitch darkness, colliding with obstacles, shedding a slipper,-but too frantic to care. She reached the bank herself and scrambled up it, dragging her dressing-gown free from a clinging bramble. At all costs, she mustn't lose him now. She climbed out on to the track and raced up it in the direction he had taken. She could hear nothing except the pounding of her own heart and lungs. She stopped for a second, listening. He must be running on the grass. "Oh, God!" she gulped, and ran on blindly until she could run no more. It was no use—she *had* lost him. In this darkness and these hills she hadn't a chance.

With a sob she turned and rushed back to the cottage. Her thoughts were in turmoil. This was worse than any nightmare—it was real, and indescribably horrible. She must have help, and quickly. She flung herself upon the phone and frantically agitated the receiver hook;

It seemed an age before the operator answered, and another age before she heard Joe Martin's voice, slow and heavy with sleep. It took him some time to grasp what she wanted, but at last he sensed her urgency and went off to wake Ben. Julie sat trembling by the phone.

At last!—the familiar, comforting voice. "What is it, Julie? What's the trouble?"

"Ben! Laurence has been here. Something awful's happening, I know it is. Please come."

"Okay, honey," he said crisply, "I'll be right over."

She dropped the receiver back on its rest with a gasp of thankfulness. For a while she was too overcome and breathless to move. When she felt a little recovered she got up and went into the kitchen. There was a broken milk bottle on the floor—that was what she must have heard upstairs and a frightful mess everywhere. She was still gazing helplessly at the scene when the jeep's engine roared outside and she went to let Ben in.

Chapter Thirteen

For a moment she clung to his reassuring bulk, her body shaking as though she had a fever. He held her tight, soothing her. Then his glance took in her torn dressing gown, her bare scratched feet, the traces of blood and bramble on the hem of her nightdress.

"Why, you poor kid . . .! Here, let's go in and get you warm." He half-carried her into the sitting-room and switched on the electric fire.

"I'm all right, Ben, really I am," she protested. "I want to tell you what happened . . ."

"It'll keep for a while," he said firmly. "You've had a pretty bad shock." He made her tell him where he could find a rug and some brandy. After he'd cosseted her a little the shivering stopped and the colour began to creep back into her cheeks.

"That's much better, honey. Okay, tell me about it."

"Oh, Ben," she burst out, "I hardly knew him, he'd changed so much. His face was quite blanched and his eyes had a terrible unearthly sort of look, and he was bearded and horribly dirty. He seemed scared of me, too—he wouldn't speak—not a word—he just rushed away."

"Tell me from the beginning," said Ben gently.

She took a deep breath and started again. "You see, I'd had a nightmare . . ." She told her story coherently now, from the moment she'd woken up until she'd lost Laurence on the hillside. "And Ben," she concluded, "I know what he came for. Food! He's taken bread, and tins from the pantry. Oh, it's too horrible—he looked like a hunted beast, Ben, like an animal caught stealing that thinks it's going to be whipped He's thin and ragged and . . . oh, my God, I can't bear it. I'd sooner he were dead."

Ben took her hands. "Now listen to me, honey, you've got to snap out of this. It won't help, and you'll make yourself ill."

"Ben, it's easy to say that, but how can I when I know something dreadful is happening to him and I can't do anything about it. You didn't see him, you don't realise—he looked scarcely human. He must have been hiding in the hills all this time, half-famished . . ." She looked pitifully into Ben's eyes, as though begging him to contradict her thoughts, and then it all came pouring out. "Ben, I'm afraid he's lost his reason. I can see now how it's been coming on—all that strange behaviour in France and that crazy business over Brenda and now this hiding away and letting himself get into such a state. He's never been a normal sort of person, but now I think he's had a complete breakdown."

Ben was silent, turning that over. "I guess that could be it," he said after a while. "Maybe it's the best we can hope for."

She looked startled. "Why do you say that?"

He didn't meet her eyes. "I've been doing some thinking this last hour or two, trying to make sense out of the bits of information we've got. We know he contacted Anstey. We're pretty sure they went on an expedition together. Immediately afterwards Anstey disappeared, and it's fairly obvious something unpleasant happened to him. But it wasn't an ordinary disappearance. His wallet was washed up off this coast but his bike was found in Yorkshire. I hardly knew where Yorkshire was until I had a look at my map to-night, but it's a heck of a way from here. That suggests some pretty fanny business to me. It suggests that Anstey came to grief around these parts and that the bike was used as a blind to conceal the truth."

Julie stared at him, but said nothing.

"And that's not all," Ben went on unhappily. "Your husband tried to cover up the whole episode. He kept his meeting with Anstey a secret, even from you. He didn't breathe a word about the plan of the pothole. And afterwards he was in pretty bad shape, as though he had a hell of a lot on his mind . . . For your sake,

Julie, I hope I'm wrong, but it seems to me that the only explanation that takes in all those facts is that he himself was responsible for Anstey's disappearance. If that's true, then it's possible to go on and explain other things. What was he doing when he came back from France and was supposed to be with that Brenda dame? I don't know, but maybe there was a body to be put away some place safe. And now, what with having to lie to you because you showed up too soon, and all the publicity about his disappearance, he feels he daren't do anything but stay in hiding . . . What do you say?"

"I can't believe it." Julie voice had sunk to a whisper. "And yet . . ."

"What, honey?"

"I remember now that when I got home from Dorset Laurence had a terrific bruise on his head and he'd smashed his watch. He said he'd run into a door, but he *looked* as though he'd been in a fight."

Ben nodded gravely.

"But it doesn't make sense. Laurence isn't like that—he's always hated any sort of personal violence. He'd be the last person to kill anyone. And why should he kill *Anstey*? Good heavens, he didn't know him—Anstey was just a casual acquaintance, someone he'd just met."

Ben shook his head. "You don't know how well he knew him, Julie. It's clear he's been holding out on you for a long while—look at those other times when he was off on some secret business. He may have had dealings with Anstey you never heard of . . ." He broke off. "Honey, I'm sorry, about this, honest I am. God knows I'm not trying to make a case—I think it's been made for us. And I think that inspector guy was on to it, too. They don't put detectives on straightforward accident cases—not with us, they don't, any way."

Julie was hardly listening any more. She was thinking of the distraught apparition in the hall. "If he did kill Anstey," she said at last, "he must have done it when he was out of his mind and not responsible."

"That could well be. If he's really gone to pieces, he may be homicidal without knowing what he's doing. Anyway, I guess we ought to let the police know about this visit of his to-night—the sooner he's found now, the better for everyone." He saw the reluctance in her eyes and got up and began to pace the floor. "Julie, I hate this, I wish I wasn't in on it. You'll be thinking next that I want to get rid. of the guy . . ."

"No, no, Ben—don't *say* things like that. I know you only want to get everything cleared up, and I do too. It's just that I can't bear the idea of his being hunted . . ."

"He's got to be found—he may be dangerous."

"He didn't look dangerous when I saw him—he just looked ill and frightened. Oh, Ben, if only we could find him ourselves!"

"That would be fine, honey, but where would we start searching? I'm open to suggestions—you know the countryside."

"Well, he can't be far away because he came here on foot. And his hiding place must be something rather special because there are still visitors about in the hills, lots of them, and if he'd been simply lying about in the open he'd have been noticed. anyone who'd seen him would have mentioned him, I'm sure—he's so unbelievably white and haggard . . . I can't imagine how he could have got like that on the fells . . ."

She looked up as Ben suddenly clicked his fingers. "What is it—have I said something?"

"I'll say you have, and we've been pretty slow not to think of it before. The pothole, Julie!—surely that's the answer? I ought to have realised when you said his face was *blanched*. Don't you see, he's been living underground all this time in the pothole that he and Anstey went looking for, and that's why no one's spotted him."

"I believe you may be right," said Julie after a pause. "In that case I don't see how anyone will ever find him."

"He'll have to come up for food again some time," said Ben grimly. "Anyway, if *he* found the place, why shouldn't we? Julie, are you *sure* you've never heard of a pothole near here—not even a rumour? There could be one, you know. This hill behind the cottage is mountain limestone—I noticed as I came up yesterday. It's just the place for one."

Julie shook her head. "There's never been a whisper."

"Well, I wish I had a clearer recollection about what was on that plan. The shape of the ground might have helped, though I guess the police would have thought of that . . . He frowned, trying to visualise the scrap of yellow paper.

"If only I knew the district! There was a sort of hollow and a bumpy slope—could be anywhere, of course. Wait a moment, though, there *was* one odd thing—I don't know whether you noticed, it was pretty well washed out, but there seemed to be something sticking up at the entrance. Could have been stone pillars or something like that—rather rare in limestone country."

"No, I didn't notice," said Julie despondently. "I couldn't make head or tail of the thing."

"They were rather an unusual shape—here, let's see if I can draw them." He unscrewed his fountain pen and made a rough sketch on the back of an envelope. "Something like that, I guess."

Julie gazed at the sketch, and the look of despondency suddenly vanished. "But, Ben, I *do* know where those are. They're what Laurence and I call the Pikes—they're about half a mile up the track behind the cottage."

"Was that the way he was running?"

"Yes."

"Then, by heck, I think we've got it!"

"But there isn't a pothole there. I know every inch of it. Laurence and I often used to go and sit . . .'"

"Spare me the details, honey! Let's quit talking and go see for ourselves."

"What, now? In the dark?"

"Why not? We can run the jeep up and turn the headlights on the place. And if we find the hole and decide to go in—well, it'll be dark inside anyway."

She looked at him doubtfully. "All right—anything's better than just sitting here thinking. I'll go and dress."

"Put some warm things on, and strong shoes. We'll have to organise this a bit. Have you got a torch?"

"Yes, it's not much good, though."

"Never mind, it'll help—I've a good one in the jeep. Can I pack up some food?"

"Ben—you don't *really* think we'll find it?"

"Sure we'll find it. You lead me to the place and I'll do the rest—this is something I know about."

His confidence drew a smile from her. "Well, you'll find all the stuff lying about in the kitchen where Laurence left it. There's another thermos in the pantry. I won't be long."

"I suppose there wouldn't be any rope around the joint?"

"There should be some climbing rope, unless Laurence has taken it. In the barn."

"Okay, I'll look."

The next ten minutes were taken up with vigorous preparations. Ben put on water for coffee and hacked some bread into sandwiches and then he groped his way out into the barn. He found the rope at once—a big coil of nylon in almost new condition—and flung it into the back of the jeep. That was a stroke of luck! He tested his torch and searched in the toolbox until he found a spare battery. He was just going in again when Julie joined him with a basket. "Laurence has the rucksack," she said. "Will this do?"

"I guess it'll have to. Everything in?"

"I think so. I've brought the brandy, just in case."

"Good for you. Right, let's go."

They climbed into the jeep and a moment later it was roaring up the track, flinging them from side to side as it bumped and bounced over the rough ground. The night was still black, but the headlights were powerful and Ben had no difficulty in keeping to the old ruts. In a matter of seconds, it seemed, they had topped the ridge and begun to drop down into the limestone bowl.

Julie pointed ahead. "Those are the Pikes."

Ben grunted and swung the jeep on to the short turf so that the ground between the stones was floodlit. "We'll soon know now, anyway." He jumped out and strode quickly to the granite piles.

"Mind your step!" he called back. "The hole must be open if he's down there." He reconnoitred the stones, walking between them and around them, flashing his torch on the scree. Then he stopped and looked at Julie in chagrin. "Hell, I guess I was wrong at that—there's nothing here." He stared at the Pikes. "I could have sworn this was the place, though—look at the shape of those things, they're unique."

He gave a disgruntled kick at the loose scree. Then suddenly he was down on his knees, examining it. It wasn't loose! His exploring fingers closed on a small stone that didn't move, and another. "Hey, Julie, come and hold my torch, will you?" he called. "There's something mighty queer here ..." She knelt down beside him, flashing the light so that he could see into the crevices between the stones.

"Good lord!" he muttered. He grasped two of the stones and heaved, and in a moment a square yard of scree had lifted and come away in one piece.

"Well, what do you know!" he exclaimed, gazing down into the hole and then at the square of scree-covered wood. "That guy of yours sure is thorough!" The outer surface of the trap had been cemented over and stones cunningly sunk into the cement so that the surface, to the casual eye if not to the moody foot, was indistinguishable from its surroundings. It was a door that could be replaced from within.

Julie crouched beside the hole, fascinated but scarcely believing. It was only the day before that she had been reclining almost on this very spot.

"What a frightful looking place!" she said.

Ben was shining his torch right down into it. "I can see the bottom. Maybe it won't seem so bad inside." He spoke without much conviction. "Look, Julie, why don't you go back to the cottage and wait there? You can't hang about up here, it's too cold, and there's not a bit of point in your coming down with me. I'll find him and bring him back."

Julie was still staring into the hole as though hypnotised.

"You really think he can be down there?"

"I haven't a doubt of it."

"Then I'd better come."

"I don't think you'll like it, you know."

"I'll be frightened to death if you go in alone. I'm sure it'll be much safer with two. I'll be all right, Ben. I'll come in just a little way and see what it's like."

"Well, for Pete's sake, be careful." He turned and slid his legs over the edge. "Got the food there?"

"Yes."

"I'll take it. Shove the rope in the basket. It's not much of a drop here—I'll be able to help you down." He hooked the basket under his arm, wedged his feet and back against the sides of the hole, and gradually manaeuvred himself to the bottom. "Okay, you can come now." He could just reach her ankles as she lowered herself over the edge and a moment later she was standing beside him.

"Well, that was straightforward enough," he said. He flashed his torch into the low passage that led out of the bottom of the hole. "Hello—someone's left something." The beam had picked out a bundle of clothes.

"Laurence's!" said Julie. "They're what he was wearing!" All her fears for his mental state came rushing back as she pictured him roaming half-naked in the bowels of the earth.

"At least we know we've come to the right place," said Ben grimly. He peered into the passage, studying the slope and wishing again that he could remember the details of the plan. "It's going to be a tough crawl, baby. Think you can manage it?"

"Of course I can," she said without hesitation. "I'm perfectly all right, you really needn't worry about me."

Her tone reassured him. "Here goes, then." He thrust his head into the passage and. began scrabbling his way down the slope, pushing the basket ahead and turning from time to time to make sure that Julie was close behind him. Very soon his torch picked out Anstey's pitons, and he came to a stop. "There's a ladder fixed here," he called back. "There must be a drop. Wait a minute." He searched around until he found a loose stone, and tossed it ahead into the darkness. Seconds later, the echoes came reverberating up from the chasm.

"Sounds pretty deep," he muttered.

Julie wriggled up to him. "The ladder looks quite strong."

He nodded, testing one of the pitons. "Okay," he said at last, "I'll go down and see what it's like."

"I'm coming too, Ben."

"Oh, no, you're not. You know darned well you can't stand heights."

"I won't think about it. Ben, I *must* go on, now I know he's here. I can't stand the uncertainty any longer. I'm going to find him now if it's the last thing I do."

"It could be, at that."

"I'll be careful. It's only when I can see I'm high up that I turn giddy. As long as it's dark I shan't mind."

He put a hand on her arm. "Why, you're trembling now," he said.

"It's only excitement. Please let's get it over."

Ben sat silent, trying to decide. He could see that she was in a pretty desperate state of mind and would take a lot of Dissuading. The ladder must be all right, since it had supported Quilter's weight. If their nylon rope proved long enough he hadn't any doubt that he could get her down safely. He didn't much fancy the idea of her going ahead, but the complete absence of light below suggested that Quilter had moved farther down the pothole, so there was no danger that she would have to deal with him on her own.

He uncoiled the rope, tied a stone to one end, and lowered it over the edge. The hole didn't seem to be so frightfully deep—when the stone touched, he had still twenty feet of rope in hand. That should be plenty. He hauled up again.

"Okay," he said. "I'll have to rope you up, though—you'll feel more secure and if anything *did* happen I'd be able to bold you. Let's see if we can get it round you."

Every movement was difficult in the confined space, but at last he succeeded in tying a bowline under her arms and belaying the other end of the rope round one of Anstey's pitons. He stuffed her torch into the pocket of the windcheater she was wearing.

"Right—over you go," he said, trying to make his voice sound as matter-of-fact as possible. "Keep your feet on the rungs and your mind on the job. When you get to the bottom, untie the rope and wave your torch. I'll draw up and let the basket down and then I'll be with you."

Julie nodded, not trusting herself to speak. She squeezed past him, turned on to her stomach and groped for the nearest rung. The gentle pressure of the rope under her arms gave her confidence. She must *feel* her way down, she told herself, and not think. She tried the rung, testing her weight on it It didn't feel nearly as rigid as an ordinary ladder, but she would have to get used to that. She took one last look at Ben, who was lying well back in the passage with the rope looped round him and his feet braced against the rock wall. As always, he looked reassuringly solid. Then she dropped below the edge. Everything was black as pitch around her; for she needed both hands for the descent. She moved very slowly, making sure of her footing, concentrating on the ladder. Soon she got into a sort of rhythm—right toe down, a scraping movement to get a foothold, a shift of the foot to get the metal rung firmly under the instep, then hands down to the next rung, and finally the other foot.

Suddenly her toe scraped in vain, as she reached the place where the side of the chasm jutted out and the wire ladder hugged the rock. She could feel nothing at all below her—it was just as though there were no more rungs. As her toe scrabbled against the rock, the violence of her movement set the ladder swaying. At once she was conscious of the black emptiness below her, and of her own inadequacy. She would never make it! A cry broke from her.

Distantly she heard Ben's shout. "Are you all right?"

"I—I don't know. Oh, Ben—Ben!" Her head had begun to swim—she knew she was going. She felt her fingers slip ping from the rung. She gave a great shriek and swayed, away from the ladder, clawing at the bulging rock.

Ben felt the jerk of the rope against the steel bar and took the sudden strain. "Julie!" he shouted. "Julie, can you hear me?" He jammed himself tighter in the passage and managed to take a turn of the rope round the second piton, though in doing so he had to let it out a few feet. That felt more secure—she should be safe enough now, if only she could help herself. "Julie!" he yelled again, but got no reply. She must have passed out. There was no hope that he could pull her up, not from this cramped position. He'd have to lower her—she'd come round at the bottom.

Suddenly the strain went off the rope, and for a fearful moment that stayed for ever in his mind he thought that his knot had given way. Then, faintly, from far below, he heard her call. "I'm all right, Ben. I'm better now. I've found the ladder."

"Okay," he shouted, and sweat poured into his eyes. "Take it easy." Slowly he paid out the rope. He could hear nothing now from the depths. The coil at his feet was getting rapidly smaller. Only a few more feet of it! With horror he realised that he'd miscalculated—the place where the stone had stopped couldn't have been the bottom, it must have been a ledge! God, this was frightful! He held on now, not daring to let out any more. He felt the tug as she tried to descend. It was no use—she'd have to come up again. But there was no way that he could tell her.

Then the rope went slack once more. He pulled, but there was no weight on it. He couldn't imagine what had happened. He wriggled to the edge and looked out but could see no fight. In desperation he was just going to start the descent himself when he saw the tiny gleam of Julie's torch.

That solved all problems for the moment. In a short time he had lowered the basket and was on his way down. The bulge in the rock gave him a bit of trouble but he was too concerned for Julie to worry about it and was soon past the worst. The light of her torch was just beneath him now, and in a matter of seconds he was beside her.

"Are you hurt?" he asked breathlessly.

"Only a bit scratched." Her voice was shaky. "I'm sorry, Ben—I nearly fainted and I couldn't hold on."

"I was a goddam fool to let you come," he said savagely. "Was the rope long enough? What happened?"

"It wasn't, quite. I had to untie it and do without it for the last bit."

"God! I ought to have my head examined."

"We're down, anyway."

"Oh, sure! Well; let's see what we've got ourselves into."

They began to move cautiously across the floor of the Funnel Chamber. Though they used both torches together, the illumination was poor and it took them a little time to find the exit on the opposite wall and satisfy themselves that it was the only one. After that they made steady progress down the steep tunnel that Anstey had roped. It was Ben, a yard or two ahead, who heard the first distant murmur of water, and he called a halt to listen.

"This is a hell of a place," he said soberly. "I wonder how much farther it goes."

They set off again, but almost at once they came across the second lot of pitons and the second ladder. This time it, took Ben longer to find a loose piece of rock. In the end he managed to prise away a big lump and rolled it into the chasm. They waited, looking at each other. When at last it hit the bottom there was a crash like the roll of thunder drowning the sound of the cascade and setting up terrifying echoes. Ben drew back, aghast.

"Well, I guess this is the end of *your* Odyssey, baby! It must be all of a hundred feet deep and we've no safety line."

She gazed into the sighing darkness and shuddered. She knew she couldn't do it—it would be suicide to try.

"Perhaps we'd better go back," she faltered.

He shone his torch on her face. "Scared to be left?"

"It's not that. I don't want you to go down there alone. I—I'd no idea it would be anything like this."

"It can't be too bad—*he* managed it. He's down there now. Hell, Julie, we've come too far to turn back now. We've got to get him. I'll try not to be long." His torch, swept the broad flat ledge on which they were crouching. "You'll be okay here, there's plenty of room . . ." He broke off with an exclamation. The beam of light had fallen-on a whole pile of stuff—mostly lamps and torches of various types, with a huge stock of spare batteries and a sledge-hammer and something that looked like a rope cradle. Tucked away in a fissure of the wall was a small blue case.

"Look, there's the radio!" Julie cried.

"Fine—you'll be able to amuse, yourself! "He bent over the dump and equipped himself with an extra torch and battery. "Right, I'd better get cracking."

"Take some food, Ben—take the thermos."

"I won't need that—there's plenty of water, by the sound of it." He stuffed a packet of sandwiches into his jacket pocket. "Now listen, honey. I'll be as quick as I can, but don't fret. These heights don't worry me much, and I'll watch my step. Look after yourself."

"I will," she promised. "Good luck, darling."

He swung a leg over the ledge, waved to her, and started the long descent.

Chapter Fourteen

Rung by rung he groped his way down the twisting ladder into the inky blackness of the chasm. The vastness of the hole was terrifying; the tumbling water was like a warning in his ears. Only the knowledge that Quilter had passed this way kept him going. If Quilter had done it, he kept telling himself, so could he. All the same, he felt scared—not so much by the depth as by the utter remoteness of the place. The one thing that cheered him was the fact that he hadn't Julie's safety to worry about any longer. That more than halved the anxiety. And being on his own would enormously simplify the meeting with Quilter—if he should ever find him.

He had been on the ladder for almost ten minutes when at last he touched down in a patch of wet clay. Spray from the cascade soaked him. He gazed up into the vaulted darkness and waved his torch in case Julie should be watching from the ledge. Then he began to cast about for Quilter's trail. His feeble lamp revealed none of the marvels which had held Anstey and Quilter spellbound, but at that moment he neither knew nor cared what he was missing. He took a step or two away from the ladder, shining his torch on the ground. Presently he gave a grunt of satisfaction. The wet floor of the chamber had been churned by repeated journeys into a track of clayey mud and broken stalagmite, which ran beside the stream as unmistakably as though it had been signposted. He followed the footprints, slowing where the ground became uneven, pressing on fast when it levelled out. His eyes were mostly on the way ahead; the only thing that caught his attention in the chamber were some bits of flat wood floating on the surface of a pool. They puzzled him.

Soon he came to the high narrow tunnel which carried the stream out of the chamber. Here, too, there were signs of much coming and going. The floor was scarred with the scratches of nailed boots and littered with snapped-off calcite fragments. He strode quickly along the passage, oppressed by the fantastic extent of the pothole and anxious only to get to the end of his journey. He crossed the third chamber with barely a pause and plunged on, still following the tracks, until he emerged into a smaller cave and was brought up sharp by a blank rock face. The stream, he saw, trickled away under a chaos of huge boulders which, judging by their bright colouring, had only recently broken away from the mass above. Where the water ran under the choke a pile of wood and debris had collected. Not far away there was a black circle of charred wood fragments on the rock floor. Quilter must have brought the wood down to keep himself warm.

Lacking any helpful diagram, Ben searched without much confidence for some other exit. It almost seemed that this *was* the end of the road. He began to wonder if he had passed his quarry in one of the larger chambers without. realising it. The thought troubled him—he didn't like the idea that Quilter might be behind him, with Julie alone up there on the ledge. He stood listening, hoping for some indication of a presence, some scraping of a boot or clatter of a stone, some beckoning gleam of fight. There was nothing—the only movement of any sort was that of the gently running stream. He clambered a little way up the rock face and swept it with his torch. He was on the point of deciding that he'd better go back when the beam revealed a possible opening.

He scrambled up to it and peered in. At first he refused to believe that this narrow pipe was a continuation of the pothole and that he would have to go through it, but as he flashed; the light he saw that the sandy floor had been scoured as, though by the passage of a body and when he looked more closely he found the toe-marks of nailed boots. It was incredible, but Quilter must be in there.

Ben went back to the stream and gulped some water and then

he sat down to eat a sandwich and smoke a cigarette. He hoped that if he waited a while, Quilter would come out. Time passed, and nothing happened. Presently he knew he would have to go in after him. He wished profoundly that he hadn't let Julie talk him into this foolhardy search. It was a job for experts. If he wasn't careful he would get himself into a hell of a jam—literally a jam, he told himself ruefully, thinking of the tiny aperture. Well, he'd got to go through with it now—he couldn't possibly go back to Julie and tell her he'd failed. He picked up his torch and once more climbed the face.

His misgivings increased rapidly as he entered the pipe. He was broader in the shoulders than Quilter, and he soon realised he'd been wrong in supposing that he could go whenever Quilter went. As he writhed forward foot by foot he had to keep his unprotected head well down to avoid the jagged points of rock that jutted from the roof, and he felt his clothes catching and ripping on the walls as he squirmed between them.

Just short of the narrowest part, he stopped. Ahead, he could see that the pipe twisted. He felt certain he could never get through. He made one last effort, inching his body forward until he could go no farther. So that was that—he'd reached his limit. Not even for Julie could he change his shape! He switched off his torch to save the battery and lay flat, his head on his outstretched arms, relaxing after his efforts. He'd have a short breather, he decided, and then back out of this hell-hole before he got stuck for good.

As he subsided into silence, he caught the faintest murmur of sound from the pipe ahead. At first he wasn't sure—his ears could have deceived him. Then it grew louder, resolving itself unmistakably into the scraping of a body through the pipe. It was Quilter!—he was coming out. Ben lay still, wondering if there'd ever been an encounter like this before. In a few moments the blackness ahead became illuminated as the rays of Quilter's lamp lit up the rock wall at the bend of the passage. The scraping was much louder now, the light much stronger. Suddenly a blinding beam fell full on Ben, momentarily dazzling him.

For Quilter, the shock was unnerving. He drew in his breath in a sudden hiss of fear and his helmet clanged against the roof as he jerked back.

Ben switched on his own torch. At once he understood why Julie had been so upset by the apparition in the cottage. The change in Quilter's appearance was staggering. His face was ashen, his cheeks hollow and bony, his eye sockets deeply sunken. A ragged beard covered his chin. If Ben hadn't known who the man was, he would never have taken him for the sprightly, youthful, sunburned figure whom he had met in the Dordogne so short a time ago. Only the bright intelligent eyes were the same.

For a couple of seconds, neither of the men spoke. Quilter showed no sign of recognition; he lay motionless, staring, as though he couldn't believe what he saw.

It was Ben who broke the silence. "Hello, Quilter. I guess I startled you."

"Who are you?"

"Benson Traill—remember, we met in France?"

The eyes gleamed. "What the devil are you doing here?"

"Looking for you."

"How did you find this place?"

"Look, Quilter, let's get out of here and then talk. It's a damn silly spot for a discussion."

Quilter looked as though he hadn't even heard. "Tell me how you found it?"

Ben's shoulders contracted in a shrug. "Okay, if it'll make you any happier. You know a man named Anstey?"

"Yes," said Quilter.

"Well, the police found a plan of this cave in his wallet."

"That's impossible!"

"It happened. The wallet was washed up on the beach, some place near here."

Slowly, the look of disbelief faded from Quilter's face. "I see," he said in a toneless voice. "So Anstey was right about the stream."

Ben couldn't make anything of that. "Is Anstey dead?" he asked.

"Oh, yes—he's dead."

Ben was staggered by his nonchalance. "There's a sort of idea around that you may have had something to do with his death. Did you?"

"In a way. I can tell you exactly what happened."

"Keep it till later, we'll suffocate in this passage. Besides, Julie's waiting back there at the top of the big cave."

"I'd sooner tell you now while I've got the chance—I wouldn't like it to be thought that I'd murdered the man. You see, Anstey came down with me to explore this place. There was a sudden storm overhead and he got trapped in what used to be a tunnel—that place where the stream runs under the boulders. I could have saved him, but I was a coward and ran for my life. Afterwards I was afraid someone might get to know I'd abandoned him, so I tried to hide all the traces of our association. And that's really the whole story about Anstey."

It was Ben's turn to stare. "You mean it was just an accident?"

"Yes."

"Then all I can say is you've been a damn fool hiding down here. Hell, you're not the only guy that's been scared. Where's his body?"

"It's still in the tunnel, but the place is all blocked up now. I didn't want anyone to find it, ever, so I brought down some explosive and blew up the entrance."

"Christ! You must have got yourself into a state. I still don't see, though, why you've been hiding all this time. What was the point? You must have known you'd have to account for yourself sooner or later."

"Not necessarily."

"I don't get you."

"I don't suppose you do," said Quilter. "It really doesn't matter."

"It matters that you've been doing a disappearing trick. Julie's almost off her head with worry. The whole country's looking for you—do you know that? I must say, looking at you now, that it's kind of hard to believe, but I gather you'd probably be a Minister of the Crown by now if you'd been around."

"Really?" Quilter couldn't have sounded more indifferent. "That's ironical, I must say. When did the message come?" "Oh, about a week ago, I guess."

"A week ago. H'm. I wonder if it would have made any difference if I'd known? I don't suppose so. I've been a bit out of touch, you know—I brought the radio down to keep a check on what was happening, but it wouldn't work properly at this depth. Even up on the ledge I could only get a murmur. Ah, well, it's all the same now."

"It's not all the same whether we stifle here or not. If you ask me, Quilter, you're ill—very ill. The sooner you're above ground and being looked after, the better. Come on, let's clear out."

"You can go," said Quilter, "I'm not leaving here."

"Of course you are. You can't stay down here—you're all in. You'll die, man."

"I've no choice now—I must stay."

"That's damn nonsense. If you didn't kill Anstey deliberately . . ."

"Anstey? Oh, he's nothing to do with it."

"No? Then what the hell are you talking about?"

Quilter gave a little smile, ghastly in its incongruity. "I'll tell you, Traill, if you like. Do you happen to know where we are?"

"I know we're in a goddam awful spot." "Do you know the location of the place we're in?"

"How would I? Somewhere in Cumberland, England. Why?"

"We're almost exactly underneath the biggest atomic plant outside America, and in about five minutes I intend to blow it to rubble."

Chapter Fifteen

Ben slowly shook his head. "Look, bud, you need a doctor. Now come on out—you'll feel better when you get up top."

Quilter gave another of his ghastly smiles. "You don't believe me, do you?"

"You're darned right I don't!"

"It's the truth, though . . . Here, perhaps this will convince you." He twisted round on to his side and with great difficulty succeeded in passing something through from behind him. Ben saw the ends of a coil of wire—and something else.

Quilter held the object in front of him. "Do you know what this is?"

"Sure," said Ben. "It's a plunger for detonating explosives."

"Exactly. You're familiar with such things, of course—it took me some time to find out about them. However, an intelligent man can soon pick up a new skill. The other end of the wire, by the way, is already connected to the detonator. I was bringing the plunger out to a safer place—it's going to be a *very* big explosion."

Ben looked at the plunger, and then rather helplessly at Quilter. This was the first time he'd ever had to handle a man who was quite so obviously round the bend.

"Of course," Quilter went on, "I had a bit of a job over the explosive." He seemed anxious to talk after his weeks of solitude. "There wasn't any difficulty about the gelignite and detonators and plunger—I got those from a shed on my own land—things they'd been using to blow up tree roots. But I had to steal the bulk of the stuff from an army dump near Lancaster—I did that while Julie was in France."

Ben stiffened. What was that he'd read in the paper about a theft of explosives from an army dump? Yesterday, it was—but maybe they'd only just found out. It *had* been Lancaster, or some place very like it. Was it conceivable . . .?

"Actually it was much easier than I'd expected," Quilter continued. "The explosive was stored most conveniently in wooden boxes in a forest by the roadside, quite unguarded.

The Army's gift to saboteurs! I happened to know about it because a colleague of mine in the House was kind enough to write to *The Times* complaining. So I drove over and took my pick. I could have had shells, grenades, anything. I chose land-mines—anti-tank mines. I had to make a lot of journeys, but it's amazing what the station wagon holds. I filled it up, night after night, and by dawn each morning they were safely hidden away underground. I flatter myself it was a most efficient operation. I lowered the boxes down the precipices in a sort of improvised sling, broke them open in the big cave, and floated the mines downstream on the bits of wood. It was really extraordinarily simple—getting them through here was the most tedious part of the business. Anyway, they're all stacked up there now behind me—hundreds of them, perhaps thousands. I don't know how many, I lost count. And the explosive force of each one, Traill, is sufficient to destroy a tank. Think of it!"

Ben ran his tongue over his dry lips. "You *can't* be serious!"

"Indeed I am. I assure you everything's been attended to down to the last detail. Anstey made a most conscientious survey of the cave—it was looking at his plan of the place, after I got back from France, that gave me the idea. When I superimposed it on a local map and discovered that the end of this passage was right underneath the plant, and not far underneath, the temptation was irresistible. Mind you, I had to do some digging—that was the hardest bit of all. I had to drive passages up at a slant through the sandstone and I'm not used to pick-and-shovel work." He held out his hands, and Ben saw that they were filthy and calloused, with black broken nails. "Still, I got where I wanted in the end. I had to work night and day, but it was worth it. In some places the mines are actually stacked right among the concrete footings of the plant—I didn't dare to go any higher in case someone might hear me. It's rather amusing to think of all the trouble they went to to put a double security fence around the plant, isn't it?"

"Sure! The whole thing's a hell of a joke. God, it's unbelievable! You can't know what you're doing."

"Oh, but I do. You see, Traill, my loyalties aren't yours. You're for American imperialism, I don't doubt. I'm on the other side—I have been for years. I've been a secret communist since 1942. Not a very good one, perhaps—I don't take very kindly to discipline, especially when it involves patience. In all these years the people I'm in touch with have given me only a couple of trivial assignments—hardly worth the effort of lying to Julie when I had to go away. The idea, you see, was to use me as a long-term investment. I was to be an orthodox member of the Labour Party, a respectable politician. Then one day I'd be offered a big job in the Government and I'd be able to operate from a key position. Well, I got tired of waiting—I even began to wonder if I was really trusted. And this Anstey affair upset me. I wanted to *do* something. I wanted to get into the fight. Suddenly here was my chance—by pure accident, by a piece of fortune that would never happen again. I couldn't turn it down. I knew it would be the biggest stroke of peace-time sabotage in the history of the world."

"It'll be a piece of monstrous treachery!"

"Nonsense, Traill. How can I betray something I don't believe in? These labels mean nothing. If some anti-Soviet Russians succeeded in blowing up a big atom plant in Russia, would your side call him a traitor? Of course you wouldn't. You'd say he was a freedom-loving democrat, a hero, a martyr."

"He'd be fighting a tyranny. You're helping one."

"Naturally I don't accept that. Believe me, my conscience isn't troubled. In the end, humanity will thank me."

"What about the poor devils working up there when your firework goes off? Will they thank you?"

"Did you Americans think of that when you atom-bombed

Hiroshima? In war, you don't stop to count suffering. This is my personal act of war."

"You're starting it—we didn't."

"It'll come, some time. It's inevitable."

"It may not be inevitable. You may be wrong. If you are wrong, this thing you're planning is just a wicked, pointless atrocity. Have you no feelings at all for the misery you're going to cause? Think of Julie, man—this'll just about break her. Does she mean nothing to you?"

"Nothing. Less than nothing, now. I've got beyond that. What does any one person matter? It may sound grandiloquent to you, but I've got a date with Destiny. I'm helping to shape the whole future of the world."

An exclamation of disbelief broke from Ben. "you presumptuous fool! Haven't you ever heard of evolution? Don't you know that the only thing that shapes the world is Time? Great God, you lie among rocks that were laid down here a hundred million years ago, and you talk of a date with Destiny because you're going to blow up one little man-made factory!"

Quilter smirked. "For a scientist, you're quite articulate." He picked up the ends of the wire and started to connect them to the plunger.

Ben strained forward in a desperate attempt to reach it, but the pipe held him and there was nothing he could do.

"I should conserve your strength," said Quilter. "You'll need it for getting out." He seemed absorbed in his technical problem; it was only too evident that for him no moral problem existed.

"Listen, Quilter—just listen to me. Even as an act of war it's not worth it. What's this plant making—atom bomb stuff? Okay, suppose it is, and you blow it up. It won't make a dime's worth of difference. We've got stacks of the things."

Quilter went on fiddling. "I hardly think your Government would agree with you! In any case, you might as well save your breath, Traill. You don't suppose I haven't thought this out? God knows I've had long enough. In the past few weeks I've thought of everything—*everything*. I've faced up to all the possible consequences. By coming down here you've altered things a little—but not much. I've made up my mind."

"You'll never get away with this."

"That's what I mean when I say you've altered things a little. I did plan to leave the country afterwards. I assumed that it would be some while before the explosion would be traced to me, and that I should have plenty of time to get away. I'd have found important work to do in Russia—even a few old friends! Now I can't hope for that. I know I can't escape. Even if I could deal with you, there's still Julie. So—I shall give myself up."

"They'll hang you."

"I expect so. Ever since you appeared, I've been trying to get used to the idea. I think I can face it. At least I shall have left some mark upon the world. I may provide a paragraph even in *your* history books. I've had a futile sort of life, always waiting and never achieving—it will be quite pleasant to end it in a blaze of execration."

"Suppose they decide you're mad, and shut you up with lunatics for the rest of your days?"

"They won't do that—they won't have enough restraint. Anyway, I'm not mad. Don't be misled by my appearance—that would happen to anyone who'd been through what I've been through. I know exactly what I'm doing and I'm completely responsible. I'm only doing what thousands of perfectly sane men have been applauded for in the past—striking at the enemy. You wouldn't think me insane if this were Nazi Germany and I were an American agent, would you?" He turned his wrist over in the sand and looked at his watch. "Well, the time has come—if I leave it any longer the morning shift will have started work, and I don't want to kill people unnecessarily."

He locked his hands together and rested them on the plunger. For a second or two he waited, but not from any doubt or regret. This was the end of doubt—it was the climax of his devoted labours, the moment of fruition. A glorious picture filled his mind—a picture of earth-splitting upheaval, crumbling walls, toppling chimneys and destroying fire. Beyond that, he saw himself proudly facing his accusers, indifferent to their hate, tranquil in his triumph. And beyond that still he could see himself walking out into a prison yard in the chill of an autumn morning, and knew he would not be afraid. He had faced and overcome his fears. He was at peace.

He strained on the plunger and the rod went down. "You crazy fool!" Ben shouted, and pressed his body down into the sand, covering his head with his arms.

Seconds passed like years. Then from Quilter there came a moaning sigh. When Ben looked at him again his face was trembling, as though he were about to cry.

"It looks like Destiny hasn't kept that date," said Ben. A trickle of sweat dripped from his elbows.

The taunt stung Quilter to frantic action. He began to fiddle with the wires, checking the connections. Then he worked the plunger up and down in a desperate attempt to get some contact. He knew he'd never really understood the thing. It had worked before, when he'd blown up the choke, but something must have happened to it. Now it was quite dead. Presently he gave up and lay exhausted, his face a wet greyness. This was the final, the unbearable humiliation. He had failed! After all his planning, all his efforts—yes, and all his talk!—he had failed. Now there would be derision not glory; confinement, not martyrdom.

He started to inch his way back. He *couldn't* fail now. He had paper and wood—he could light a fire under the gelignite—surely that would set the thing off? He straggled to adjust his mind—to face the thought of being blown to fragments, of private, lonely death, without abuse or acclaim. It wasn't how he had planned it—it was the lesser evil now, that was all that could be said for it. There was no acceptable alternative—no other way. At least . . . Suddenly he stopped again and lay still, thinking.

Ben's voice broke in harshly. "Give it up, Quilter. Accept the verdict."

Quilter raised his head. "Why should I? I can start a blaze back there and go up with it."

"Don't be a fool, man. Give it up. Come on, let's get out."

Quilter didn't move. "That's not much of a proposition, Traill. What happens to me if I do? Arrest, and a life sentence."

Ben thought of the heaped explosive and the size of the stake. "I guess you could still leave the country," he said. "If you come out now, I'll keep my mouth shut until you're clear."

"You swear that?"

"So help me God!"

There was a long, nerve-racking moment of indecision. Then Quilter stirred. "Very well. On that condition, I accept."

"Right—let's get moving." Ben started at once to back out of the pipe, his only thought to get Quilter away from the dump as quickly as possible. It was a slow, laborious journey, punctuated by moments of horrible suspense when Quilter seemed to lag. The man could still change his mind! Only when they had both emerged and were standing upright by the exit did Ben breathe freely again.

"You'd better go ahead," he said curtly. "You know the way better than I do."

Without a word, Quilter set off along the straight passage.

He had the advantage of a headlamp as well as a strong torch and he walked with such speed that Ben had difficulty in keeping up with him. In ten minutes they were entering the Cascade Chamber and Quilter was leaping and striding from clay to rock and rock to stalagmite with the confidence of long practice. He might look like a pallid ghost, but it was clear that his physical strength was far from exhausted.

"Easy, there." Ben called sharply.

Quilter slowed without turning, and Ben came up with him. A few more steps, and they were at the foot of the ladder. Far above, Ben could just make out a moving point of light and waved his torch in greeting. "Who goes first?" asked Quilter. "You do, bud. I'll be on your heels."

"You'll have to wait till I'm up. Those pitons won't stand the weight of both of us together."

For a moment, Ben hesitated. The man might be sane after his fashion or he might not, but sending him up to spend five or ten minutes alone with Julie on a narrow ledge wasn't a very attractive way of putting the matter to the test. Yet to go ahead himself and leave Quilter free to go back to the dump if he suddenly felt like it was unthinkable.

"Okay," said Ben, "I'll wait. But if you try any funny business, Quilter, I'll personally tear you apart. Up you go—and signal when you're off the ladder." He stood watching until Quilter had disappeared into the blackness of the cavern.

Up on the shelf of rock, Julie waited. She had had a long and exhausting vigil and she felt inexpressibly thankful that it was over and that none of her fears had been realised. Ben was safe, and Laurence had been found, and now everything would be sorted out. Not even the sight of her husband's gaunt and dreadful countenance coming up to the ledge could lessen her sense of relief. She had no fear of him—however ill he was, he couldn't wish her harm. Compassion filled her. She leaned forward to grasp his arm and help him off the ladder. He turned to wave his torch over the chasm and then, without a word, threw himself down on the floor to rest. Julie stared at his canvas overall and strange headgear—just, one more of the many things she didn't understand. "Are you all right, Laurence?"

"Yes," he said tonelessly.

What *have* you been doing?"

"You ask too many questions, Julie—you always did." He flashed his torch round the ledge, and focused on her basket.

"Is there anything to drink?"

"There's a little brandy." She passed him the flask and he took a mouthful and gave it back to her. Then he sat with his chin on his knees, paying no further attention to her.

Reluctantly, she decided to let him have his way, and leaned over the edge to see if there were any sign of Ben. His torch was off, but the movement of the ladder told her he was coming up fast. Soon he was within hailing distance, and she heard his shout—" You okay; Julie?"

"Yes, everything's fine."

"Keep it that way—I'll be right up."

A few seconds later he scrambled up on to the ledge.

"Well, we made it, honey. Sorry we were so long." He glanced across at Quilter's silent, sphinx-like figure; then looked at Julie and gave a significant headshake.

She gripped his arm. "What happened, Ben?"

"Tell you later! Come on, Quilter, let's get moving. Okay, Julie?"

He took her by the elbow and steered her away from the precipice and into the darkness of the roped passage. "You'd better lead up the slope—keep tight hold of the rope and you'll be okay. Now what the devil is that guy . . . ?"

He broke off as sounds of sudden activity came from behind them. In an instant he was back on the ledge, flashing his torch around. "My God, he's gone!" he shouted. He rushed to the edge, flinging himself down flat. There was no light, nothing. For a moment he thought that Quilter must have thrown himself into the abyss, and braced himself for the crash. Then he saw that the ladder was moving. He shone his torch down and caught a grey figure in the beam, twenty feet below and descending rapidly with an odd, lop-sided motion. Quilter had his left arm hooked through something. Surely—yes, it was the handle of the radio.

The radio! At once Ben understood everything. He turned on his belly and gripped the ladder. Julie was crying "What is it? What's happening?" but he barely heard her. He was remembering what Quilter had said about the pitons—that they wouldn't support two. He looked down into the pit and knew there was no point in risking it. Quilter was already out of sight. With his skill and knowledge he would be back in the pipe long before anyone could catch him. There was only one other way to stop him.

With a hard, set face Ben scrambled back on to the ledge and began heaving at the ladder where it was held by the pitons.

Julie grabbed his arm. "Ben!" she shrieked. "What are you doing? Are you crazy?"

He strained at the ladder, shouting back, "He's taken the battery—the high-tension battery. It'll detonate the charge. Christ, where's that sledgehammer?" He groped around in the dim light. "Got it! Stand back, Julie—it's the only way."

She flung herself at him. "You're mad. You'll kill him. Oh, God, what's happened to you?"

He thrust her away from him and struck at one of the pitons. "He's going to blow up the atom plant!"

It seemed that she didn't hear. As he lifted the hammer again she clawed at him, pummelling his back. "No, Ben, *no, NO!*" She was beside herself, fighting like a tigress, hampering his movements so that he couldn't lift the hammer. He swayed away from the piton, trying to shake her off. She fell and rolled and he caught her on the very edge of the pit with a gasp of anguish. He picked her up bodily and carried her to the rock wall, pinning her to the floor. She was sobbing and struggling. "No, Ben, no!"

He shook her. "Listen!—listen to me! He's going to blow up the atom plant, do you hear, blow it up! He's been carrying explosives down for weeks. He'll kill hundreds of people. I've *got* to stop him."

Something of what he was saying seemed to register at last. She went limp, with an awful moan. He let her go and seized the sledgehammer again and cracked at one of the pitons with all his strength. He saw it move a little and aimed another blow at it and then he hit the second one, and suddenly both of them shot out of their rock crevices and the end of the ladder went sliding over the precipice, carrying debris with it that echoed and ricocheted as it fell.

He dropped to his knees and peered down. All was silence now, except for the murmur of the cascade. No sound, no sign of movement.

"You've killed him!" said Julie, her voice a whisper.

Then, far below, a fight flicked on, and a second light, and the two of them began moving like will-o'-the-wisps across the cavern floor.

You're wrong," said Ben in a solemn tone. "There he goes—back to his dump! He must have been almost at the bottom when the ladder went over." He groped for a cigarette and lit it with fingers that trembled a little. "Well, I guess there's nothing more we can do."

Helplessly he stared into the chasm. Almost at once, it seemed, the lights disappeared—Quilter was wasting no time. By now he would be hurrying through the long tunnel. Say seven or eight minutes to reach the pipe—a few minutes to crawl through it to the wires . . .

He waited, tense and silent. Presently Julie came creeping out of the shadows and knelt beside him. He could feel her body shaking and her hand on his was icy cold. "Ben, I'm so frightened. Hold me—hold me tight!" He put an arm round her, trying to comfort her. There was nothing he could say. Slowly the minutes passed.

After a while he felt the cigarette burning his fingers and stubbed it out. Any time now, he thought. Unless . . . He wondered if it was possible that Quilter would make a hash of it again. You had to know how to fix detonators to gelignite—maybe, that had been the trouble before. If things didn't work out this time, maybe he'd go on hanging about for a while, trying to make up his mind to blow himself up . . .

Suddenly Ben jumped to his feet. "There may be time after all. If I can get to the top and ring the plant from the cottage . . ."

His words were cut short by the explosion. It reached them first as a violent thud, a concussion that made them doubt the solidity of the ledge on which they stood. Then there came a rumbling sound like the muttering of a distant storm. The air began to stir around them and the sound swelled until the whole cavern was singing and vibrating with noise. Then, little by little, the echoes died.

"So he's done it," said Ben in a flat voice. "Let's go."

Julie moved away up the slope without a word. Her senses were numbed by the shock, and a deadly fatigue made all her movements automatic. Her brain seemed to have stopped working altogether. Once, in the steep roped passage she slipped and let go of the rope and came slithering down on Ben, who himself had barely the strength to hold her. He started her off again with words of encouragement, supporting her from behind his spirits sank with every flagging step. She had been tried too much. He knew he would never be able to get her up the second ladder. Even if he roped her he couldn't pull her up single-handed. In his present state he doubted if he could even hold her. He had already resolved to leave her and go for help when, just as they reached the foot of the ladder, she gave a long sigh and slumped back into his arms.

He laid her on the floor and chafed her cold cheeks. Her whiteness frightened him. He was fumbling for the brandy when she stirred and opened her eyes. "It's—no good Ben" she murmured. "You—go."

"Okay, honey. You just lie still—I'll be back soon."

She smiled, and her eyelids flickered, and presently she seemed to be asleep.

He flashed his torch around making sure that the ground where she was lying was flat and safe. He left her own torch on, and a spare one beside her in the basket with some food and the brandy flask. He covered her with his jacket. Then driven by a new sense of urgency, he struggled up the ladder. Even the fate of the plant had become a secondary matter. His one thought now was to bring help before Julie's remaining strength was undermined by cold and loneliness and fear.

Chapter Sixteen

Ten minutes later he stumbled out on to the turf beside the Pikes. The air was acrid with smoke. He glanced down towards the coast and saw that a grey haze was slowly drifting over the hillside. It looked as though Quilter had made a job of it.

He stopped at the cottage to sluice his face and get himself a drink. He knew he was just about all in. His hands were still trembling from the strain of hauling himself up the ladder and most of what was in the whisky bottle went down his shirt, but he saved enough for a stiff shot. When he'd knocked it back he felt better. He grabbed the phone and impatiently flashed the exchange. Minutes passed, but no one answered. In the end he gave it up and drove down to the Plough at reckless speed.

The innkeeper's wife was standing at the door, looking out towards Blean. She turned as she heard the jeep. "Why, Mr. Traill . . .!" she exclaimed, staring at him.

"Is Mr. Martin about?"

"No, they're all down at the plant. You've heard about the explosion . . .?"

He slammed in the clutch and drove on. Better to go straight to the police, he thought—they'd be able to organise everything. He trod hard on the gas and the hedgerows rushed by.

Blean was seething. Half the population seemed to be making its way towards the plant, whose chimneys, at least, still stood. A fire-engine dashed past, clearing the road with its bell. Another followed close behind. The resources of the district were being mobilised.

Ben stopped by a knot of women on a street corner. "Say, could you direct me to the police station?"

One of them pointed across the Square and he saw the blue lamp and drove across. He stopped the jeep with a squeal of tyres and stumbled up the stone steps. The station was empty except for a burly, heavily-moustached sergeant who was talking on the telephone. In the corner of the room another phone was ringing.

Ben lurched heavily against the counter. "Officer . . .!" he cried.

Sergeant Barrait gave him a cold stare and went on talking. When he'd finished he turned and walked slowly to the other phone. Ben drummed on the counter, glanced at the door, wondered if there was anywhere else he could go. The fire station, the hospital . . .? No, he'd get no help there, not at a moment like this.

At last the sergeant came back to the counter. "Well, what is it?"

"Officer," said Ben with desperate earnestness, "I know how this atom plant was blown up. It was done from a pothole and there's a woman still down there. I need your help . . ." He lolled forward on to the counter.

Barratt looked him slowly up and down, noting his torn shirt, his tousled hair, his drooping eyelids. He sniffed suspiciously.

"You've been drinking."

"Only a mouthful—I spilt it down me."

"I've heard that one before. The best thing you can do, young fellow me lad, is to go and sleep it off."

"Don't be a bloody fool, I'm stone sober . . ."

"Now look here . . .!" began Barrat in a threatening tone.

"You've got to listen to me. My name's Traill, I'm an American. I'm not drunk, do you understand—I've spent the last twelve hours in a pothole with a madman, that's why I look like this. Up there on the hill—it runs right down under the plant." He looked hopelessly at the sergeant's wooden face. "Christ, I thought English policemen were wonderful! You know what a pothole is, don't you? I tell you I was with the guy that blew up the plant, and his wife's still there in the hole and she'll probably die . . . Officer, you've *got* to do something—I need men, ropes, an ambulance . . ."

Barratt looked at his wild, bloodshot eyes and slowly shook his head. Then he shrugged and drew an open ledger towards him. "What did you say your name was?"

"Traill—Benson Traill."

"How do you spell it?"

"Oh, for God's sake, officer . . .!"

"Now see here," said Barratt, "do you want me to take particulars or not?"

Ben groaned. "Okay!" He spelt out the name, fuming.

"Address?"

"The Plough Inn."

"Ah! Barratt sounded as though he might have a word to say to the proprietor of the Plough Inn. His pen scratched slowly over the paper. "Now then, you say you know who's responsible for this explosion, eh?"

"Yes, it's a guy named Quilter—Laurence Quilter. He's an M.P. He's down there now in the pothole . . ."

Barratt flung down his pen. "You're drunk, all right. Come on, now, get out of here or you'll find yourself in a cell. We've got enough on our hands this morning without being bothered with people like you . . ." The telephone rang again and he picked up the receiver and said, "Station sergeant here," jerking his head at Ben and indicating the door.

Ben fingered a moment, then saw that it was hopeless and staggered out. If only he'd been a bit more coherent!—but he was so tired, so desperately tired and anxious. With the whole town in ferment, probably no one would listen to him . . .

His eye lit on an empty telephone kiosk across the road and suddenly he knew what he must do. He rushed ever, grabbed the receiver, and dialled 0. The ringing seemed as though it would go on for ever, but when he'd almost abandoned hope the operator answered.

"Say, miss, will you get me the United States Embassy in London? I don't know the number offhand but it's terribly urgent . . ."

"Is it a priority call?"

"Sure, top priority."

"Who are you, please?"

"I'm an American—it's a matter of life and death. I must get through . . ."

"I'm sorry—the lines to London are all busy." She rang Off.

Ben dropped the receiver and sagged against the side of the box. There must be *some* way. He had a picture of Julie waking at the bottom of that cold dark chasm, alone and frightened, wondering what had happened to him. God, she might try to climb the ladder by herself! He rushed frantically out into the street. People were still moving towards the plant. Maybe he'd better go there, too—that was where everything was happening. There'd be security officers attached to the place and they might listen to him. He jumped into the jeep and started to honk his way through the crowd. Soon there were so many people that he had to leave it and continue on foot. There was a huge throng beside the first line of wire—they were packed tight, hundreds of them, waiting for news. A dozen policemen were on duty by the entrance, keeping the road clear. The double iron gates stood ajar, with a uniformed guard just inside and an inspector outside. Ben could see a sentry box and a guardhouse beyond. A huge notice said, "All passes must be shown."

He shouldered his way forward almost to the gates. Then a constable stopped him. "Where do you think you're going?" he demanded.

"I've got some information," Ben said. "I've got to see the security people."

The inspector heard him and strolled up. Again Ben felt cold, critical eyes surveying him; again he heard that suspicious sniff. "Have you a pass?"

"No, but it's vital I see someone. I can tell you . . ."

"No one comes in without a pass. Stand back!"

At that moment an ambulance drove up and two policemen pushed the gates wide.

The engines roared and the ambulance slid forward. As it went through Ben slipped in beside it. From somewhere a hand shot out and grabbed him and swung him round. "Oh, no, you don't—what's the idea, eh?" Somebody seized him by the collar and began to march him towards a van. God, they were going to take him away now! Suddenly he saw a man approaching whose appearance seemed familiar—a man in a soft hat and a raincoat.

"Inspector!" he shouted. "Inspector Ford!" The man stopped.

"Inspector, you know me! Can I speak to you?" Ford came up to them. "What's going on?"

"Obstructing the police, sir "said the constable, "Drunk, I reckon."

"My name's Traill," said Ben desperately. "Don't you remember—I was with Mrs. Quilter that day you called at the cottage."

Ford stared, sniffed, looked him up and down. "Yes, I remember. What are you doing here?"

"I'm trying to get somebody to listen to me." Ben was almost weeping with frustration. "It was Quilter who blew up the plant. I was there. He did it from a pothole . . ."

"A pothole!" Ford suddenly took his arm. "All right, constable, I'll see to him. Come with me, Traill."

Ben hardly knew what happened after that. He was going through the wire, and through some more wire and then he was in a small brick hut and there were plain clothes men around, and someone was handing him a cup of tea and then he was telling his story and people were actually listening . . .

There was no more trouble. Ben was vaguely aware of sharp instructions being given and preparations being made, and soon a convoy of vehicles was threading its way out of Blean—a police car, another police car, an improvised ambulance, and a lorry with a squad of heavy rescue workers from the plant. Ben sat with Ford in the leading car, giving directions in a voice he hardly recognised as his own. In a matter of minutes the convoy had turned up the track and ground to a standstill by the Pikes.

They wouldn't let Ben go down again, and waiting was agony, but Ford reassured him. The men had got all the proper tackle, he said, and they knew what they were doing. Mrs. Quilter would be all right. Half an hour passed—the longest half-hour Ben could remember. Then a helmeted head emerged from the hole, and another, and they were hauling Julie out.

He dropped down beside her on the grass and took her hand. "you okay, honey?"

She gave a faint smile. "Yes, Ben," she whispered. "I'm—okay."

He smiled back and they lifted her and put her in. the ambulance and he watched it drive away down the hill. Then he blacked out.

Chapter Seventeen

He woke in darkness and for a second thought he was back in the pothole. Then he discovered he was lying on something soft with a rug over him and realised that he was in the sitting-room of the cottage. He got up and switched on the light. He was still filthy and smelt abominably of stale whisky.

The door opened and a man came in, grinning. "Ah, so you've come to life, sir! How are you feeling?"

"Scruffy. Have I slept long?"

"Twelve hours. My name's Howlett, by the way—I'm from Special Branch. Would you care for coffee, bacon and eggs?"

"*Would* I? You my male nurse or something?"

"Just for the moment, sir. I'm really here to get a full statement from you, but there's no hurry."

"How's Mrs. Quilter?"

"She's fine. They're keeping her over at the hospital to-night, but she'll be back in the morning. It was just exhaustion. Right, I'll get the coffee in."

Ben went to the bathroom and cleaned himself up. When he came down again the food was ready.

"My, that smells good," he said. "I see I was wrong—the police *are* wonderful." He sat down. "Any news of Quilter?"

"There is, indeed. He's dead."

"Oh! "Ben was silent for a moment. "What happened to him?"

"They tell me he was in a very narrow passage when he fired the charge and the force of the explosion jammed him in there like a cork in a bottle."

"They've been down there, have they?"

"From the top end. There's a huge crater and the tunnel's exposed."

"I see. Well, I guess it was a quick death."

"I rather doubt that, sir, from what I hear."

Ben pushed back his plate. "Does Mrs. Quilter know about it?"

"I don't think so, not yet. They were going to tell her to-morrow."

"I hope they'll tell her it was quick."

"They always do, sir. I shouldn't worry about that."

"What about the plant? Some of it seemed to be standing."

Howlett smiled. "Good lord, sir, it's hardly touched. The explosion was underneath one of the lavatory blocks—completely destroyed it, of course, but the main buildings are intact except for the windows."

"Anyone killed?"

"Three chaps—two workmen and a lavatory attendant."

"The whole thing was a fiasco, in fact?"

"Yes, but it might not have been. The engineers say that Quilter made the mistake of exploding his charge too near the surface, so the force of the thing was mostly wasted in the air. If a mine like that had gone off in solid ground it would have had the effect of a small earthquake and the shock waves might have made the main production block unusable."

"As near as that, eh?"

Howlett nodded. "Quite an achievement for an amateur!"

"He had guts," said Ben. "I'll say that for him. I couldn't have done what he did in a million years." He lit a cigarette. "Okay, what about this statement?"

Chapter Eighteen

First thing in the morning, Julie came back. She was pale and very subdued, and it was obvious the whole episode had hit her hard. They sat on the bank in the sun and they talked for a long time. There was much that she still didn't know and Ben filled in the gaps.

"I suppose," she said at last, "that I was wrong to try and stop you on the ledge?"

"To stop me? Oh, that! He shrugged. "It was natural enough."

"Three men died, though, and it might have been more."

"You don't have to answer for that. Anyway, you know darned well that what I was saying didn't register."

"It wouldn't have made any difference if it had I couldn't think of anything but that ghastly drop and Laurence falling down and down into the darkness and being smashed."

Ben took her hand. "Forget it, honey—please! You did what anyone would have done. I know how you felt."

"I wonder if you do. It wasn't that I still loved him—at least, I don't think so. I'd finished with that. I didn't really feel anything at all about him consciously, except that—well I somehow felt responsible for him."

"That's what I told you in France—unsatisfied maternal instinct. You ought to do something about it."

A flicker of a smile crossed her face. Then she became solemn again. "The trouble is, Ben, that I can't really blame him. Oh, I know it was a terrible thing he did but it grew out of what he was—I don't think he could help himself."

"That lets us all out."

"Yes, but he wasn't normal—he was different."

"He sure was. Still, honey, don't imagine I want to strike a moral attitude. What was that crack some Frenchman made I've never investigated the soul of a wicked man, but I once knew the soul of a good man, and I was shocked."

"Oh, Ben, you *are* tolerant."

"Sure—now he's dead."

"That's better than gloating. I heard some people talking in the town as I left the hospital—oh, I don't blame them of course, but it was horrible. They never really knew him when they thought he was so wonderful, and they still don't know him. Why must everything always be black or white?" Her eyes filled with tears. "He was never happy, never at peace with himself. He wanted to be strong—he hated his weaknesses. He never trusted himself, never felt secure—he always wanted to be reassured. I suppose that's why he became a communist. He spent his whole life trying to prove to himself that he was as big a man as he wanted to be, and failing." She looked across at the smoking chimneys of the plant. "He failed in this last thing, too—and thank God for it! But I'm glad he doesn't know."

Ben squeezed her hand. "Poor kid!—you've had a hell of a time. You'll have to try not to think about it any more, though, honey."

"I know, Ben."

"I had a long talk on the phone this morning with the doctor at the hospital—the guy who gave you the once-over." She looked startled. "Why? I'm all right."

"He says not. He says you're very run down and he recommends a sea voyage. I said what about a voyage to Trinidad and he said that was just the right length. What about it, Julie?"

She smiled up at him. "Oh, Ben, yes."

Printed and bound by CPI Group (UK) Ltd, Croydon, CR0 4YY

18/03/2025

01834158-0001